A DEEPER SONG

REBECCA BRADLEY

PROLOGUE

I f I'd heard correctly, the girl hadn't bolted the door behind herself properly. All I had to do was bide my time and wait for everyone to settle down for the night. Not that I knew how many people there were here but I would wait until it felt right.

There was no clock in this room. No sense of time.

I had no idea how much trouble the girl would get into for leaving the door insecure but that wasn't my problem. I had one thing on my mind and that was to find a way out of this place.

I trusted my team and knew they would find me but I also had to trust in myself. I had the control here this evening and I would grasp it with both hands. All I had to do was get out of the building. Once out I could find a passing car on a nearby road – not that I could hear cars from here, but I would run until I reached one. Or a neighbouring house with a phone. That was all I needed, a phone and I could make contact with Aaron, alert him to where I was and I'd be safe again.

I had no idea what was happening here. The girl hadn't told me anything. I got the feeling she was afraid and was simply doing as she was told. I'd be able to help her once I was out. I'd come back for her and get her out, as well as finding whoever was behind this.

Tonight, I'd be breaking free from this place and I'd be going home. No more locked rooms. No more scared girls feeding me. Tonight this was going to end.

1

I fretted at the piece of skin, pulling it away from the side of my nail as my dad walked back into the living room. Tugging at it with my teeth. Feeling my way along it with the tip of my tongue. It would be sore if I pulled it off, but leaving it there meant I would be distracted by it for days to come.

Dad placed the mug down on the coffee table in front of me. Steam curled out and whispered away to nothing. Dad returned to his seat. He'd brought me here this evening and ambushed me.

I looked across the room to my sister Zoe. She was pale and looked smaller than I remembered her from the last time I'd seen her. I tried to avoid my sister and saw my dad when I knew she was out, or arranged to see him out of the house. I was a detective inspector with Nottinghamshire police working within EMSOU – MC (East Midlands Special Operations Unit – Major Crime) which was a five force collaborative unit comprising Nottinghamshire, Derbyshire, Leicestershire, Northamptonshire and Lincolnshire, and Zoe was a drug user who had been arrested, charged and sent to prison for possession with intent to distribute. Not only that, but she'd been staying at my place at the time she'd been arrested and had stashed drugs in my apartment. My home had been searched, the drugs located and I'd been placed under investigation. I'd seen my whole career flash before my eyes. Eventually I was cleared but I hadn't forgiven Zoe.

Her eyes looked huge as she gazed back at me, arms wrapped around her body, hugging herself tightly as though she were cold. Hair pulled back and tied in a knot at the top of her head, face pale and drawn. She'd barely spoken. She'd left most of the talking to Dad. Knew I wouldn't explode at him, or not to the extent I would if it had been her explaining the circumstances to me.

My tongue wiggled the piece of skin, and my finger tingled, indicating how sore it would be should I pull the loose thread off. Would a quick and ruthless tug be better than days of picking and messing about with it?

'Drink your tea,' said Dad. 'I bought green tea especially for you.' He attempted a smile but it fell somewhere short.

Still Zoe didn't speak.

I pulled my finger out my mouth. 'How long?' I asked eventually.

He furrowed his brow. The question could mean many things. How long had they been hiding this from me? How long had they been plotting to tell me? How long did I have to decide? How long if I said no?

I wasn't even sure myself which of those questions I wanted answering. I needed all of them to be addressed for sure but, right at this moment, which was the most pertinent? Or pertinent to me?

I looked from Zoe to Dad. 'Has it been going on?' I decided.

Dad ran a hand through what was left of his hair. It was thinning on top, a deep widow's peak over his forehead accentuating the lines that told the story of his age and his worries. There was a small patch at the back of his head that was balding, but he was doing well to hold on to his hair, the silver shining under the light that he'd turned on when I came in. He blew out air through pursed lips and looked to Zoe who had the decency to look sheepish and bowed her head. 'I'm sorry, Hannah. Zoe wanted to try to connect with you properly, make amends for what happened before she came to you with all this. I went along with her because it was what she needed.'

Zoe had attempted reconciliation when she was released from prison and I glared at her now. She still hadn't yet looked up from her knees. This was all Zoe's fault. I caught myself. It wasn't exactly her fault. But how she had dealt with it was. How she dealt with anything was always the problem. Once caught with the drugs in my home she told me they were supposed to have been a temporary thing, a between-drugs home thing, a one-night-only affair, but it had gone wrong and she'd been caught before she'd had a chance to move them out. She had never meant to involve me in her problems.

And here I was, again, in the middle of Zoe's problems.

My heart twisted in my chest. I was being harsh. But I couldn't forget what she'd done. How she'd torn Dad's world apart by going to prison not long after Mum died. It was always about Zoe and now it was about Zoe again and Dad was asking for my help.

Zoe was asking for my help through Dad.

She'd barely said a word.

I looked at her. Stared hard at her. Angry at her for putting me in this position. For making me this angry at her. Finally she lifted her head and met my eyes.

'You don't have to, Hannah. I understand.' Her voice was quiet.

I waved a hand over towards Dad. 'You think he's going to accept that?'

'Hannah...' he spluttered.

It wasn't fair. I know. But he wouldn't.

'Dad'll get over it,' she said. 'This is between me and you and I've done a lot to hurt you. It's expecting a lot. To ask this of you. I accept that. But you have to believe I'm clean. I've been clean for months. I stay away from people in my old life. I'm making an effort, Hannah.'

Dad stayed silent. Letting us thrash it out.

'And Dad's been tested?' I asked, trying to bring my fury down a notch or two.

'He's not a match.'

I looked over at Dad and watched him slump into the sofa. He'd do anything for his kids. Even if we were no longer kids and no matter what we put him through. It pained him so much that we were at loggerheads the way we were. All he wanted was for us to be sisters again. To not be able to help Zoe in her time of need must be killing him. I reached over to him and squeezed his hand. He forced a smile but it was lacking.

I returned my attention to Zoe. 'So you had to come to me.' It was a statement rather than a question.

'Trust me, I'd rather I didn't have to. I've put on you enough.'

I barked out a laugh. 'That's an understatement.'

Zoe bowed her head.

I tried again. 'If I do this, what's involved?'

She shrugged. 'Not much to be honest. There are two options, one is you're hooked up to a cell-separator machine where you have a needle in each arm. With that I think they have to give you an injection every day for four or five days in the run up to the process.'

'And the other option...'

'They drill...' she shrugged again, 'down into your bone and remove some marrow and give it to me. You'll be a bit sore but other than that, you'll be fine. You'll only need about a week off work to recover and that's because you'll be sore and to prevent infection, I think.'

'And you?' I asked flinching at the thought of the drilling.

'They say with a bone marrow transplant I should be as good as new.'

I studied her face again. Saw how pale she was. I'd noticed this last time I'd seen her but thought nothing of it. When she was on the drugs she had never been the healthiest-looking person in my life, so when she was genuinely sick it passed me by. I leaned forward and picked up the tea. The warmth of the steam prickled my nose. I sipped the familiar calming drink and tried to think.

I'd been angry with Zoe for so long it was ingrained in me. I struggled to feel anything else. Of course I didn't want her to die. She was my sister when all was said and done, but so much water had gone under our bridge I didn't know how to go about repairing our relationship. On one level it felt that I was here because she needed something from me again, as she had back then when she'd needed a place to stay and she'd brought her drugs with her. It was this that drove the irritation and fury that bit at my heels. On another level, she was sick and no one could help getting sick. Not even Zoe. Though I wouldn't put it past her if it was a possibility, a way of wheedling her way back into my good graces. But here we were. She needed me.

I stuck the tip of my finger in my mouth, felt for the loose skin. Touched my tongue to the edge of it, then clamped down with my teeth and pulled it away, clear and free. A sharp sting ran to my brain and I winced.

2

The car was a quiet relief compared to the compressed stress of Dad's house. I turned the radio off, cracked the window a little, let the air circulate and blow through the emotions rattling about in my head and steered myself home.

It was early April and the weather was unpredictable but this evening it was fine and clear.

I'd left the house with a promise to think through Zoe and my father's request, though everyone knew I would end up saying yes eventually. There was no way I would let my sister die. Not because my father would never forgive me but because when it came down to the wire, she was my flesh and blood. My mother would turn in her grave at the state of us at the moment. Yes, I was angry at Zoe. I'd been angry for a long time. So angry and so long that I didn't know how to let go of that anger. It was like a balled-up fist of knots in the bottom of my stomach, that had been there so long it had bedded itself into me.

Traffic was light, barely another car on the road. I was grateful for this. My mind was a mess and I wasn't best placed to be driving. I wanted to be at home in my apartment at the base of Nottingham Castle with a glass or two of red wine and a couple of painkillers. My arm was throbbing. An old injury I'd sustained on the job eighteen months ago when a woman had sliced me with a knife during an operation that had gone badly wrong. After that I'd needed some time off work but had returned as quickly as I could because my team needed me. My GP had been helpful in providing me with prescription medication to control the continuing pain the wound caused me. He was cautious and reviewed it regularly but understood the pressures of the job meant I needed to concentrate.

As far as I understood it from this evening's discussion I would not be off work more than a couple of days, a week at the most if I donated my bone marrow to Zoe. I could cope with that.

I was in the inside lane on Canal Street, taking it steady when suddenly he was there. As if magicked into place. In front of the car. On the road.

In front of my moving car.

Stumbling. Falling.

Arms wheeling like he was trying to grab hold of something.

His head jerked sideways and he looked in at me. Eyes unfocused but the clearest blue I have ever seen. Lit up by my headlights bearing down upon him.

I hit the brakes. Forcing my foot down hard. The tyres squealed as they skidded on the asphalt. My arms locked, and my head slammed forward. The airbag inflated and the breath was forced from my lungs with a violent grunt as it smashed into me at full throttle. I coughed and choked trying to regain breath, sucking up air.

Unable to see out the windscreen as the airbag blocked my view.

What the hell?

I couldn't see him. He wasn't standing in front of the car and I couldn't see him running down the street in front of me or in my rearview mirror. Dread shimmied its way up my spine.

As I pulled on the handbrake a soft beige powder covered my hands. The airbag, now deflated, sagged in my lap. I patted my trouser pocket for my phone and jumped out of my Peugeot. A car passed by on the other side of the road. No one had noticed what had happened. No one had noticed the young man come flying from Trent Street junction into the middle of the road.

My heart was slamming into my chest wall. My ribcage felt too fragile to hold it in place as I moved to the front of the car.

And there he was. Laid on the ground, the lower half of his legs out of view under the Peugeot 308. His face so pale in the amber glow of the street light I feared he was dead, but his wide blinking eyes looked at me with such intensity my thudding heart nearly stopped.

He was covered in blood. His T-shirt and jeans were smeared with the stuff. I could see it clearly in the bright light of the car's head-lamps. This was serious.

I pulled out my phone and crouched down beside him, calling an ambulance and reassuring him that he would be okay, but telling him that he wasn't to move. I was terrified of what injuries he may have sustained and didn't want to make an already disastrous situation worse. My heart was now in my throat. I dialled the control room but didn't know if I would be able to talk, to inform them of what I had done. The call was connected and I found myself stuttering and stam-mering, making clear I needed supervisory support as I'd been involved in an accident. As was always the case with control room they were professional and prompt, checking to see if I needed medical assistance and then reassuring me that support was on its way.

'What's your name?' I asked as I sat on the cold concrete ground next to his head. Frightened for him.

'I don't know.' He blinked at me. There wasn't a scratch on his face.

'You don't know your name?'

He blinked again and bent his arms, forcing his elbows onto the road, then tried to push himself upright. 'No. I don't... I don't know.' A look of panic crossed his face, it paled even further and he looked grey.

I took his hand. Like the rest of him, it was smeared in blood. 'Stay where you are, there's an ambulance coming. Stay there.' Gently I rubbed my fingers over his hand but there were no injuries that I could feel. No bones broken beneath my touch, no open wounds.

He tried to push himself up again but pain spasmed through his body.

'What is it?' I asked, trying to keep my voice calm, fearing he was about to do himself further harm. He'd obviously hit his head but I wasn't sure what other damage might have been done and it didn't look good.

He rolled his eyes upwards. 'My leg, I think one of my legs is broken.'

A car horn sounded behind us, the driver unable to see a driver in my vehicle or me and the young man on the ground in front of the car. An impatient, angry sound ripping through the cool night air as I gripped the man-with-no-name's hand. I looked up at my car and realised in my rush to get out I hadn't put my hazard warning lights on. The vehicle was stationary in the middle of the lane. I twisted and stretched my arm out, waving it in the middle of the road, hoping the impatient driver would see what was happening. There was a rev of an engine and a slow manoeuvre as a black Fiat pulled up at the side of us.

The driver slid his passenger side window down. A young man with serious looking glasses leaned over. 'Need a hand, love?'

'No, thanks. I've called an ambulance. It's on its way.'

He didn't move.

'You all right, mate?' he tried again, this time asking the young man lying under my car.

He looked at me, a question on his face. I gripped his arm tighter. He was frightened.

'Yes, I think I am.' He didn't look towards the driver of the Fiat but kept his gaze locked on me. He needed something to cling to in this moment of uncertainty.

'Okay then.' The Fiat driver drove away.

'I need to put my hazard lights on so drivers know to go around us.' I let go of the lad and his eyes widened in panic. 'I'll be a few seconds, that's all. I'll be right back.' The fear didn't leave his face.

I jumped up, moved to the car and switched on the orange. The car needed to be left where it was so accident investigation could check out what had happened.

Back on the ground I asked, 'How do you feel? Does anything else hurt?'

He blinked at me. 'I don't think so but why don't I know who I am?'

I didn't have an answer for him.

In the distance I could hear the two-tones. Help was on its way. I looked down at the hand in mine, the bloody smeared hand, and realised the blood was dried. It wasn't from the accident.

3

It now looked more like the scene of an accident with blue lights slicing through the night. An ambulance and marked police car were parked up, stippling the night with their blues. People gathering in groups as close as they could get, wanting to see events unfold, wanting to know what had happened. Who knew where they had appeared from when the area had been silent not fifteen minutes earlier? My car still in the middle of the road, waiting for the uniformed officer to give me the okay to move it. I thanked my lucky stars it was a plain car and not a marked police vehicle as that really would have the rubberneckers talking. John Doe was in the ambulance having been lifted in by the paramedic and technician and I was talking to the uniformed inspector, Scott Cooper. He spoke incredibly gently for a man so tall and well-built.

Being a DI myself, they had sent someone out of equal rank to deal with the RTC. I was breathalysed. Cooper was matter-of-fact about it and as expected I blew clear.

'I'll follow John Doe to the hospital, see if I can't clear up his details,' said Cooper.

'Actually, Scott,' I looked into the ambulance, at John Doe and the dried blood covering his clothing, 'I think I'm going to stay on and follow this up if you don't mind?'

'Mind?' He laughed. A genuine roar from his stomach. 'You're more than welcome. I've got plenty to be getting on with and if you're happy to stay on and attempt to ID our John Doe, then I'm thrilled. I'll submit the RTC paperwork and leave the rest to you. Let me know when you have some personal details for him.'

'That's settled then.'

Cooper paused. 'You're sure you're fit to stay on, though? You've had a bit of a fright yourself this evening.'

I smiled at him.

'Okay, I get it.' He laughed again. 'Give me a shout if you change your mind and I'll get one of my shift to come to the hospital to take over.'

I moved my car to the side of the road, and climbed into the ambulance.

'How you doing?' I asked as I looked down at the man strapped to a long board with a C-spine collar on for precaution. 'Any luck in remembering your name?'

'I'm sorry.' He frowned.

I could see him properly in the light of the ambulance interior. John Doe looked to be about seventeen to twenty-five. Slender build with a mop of brown hair that hung down towards his blue eyes, which were huge in his pale narrow face.

'Don't worry, we'll figure it out. I do have to ask you though, do you know what happened to you? Where this blood has come from? Do you have an injury, from before tonight?' I was throwing multiple questions at him.

He blinked at me again his face ashen. At his side a machine beeped through the silence. A wire ran from it to a small clip attached to the end of his right index finger.

'I don't know. I don't think so.' He pushed the front of his T-shirt up, looked down at his stomach which appeared sunken, hollowed. The beeping increased.

'I'm sorry, we need to take him,' the paramedic said, bent over in the confines of the ambulance from her position opposite, where she had been filling in a form.

'I'll meet you there and don't worry, we'll figure it out,' I told him as he rubbed at his stomach.

It was another forty-five minutes before I was able to take my car. The Accident Investigation Unit had to take all the measurements from the skid marks before they would release it from the scene. Once they had all the information and photographs they needed I was free to go. I pulled on my seat belt and started the car. Who was this boy and who did all the blood come from? I hoped to find out some answers at the hospital. I dialled the control room again and requested a CSI meet us there, updating the incident log with my reasons and needs.

Queen's Medical Centre is part of the Nottingham University Hospitals group and is the main hospital that services Nottingham patients. It sits on Derby Road, a main artery in and out of the city.

I abandoned my car where it shouldn't be parked and left a police sign on the dashboard. The emergency department was never quiet and tonight was no exception. I weaved my way past a group of girls who only looked about thirteen but were dressed as though they were much older in revealing clothes and lots of make-up, but behind all that you could see the immaturity. Hovering in a group by the door, they looked anxious and confused.

A woman sat on the chairs, her face set like stone as a man a couple of chairs away swore continually into his phone. He wasn't happy at someone who had failed to collect some cash a friend owed. And an old man leaned back in his chair with a cap pulled down over his eyes as he tried to block it all out.

I couldn't say I blamed him. Along with our jobs, emergency departments saw people having a pretty bad day in their lives and the people weren't often polite about it and, unlike us, the staff weren't equipped to deal with antagonistic patients. I had a lot of respect for the teams that worked here.

I walked up to reception and waited my turn. The noise from all the voices in the department melded into one wall of sound that I tried to block out.

Eventually I was shown round to where John Doe was being treated. He was still strapped down on a long board and had his C-spine collar on; there was an IV drip going into his arm and medical staff were hovering over him.

Under the glare of the hospital strip-lighting it was a very different image to the one I had seen in the street lights and inside of the ambulance. Here, nothing could be hidden. Every smudge of dirt and trace of blood was visible.

John Doe had been stripped of his clothes but they were in a pile on the floor at the side of him. It looked as though he had been working in a slaughter house without an apron on. His T-shirt was, or had been, white with an image of some description in the centre, he had faded denim jeans but I couldn't see any footwear. Had he been wearing any? He had nothing on his feet at all. How could I have missed that?

The blood on the pile of clothes looked as though it had been thrown at him. His T-shirt was covered and from what I could see his centre mass was where the bulk of the blood was. On his person, dried blood spatters were on his arms and hands, with some on his face. I looked back down to the pile of clothes. Saw a puddle stain in his groin on the jeans and running down his legs. Or it had done. Now it was dry.

A couple of nurses were stood over him as well as two doctors. It all looked very serious and I was worried. He was conscious and talking though, so I took that as a good sign.

I informed one of the nurses that we would be needing his clothes. I could see no visible injuries on John Doe, no open or healing wounds, so we needed to know whose blood it was and what had happened.

My phone beeped. The CSI was here and in the waiting room. I excused myself and went to speak to them.

Aditi Upreti was waiting with a large bag in her hand. She smiled as I approached. I envied her ability to never look tired, no matter the hour or how long she had been working. 'You're not busy enough at work?' she asked when I reached her.

'It seems not,' I admitted. I told her what we had, that we needed John Doe's fingerprints, photograph and DNA if he consented and his clothing should be seized and the blood tested to see what it could tell us. I was concerned by how much there was. I talked as we walked back to the treatment area, keeping my voice low to maintain confidentiality.

'He really has no idea who he is? Nothing at all?' Aditi's high ponytail swung as she walked.

'No. Nothing. It may be to do with the accident.' She pulled a face in sympathy. 'Or, looking at the state of him, it could have something to do with whatever he's been through.'

'We'll do what we can.'

We watched as the C-spine collar came off and then the back board was removed. X-rays were showing no spinal injuries, but one of his legs was broken. As we waited for further treatment we moved closer and spoke to him.

'What's the last thing you remember?' I asked.

John Doe looked around the room as though it would hold the answers for him, then he shifted his gaze to me. 'I'm not sure. You, you're the strongest memory I have.'

'Strongest?'

He blinked at me. Assessed the room again. Looked to Aditi. Blinked some more. He looked frightened. 'Only,' he whispered.

'Nothing else at all?'

Tears filled his eyes. John Doe looked five years younger. A child. 'Who am I?'

I stepped closer to the bed, put my hand on his arm. 'Don't worry, we'll find out and we'll find out what happened. Will you let us help you?'

'I'll do anything.'

I told him why Aditi was here and that we needed his permission. John Doe was now in a gown and a nurse had put his clothes into a plastic bag. Aditi gloved up and moved them into a paper bag. The plastic would sweat and destroy the blood evidence. She wrote and signed an exhibit label and sealed the bag. We had no idea what we were dealing with and Aditi was a pro.

'How do you feel?' I asked him.

'My head and my leg hurt. I feel shaky and weird.'

'You don't know why you ran in front of the car?' Why was I asking him the same question again? Hoping for a different answer.

A tear slipped down his cheek.

'Okay. I'm not going to ask any more. We'll get what we need to check our systems and leave you in the capable hands of the staff here. I'll come back and see you again in the morning. You can get some rest.' I watched him for a reaction. Any reaction.

There was nothing.

'Okay?'

'Thank you.' It was quiet and subdued.

Before I left Aditi to finish her work I took my phone out of my pocket and took a quick photograph of John Doe and slipped my phone away, then I went in search of the doctor.

Doctor Jun Yang was one of the most petite women I had ever seen. She must have been only four foot ten and carrying no weight at all. 'We'll be keeping him in at least a couple of days, but beyond that I can't tell you more until I've seen his CT scan.'

'You're admitting him though?' I confirmed.

'Absolutely. With a head injury like that, where he doesn't know who he is, we need to keep an eye on him. He'll be going for his CT shortly, he's listed as urgent.'

'Why doesn't he remember anything?'

'If the amnesia occurred at the time of the accident we're most likely looking at retrograde amnesia, which means everything before the accident is lost.'

I thought of the blood he was covered in. 'Will his memory return?'

'It's possible, with time and some stimulus of people and places he knows, yes, it can come back.' She gave me a serious look. 'But I have to warn you, it doesn't always.'

Again, I thought of his bloody clothes and who that blood might have come from. We needed to find out who John Doe was and in turn whose blood he was covered in.

4

The detective and CSI had left. John Doe found himself alone in the cubicle as he waited for his tests. Waiting for a CT scan on his head. His leg was easy enough, it was broken. They said they would give him better pain relief when he'd had his scan, but for now he was making do on stuff they were happy to give him.

He'd had an EKG done and bloods taken as well, and as far as he could figure out, they were putting a rush on the results.

It was his head he was worried about. How could it be that a person couldn't know who they were? Wasn't it an absolute for every human? Strip their name away and you strip away who they are.

There was a small square mirror on the wall at the side of him. He needed to move back a little to get a view. At this point he wasn't even sure what he looked like. He couldn't summon up an image. Maybe if he saw himself he would know who he was. After all, that would be him staring right back, he was bound to know himself then.

John Doe pushed his bum further up the bed. Pain tightened like a vice around his leg. Squeezing and digging in, throbbing deep inside so his stomach contracted and he clamped his eyes shut. He waited the wave of pain out and tried again, gritting his teeth down hard and pushing his body back. He had to get to the mirror. To see himself.

To find himself.

His leg screamed out at him. While he'd been still the pain relief had been doing its thing, but now he was fidgeting it was as though his leg was made of broken glass. But regardless. This was important.

He kept his jaw clenched. He wouldn't cry out. He didn't want to be stopped.

No matter how much he pushed himself up the bed the mirror was still out of view. He needed to move back a foot.

John Doe tightened his jaw, clenched a fist, took a deep breath through his nose, the tang of hospital disinfectant seeping into his brain, and twisted at the waist so he was looking behind the bed. All he had to do was push himself back a little and he could see in the mirror.

He listened for the sound of footsteps on the linoleum floor, for the sound of a nurse or porter coming to collect him for his tests or simply to check on him, but all he could hear was a wall of voices, chatter. Nothing he could make out, just a knot of sound.

With a last twist and push he was there, level with the mirror.

The face that peered back at him was grey and narrow with large blue eyes. It was smudged and dirty. Tired-looking. Was he always this thin? The face had a familiarity to it; a sense of self settled over him, until he tried to think of his name to go with the image he could see.

There was nothing. His mind was empty. It was like someone had come along and scraped the inside of his head out. The muscles in his stomach twitched and ached. John Doe relaxed as he lay back down. Looking around the room he could recognise and name everything in here that didn't have a weird medical name, it was his life he had no concept of.

Just his life.

5

My apartment was cold by the time I got home, the heating timer having long ago clicked off. It was two-thirty a.m. A few hours in bed and I'd be back at work feeling as though I'd never left the place. A deep throb in my upper right arm reminded me I needed some painkillers. Pulling them from my bag, I walked to the kitchen, poured a glass of red wine, swallowed the pills and took the wine through to the bedroom where I placed the glass on the bedside table before slipping off my clothes and dropping them on the floor.

It had turned into a long day and I was exhausted. I couldn't remember what time it had been when I had last taken painkillers and my arm was reminding me.

The wine was soothing, rich and deep. I leaned back on the pillows and relaxed. Now was when I wanted to phone someone, talk to them about what had happened this evening, but for one thing it was too late; for another, who would I call?

My best friend, Evie Small, who, as well as being my best friend, was the team's analyst, wouldn't appreciate me disturbing either her beauty sleep or her love life, depending on which it was she was engaging in.

My dad would happily be there for me, but I'd feel a debt was owed if I made that call and it was a debt I couldn't pay. Besides Zoe was living with him now she was out of prison and I didn't want to burden him anymore than he was already was.

I drained the rest of the wine. Tomorrow we'd find out who John Doe was and hopefully who the blood belonged to. But, I couldn't settle, couldn't rest. All I could see was John Doe in front of the car, his pale shocked face gleaming in the headlights before disappearing from view. His rounded blinking eyes, fearful and nervous. The silent tears shed at not knowing who he was. What that must be like, I couldn't imagine.

I dialled the hospital. The phone rang for so long I thought it was going to ring off. The sound in my ear starting to blend into a constant drone. Then a male voice answered, 'Hello, QMC ED.' If you didn't know which department you had asked to be put through to specifically, you would have no idea from a bunch of initials.

I informed the person who I was and asked after John Doe. He was waiting for a bed on a ward and that was all they were willing to tell me over the telephone.

Did he remember his name yet? I pushed.

No, Detective Inspector. It doesn't work like that. And that is all I can say, was the response.

I closed my eyes. My half sleep splintered with images of blood and bones and wide frightened eyes.

I was first in the office, having set my alarm early. I made myself a green tea, woke my computer and emailed forensic submissions with a cc attachment for Aditi. I wanted to know as soon as any results came in. I wanted a rush putting on the blood on the clothing. I wanted to know about the quantity, if someone could survive with that amount of blood loss, and I wanted a blood DNA type so we could maybe get an ID if they were in any of our systems. Second in urgency was the ID of John Doe, but that was something we could work on as well as forensics. They'd have to test his DNA and submit his prints to the fingerprint department but we would check the files to see if he had been reported missing overnight.

Aaron Stone, my DS, knocked on the door as I stared at the computer monitor.

'You're in early.' He was usually in before me. He liked to get himself settled before the rest of the team came into work.

'Yeah,' I agreed, 'there was an incident on the way home from my dad's last night.'

Concern crossed his face and he stepped into my office and pulled up a chair. An invitation for me to tell him more.

'I was driving home,' I shook my head as the image of John Doe diving in front of the car invaded my mind, 'and a young man ran in front of me.' I looked at Aaron. 'I hit him, Aaron.'

'Shit.'

'Yeah.'

'How is he?'

'I won't know much for definite until I go back into the hospital this morning, but he's got at least a broken leg and...' How could I say this? What I had done? The words were like barbed wire in my throat. 'He can't remember anything before the accident. He doesn't know who he is. They were doing a CT on his head.' I wanted to weep. 'He's only a young lad, Aaron.'

My DS leaned back in his chair. 'Do you want me to come to the hospital with you this morning?'

I did. I really did. 'That would be great. I need to let Catherine know before we go.' Catherine Walker was the detective superintendent of our unit and she ran a very tight ship. She hated negative publicity and would not be happy with this turn of events. 'Let's get the team up to speed and get them working on trying to identify John Doe.'

Aaron rose from his chair.

'There's one other thing that is a major concern from last night.'

Aaron looked at me.

'John Doe was covered in blood that wasn't his.'

Catherine Walker was a slim, neat-looking woman. Never a hair out of place or a tired line on her face. I wasn't quite sure how she did it. She was sat behind her desk when I entered, writing in a notebook, a look of concentration on her face. The room smelled sweet, feminine. As though she had just wafted through it.

'What can I do for you, Hannah?' she asked without looking up.

I closed the door and she lifted her head, raising a plucked eyebrow. She placed her pen on her notepad and waited for me to speak. She was formidable without the need for her to say much. I bit back the nerves and updated her on John Doe and the concern over the blood on his clothing. Catherine listened without interrupting as I relayed all the facts to her.

'And what have you prioritised?'

'The blood on the clothing. It's not from John Doe so we need to know who has been injured and quickly. Then we need to identify Doe himself.'

'Good.' She opened her notebook, turned the page over, dated and timed the top of the page and started writing notes. 'It doesn't sound as though you could have done much about it, Hannah, but we need to sort it out and move on. I'll get in touch with the accident investigation unit, make sure everything is okay with them. But, other than that, I'll leave it in your capable hands.'

I'd expected trouble but the thing with Catherine was that she never gave you what you expected and I felt a little lighter than when I went in.

OVER THE NEXT fifteen minutes the team filed in, made drinks and opened their computer terminals, chatting about home and the previous evening's television. At eight-thirty a.m. I briefed the team on John Doe.

'Bloody hell, boss, are you okay?' was the first question out of the mouth of Martin Thacker, the longest serving and most dependable, unflappable DC on the unit. He'd been leaning back in his chair, arms crossed behind his head, his usual position, but was now leaning forward watching me.

'I'm fine. Thank you.' I reassured him. 'It's the blood on his clothes we need to worry about.'

'You think he's killed someone and that's what he was running from?' asked Ross Leavy, a young and hardworking DC on the team. He didn't do shades of grey very well though. If you were the bad guy, you were the bad guy.

'I don't know what to think. To be honest, our John Doe seemed pretty frightened himself. Like he was running from something. Looked the worse for wear. But, yes, we do need to get to the bottom of this.'

'What do you want from us, Ma'am?' Pasha Lal asked. Pasha was new to the department. Young with a hunger and drive to get ahead.

'Aaron and I are going to the hospital this morning to see John Doe. I want anyone that isn't running out the door to court to check our missing persons database, see if a male between the age of about seventeen and twenty-five was reported missing yesterday or maybe a little further back. I've forwarded his photo on to all of you. You can compare it with the missing persons files. Liaise with the fingerprint bureau and see if we have a match or how long it will take. Then let me know if we manage to ID him.'

'Do you believe the amnesia thing, boss?' asked Ross, not looking so sure himself. 'It seems a bit convenient, doesn't it? If he's covered in someone else's blood when he's hit by a cop's car.'

'Such a cynic, Ross.'

He had a point. I thought back to the previous night, did he deny knowledge of who he was before or after I identified myself?

6
_____

The ward was quiet. It wasn't yet visiting time and the patients were either in their beds or on the chairs at the side, reading, with earphones in or simply staring silently into the distance. There was the odd stilted conversation but it was funny how people pretended the others weren't here on the ward with them.

Nurses were at the nurses' station, or dealing with patients, handing out the morning medications.

John Doe had been placed in a side room, the concern about his lack of identity status giving him that extra care.

I knocked and entered. John Doe lay on his back, one leg in a plaster cast above the sheets. He was staring up at the ceiling. As we walked through the door he turned and looked at the intrusion.

'Morning.' I grabbed a chair from the corner of the room. 'This is Aaron Stone, the detective sergeant on my team. I hope you don't mind him coming along.' It wasn't really a question.

Aaron said hello. There wasn't much of a response from John Doe. He looked disheartened this morning.

'How are you?' I asked.

'I didn't sleep much.' He looked back at the ceiling. 'And no, I still don't know my name or where I live or who I live with. I don't remember anything.'

There was a grit in his voice that wasn't there last night. I pushed the chair closer to the bed and sat. Aaron dragged the second chair over.

'It's okay, there's no rush. You're not in any trouble. We're concerned about you. What have the doctors said?'

He looked back at us. 'My leg's broken.' He barked a laugh as he waved his hand at his potted leg.

I smiled. 'And your head?'

Now it was John Doe's turn to smile, but it didn't travel to his eyes. It was flat. Sad. Distant. 'There was nothing on the CT. Nothing physical. They say it's retrograde amnesia, likely caused when I hit my head on the road. Memories will come back or they won't. It will take as long as it takes.' He looked back to the ceiling. But not before I saw the damp in his eyes. 'Or not.'

I shuffled my chair closer and leant on his bed. I could smell damp and soil. They'd taken care of his medical needs during the night, but he was yet to be cleaned up. 'Don't worry about it, I'm sure that won't help the process. We're working on figuring it out. You don't have to deal with this alone. You have both us and the medical profession to help you.'

'And what happens when you can't find out who I am?'

I didn't have an answer for him.

7

M artin and Pasha were out at court when we arrived back at St Ann's police station. Ross was glued to his computer screen.

'Found anything?' Aaron asked as we walked in.

'Nope. We have a few missing teenagers and adults, but none match our John Doe. Has he remembered anything?'

'No, and he's not happy either,' I answered.

'We believe him?'

'The doctors back him up that it's feasible, so no reason not to.'

'Other than the blood you say he was covered in.'

'Other than that, of course. Have we heard from forensics yet?'

'No, but I did get in touch with the fingerprint department who ran his prints and have said he's not in our systems for anything. All we know is that he's not been arrested. So, with that, it's unlikely his DNA will come back a match for anything. Not unless he was arrested and for some strange reason they forgot the fingerprints.'

I ran my hand through my hair. 'Yeah, that's unlikely. Hopefully we'll get some answers on the blood on his clothing and that will help identify him, as well as the person to whom the blood belongs.'

'Hannah!' A voice boomed behind me. Our DCI, Kevin Baxter. 'I hear you've been trying to create your own workload.' He laughed at his own wit. 'But failed miserably and now the poor guy doesn't know who he is.'

I sighed. 'Something like that, Sir. He ran out in front of me. There was no way to miss him and we're doing everything we can to figure out what's going on.'

Aaron moved away to his desk and opened up his computer.

Baxter straightened his face. 'In all seriousness, this issue with the blood sounds concerning. What are we doing about it?'

I walked towards my office in the hope Baxter would follow me and we could have a discussion in there. 'Forensics are working on the blood that was on the clothing...' I stopped, Baxter hadn't moved from the spot he'd started talking from. He was stamping his authority. He wasn't going to simply follow me because I'd moved. I let out a breath and turned to face him. 'They'll do a DNA test on it, run it through the system, see if we can come up with a match.'

'Anything else?'

I looked to Aaron. 'I'm going to get the team to check for CCTV around the accident, from the direction John Doe came from, see if we can follow him backwards and work out where that gets us.'

Baxter twisted an ear, still listening.

'The problem is, the further out of town you go, the less opportunity for CCTV we have. But we'll check private premises as well as street ones.'

'You need to get on top of this, Hannah. Think of the blowback if there is a serious GBH, or God forbid, a body turns up that he's responsible for and we haven't investigated properly.'

Did he think I wasn't considering that there was someone in trouble somewhere? 'Yes, Sir. We're taking it seriously and are doing all we can for John Doe and the surrounding circumstances.' I ran my hand through my hair again.

'I'll leave you to it then. Please keep me updated.' And with that he walked out as quickly as he'd walked in. I'd have cursed him out loud but it would have been unprofessional in front of subordinates, like Ross. I longed for the days of our old DCI Anthony Grey and his dithering. Grey used to worry quietly while he supported you. Baxter was young for a DCI; he wanted to climb his way up the career ladder. He was interested in data analysis and interpretation, and cross-organisational meetings, which is what I hated about the job. It was why I didn't want to go for promotion again. I preferred to get my hands dirty, to get involved in investigations. Something I did far more of than most DIs and far more than it seemed Baxter liked me to.

'Ross?'

He looked at me with barely disguised disgust on his face. He was not happy Baxter had talked to us as though we didn't know what we were doing.

'Can you come to my office, please.'

He followed me in and I opened maps and showed Ross where I'd been, where John Doe had run out from. 'I want you to collect CCTV.' He peered over my shoulder. 'Working backwards from here. I was travelling along Canal Street and he came running out of Trent Street.'

Pasha and Martin came back from court together. They'd been at court for a domestic murder. The woman was pleading guilty; she'd had a baby six months earlier and was suffering from postnatal depression and had lashed out in an exhausted moment without realising she was holding her steak knife in her hand. It had struck her husband in his throat, catching his carotid artery. He'd bled out before the ambulance had arrived. She was distraught. Martin had handled her sensitively and had been quite subdued during the investigation. The baby had been homed with the woman's sister who had two boys of her own and had been more than happy to take the little one in. Social care had agreed and baby had settled. But it was an awful set of circumstances. By all accounts the family had been happy. The husband and wife had been young and in love and had been trying for a baby for a couple of years and had been about to try IVF when the wife had got pregnant naturally.

Now her husband was gone and her life was in pieces around her. How fragile life is.

'Anyone for a drink?' Martin asked as he walked in.

'I'd love a green tea,' I said.

Pasha and Aaron answered in the positive and I walked to the kitchen with Martin.

'How you doing?' I asked.

'I'm okay.' He filled the kettle with cold water. 'It was the last day today. The jury have gone to deliberate. Who knows how long they'll take.'

I got the mugs out. 'You've done a good job, you know.'

'Yeah. I'd say I wish I could have done more, but that would have involved me not being involved.' He stared at the milk carton he was holding. 'If you know what I mean.'

Pasha came to the kitchen door. 'Ma'am, forensics are on the phone for you, say it's urgent.'

'Thanks, Pasha.'

I looked to Martin. 'I do. But, you've done the best you can in difficult circumstances.'

He sighed. 'Yeah.'

I headed out the door to my office to see what forensics had.

My phone was ringing as I reached my office. I picked up the receiver. It was Aditi.

'I don't suppose you've had much luck identifying your John Doe, have you?' she opened with.

'We haven't. He doesn't match the description of anyone who is currently reported missing.'

'There is one person,' she said.

I thought back to the discussion we'd had. To the adult men between the age range we'd put him between. I didn't think we'd missed anything. 'What do you have?'

'Matt Harper.'

I was about to say the name didn't ring a bell but there was a distant sound somewhere in the back of my head. 'Why do I recognise that name, Aditi?'

'What were you doing eleven years ago?' she asked.

'I was a DC in CID, why?'

'Remember the mother and child who went missing and there was no sign of them? No leads, they disappeared off the face of the earth. There was a huge search for them that went national.'

What was she telling me? It couldn't be, not after all this time. 'He's Matt Harper?' I leaned back in my chair.

'We've got his DNA on file. I thought you'd want a rush putting on the search because of the blood at the scene. That's going to take a little longer to process.'

'But the lad I ran over last night is definitely Matt Harper?'

'Yes. There's no refuting the genetics. It seems he's reappeared after all this time. It would be nice to know where he's been.'

I thought back to the case. I hadn't worked it but everyone was aware of it. He'd only been nine when he and his mother had been reported missing by his aunt, leaving an older brother at home alone. They'd simply disappeared into thin air. And now he was here, falling in front of my car, covered in blood, with no recollection of who he was or where he'd been or whose blood he was covered in. Aditi had called with answers but there were now more questions than before.

8

'There's something I haven't told you,' I said to Aaron as we travelled to the aunt's house.

Aaron kept his eyes on the road as he drove. 'What is it?'

'The reason I was at my dad's.'

Aaron stayed silent. Waited for me to spill.

'Zoe has leukaemia and needs a bone marrow transplant. She's asked me to be a donor as Dad isn't a match. They've been dealing with this for months without telling me.' I looked out the side window at the pedestrians going about their business in the rain. Umbrellas up, faces downturned. Shoulders hunched. A picture of grey.

'I'm sorry to hear that.'

He wouldn't say anything else. If I wanted a conversation about it with him I'd have to give more myself. Aaron was autistic. High functioning, what they used to call Asperger's but now named it all autism. He was great at his job but sometimes he wouldn't connect.

'I'm still so angry with her,' I said.

'She paid her dues, Hannah.' He indicated and made the manoeuvre.

I sighed. 'I know she did. But she's family and she could have destroyed my career, the one thing that's important to me. She should have known what she was doing but she didn't care. All she cared about was herself. Now she wants me to do this for her.' The frustration was mounting again. I sighed. 'It doesn't matter.'

'Who are you hurting by holding onto this?' he asked.

He was so damn practical. If I had a pencil in my hand I would stab him in the thigh with it right now.

'I'm going to do it. It's the right thing.'

'Is there a risk to you?' He glanced at me.

I shook my head. 'No. I think there's a small risk of infection as with any invasive procedure, but that's minimal. I'll be back at work in a couple of days maybe a week.'

He returned his concentration to the road, indicated again and pulled over and parked in front of a small, neat two-bedroomed property which was called a townhouse but was code for rabbit hutch, on Nicholas Road, Beeston.

'Thanks, Aaron.'

He turned the engine off. 'What for?'

'Listening.'

He climbed out of the car and walked to the front door. I followed him.

There was a plant pot filled with flowers at the side of the door. This was someone who took care of her home. Appreciated where she lived. I never seemed to have the time to put this level of attention into my own home. I was always too busy at work and too tired when I got home. My work/life balance was definitely skewed towards the work end of the spectrum.

Someone approached the door on the other side, the details obscured by the frosted glass. The door opened and a petite lady with short dark hair peered up at us. I introduced Aaron and myself and her brows furrowed.

'Can we come in?' I asked. 'It might be better if we discuss what we've come for away from the street.'

Tara Chapman stepped back, allowing us access. The rest of the house was as cared for as the front had indicated. Everything had a place. There was little in the way of knick-knacks but a busy book-shelf was filled with fiction and non-fiction and on the windowsill was a huge vase of flowers. She obviously loved the beauty of nature.

She ushered us towards the sofas and we sat. Tara sat opposite, clasped her hands together in a tight knot and waited for us to speak. I needed to break her fear of the worst case scenario quickly.

'Mrs Chapman—'

'Call me Tara.'

'Tara. You reported your sister and her youngest son missing about eleven years ago.'

Her hands twisted in her lap. Her lips thinned.

'Have you heard from either of them in the time they've been missing?'

Her mouth parted before she spoke and she paused. 'No. No, I would have informed you.'

I believed her. She was waiting for me to tell her we had found their bodies. 'Yesterday a young man ran in front of a vehicle.'

Her eyes were wide with fear.

'He sustained a leg injury and a head injury, which has resulted in retrograde amnesia.'

Her brows furrowed. Her face was pale.

I carried on. 'This means he can't remember who he is or where he's from or anything from his past.'

There was a sharp intake of breath from Tara.

'There are some issues surrounding this man that need investigating, but we have taken his DNA and we have identified him as your nephew Matthew Harper.'

The twisting of hands stilled. Silence filled the room as what I had imparted seeped through years of loss and grief.

When it came, Tara's voice was a whisper. 'You're sure?'

'We are.' I leant forward. 'The young man who ran in front of my vehicle last night is in fact your nephew, Tara. He's back.'

The information started to sink in. Tears filled her eyes as she stared hard at me. Boring into me for something else. Another sentence that would tear this all away from her.

'We need to investigate where he's been, where his mother is. He was covered in blood that wasn't his. Something has happened to him and we need to find out what it is. But your nephew is back.'

Tara swiped at her face with the back of her hand, a knuckle digging into her eye socket to stem the tears. But there was no stopping them. This had been a long time coming. 'You said he's hurt?'

'He ran in front of my car last night and has a broken leg. Other than the amnesia, there are no other physical injuries. The hospital are keeping him in a little while to keep an eye on him though.'

'I can see him?'

'That's something you need to discuss with the doctors. I can give you the ward number and the name of the doctor who is caring for Matt.'

'You've seen him?' She was desperate for information. I didn't blame her.

'He looks well considering. He's a healthy weight. He was shaved and had a haircut.'

'Sharon?' Her sister.

'I'm sorry. There was no sign of your sister and Matt doesn't remember anything. The doctor has said this should hopefully be temporary though.'

There was a huge juddering intake of breath and then she broke down, great wracking sobs taking control of her body. 'Eleven years.' I heard through the tears. 'Eleven years I've thought they were dead. I held on to hope as long as I could, but in the end I gave up and thought they must be dead. How could I?'

Aaron stood and found his way to the kitchen. He'd make her a drink for when she was ready. I would sit with her as the emotion ran its course.

'I gave up on them and continued with my life. What will he think of me? That poor, poor boy. He'll think I abandoned them.' She swiped at her tears again but her hand wasn't enough. I reached into my bag and brought out a pack of tissues and handed her a couple. She screwed them into a ball and dabbed at her face. 'What of his mother? And what has happened to him?' The sobs became louder again as the prospect of what he may have had to bear flooded her mind.

Aaron walked back into the room carrying a couple of mugs. He pushed one towards Tara and she looked up at him, surprised, her face streaked with tears. She hiccupped, swiped at her face once more then held out a hand and took one of the mugs. 'Thank you,' she said.

He handed the other one to me.

We waited with Tara another half an hour before she was in any state to calmly talk to us about her sister and nephew. We needed the details of what happened when they went missing. We needed more than what had been written in the missing report. We needed to know from someone who had lived it and Tara was it.

'She was bringing the two boys up on her own,' she said, mug of sweet tea empty but held in her hands like a comfort blanket. 'I did as much as I could for them as I didn't have children of my own and we were pretty close. Or I thought we were. Until she went missing. The police suggested she had walked out of their lives but that theory was discarded when no money was taken from her bank account after she left.'

'Why did they think she'd walked out of her life then?' I asked.

'There'd been some rather large withdrawals before they went missing but there was still money in her account and it was never touched afterwards. It was as though they dropped off the face of the earth.'

'But she had two boys,' Aaron said.

'I know. That was another reason her leaving of her own accord was discounted pretty quickly. It was only Matty, the youngest, who went missing at the same time as she did. Lucas was eighteen at the time they went and he was left at home. The police thought it was unlikely a mother would take one and leave one.'

'What happened to Lucas?' I asked.

Tara spun the mug around in her hands. 'He stayed with me for a couple of weeks initially, then as it dragged on and it didn't look like they were coming back in a hurry he decided he wanted to stay in the house and look after it in case they came home one day. He was working and took on the bills and mortgage payments without letting on to the bank that his mum had gone. Even if they figured out it was her in the news, what were they going to do, take her house while she was missing? Eventually he had to downsize to something smaller, he couldn't keep up the payments. He hated that he had to do it. If Sharon and Matty came back and went home he was afraid of what it would do to them. But he had no choice. A boy his age couldn't maintain that level of finance. I tried to help him for as long as I could but I was starting to get into debt to keep their home afloat. It was heart-wrenching when it was repossessed in her absence.' She trailed off, lost in memories of a time past.

'And where is Lucas now?' I asked. 'What did he do with himself during the eleven years his mother and brother were missing?'

Sorrow seeped from her pores. She shook her head. 'I didn't see much of him once he'd moved. He became isolated. Didn't want to see me. Didn't want reminding of family and what he'd lost. He built himself his own life I imagine. I have an address for him you can have.' She rose, looked around the room as though she was orienting herself. I couldn't imagine how she was feeling. I had done more than my fair share of death messages. Visits where I informed loved ones that family had passed and they would never see them again. It was always heart-breaking. A part of the job you never got used to. The emotion of the task burrowed deep into you and sucked another piece of your humanity out. This was something altogether different. We were here informing this woman that the boy she believed was dead was very much alive. It was new for all of us.

But no less emotional.

How did she wrap her head around the fact her nephew had returned from the dead?

Tara hadn't moved. She hovered on the spot, eyes unfocused, face streaked, hands shaking.

I stood and moved in front of her. 'What do you need, Tara? What can I do for you?' I touched her arm. She jumped and her focus was brought to me.

'I'm... I'm sorry. I was, his... Lucas, his, I was getting a piece of paper for his address.'

I held her hands in both of mine. 'It's okay.' I said, keeping my voice low. 'We have a notepad. You can give us the information and I'll write it down.' The facts we had given her were huge and she was struggling with it. Matt was back but we had no news on her sister. She was in a no man's land between elation and fear for her sister. But also hope. That if Matt had returned then so could Sharon.

Tara dropped back into the chair behind her. 'I need to see him. I need to know what happened to him, to his mother.'

I had no idea what the doctors would do in these circumstances. I couldn't make promises but neither could I imagine they'd withhold Matt from her. 'The doctors are very good and have his best interests at heart. Talk to them. Work with them. Having him back like this is amazing after all this time. He's scared though. He has no memory of where he's been or who he is. You have to take it slowly with him, Tara. Like I said earlier, I'll give you the doctor's details and you can go from there.'

She pulled her sleeve down and scrubbed at her cheeks.

I needed more information from her but it was proving difficult.

'Tell me about the last time you saw your sister, Tara.' I leant forward, elbows on knees. This was all in the original missing report, but eleven years later, a recounting might bring up details that were missed at the time.

I picked up the mug from the floor at the side of the chair Tara was sitting on and handed it to her. She needed something to do with her hands. Something to calm her so she could go back in time and bring up the information we were after. She took it and cupped both hands around it.

'I didn't know it was going to be the last day.' She looked up at me. 'You understand that?'

'Of course.' I moved back to my own seat.

'She came to the house and had Matty with her. She asked me if I could look after him for a couple of days. Said she wasn't feeling well and needed some time in bed to recover. I looked at her and she seemed fine. Told her so. Told her she wasn't fobbing Matty off on me. I was tired of my own life, I was all for helping her but not like this.'

Tears began to fall down her face again.

'If I'd have taken him she'd have gone on her own. He'd have been safe here with me. Him and Lucas. It's my fault Matty went.'

9

'What do you think?' I asked Aaron as we walked to the car.

'I think she's going to carry a lot of guilt with her. She has for a long time and whatever that boy has been through it's then going to weigh heavily on Tara.' He clicked the car open and we climbed in.

'Do you believe she had no idea what Sharon wanted to do while Tara had Matt?'

'We can only work on the facts, the evidence, and the investigation at the time didn't pull up anything suspicious on Tara.' We pulled away from the house.

Aaron was never going to tell me his gut feeling on a case, on a person. I don't know why I asked him.

'She seemed genuine enough,' I said. 'She was certainly emotional. I'm not sure you can fake that level of emotion. I couldn't.'

A silence played in the car as we moved through the streets. I thought through the interview we'd conducted. We were no further forward. 'We're going to have to look through the original missing person investigation and see if there are any lines of enquiry we can pick up on now.'

'You're hoping to find mum?'

'I'm hoping to find mum. Why not if Matt has returned?'

Lucas supposedly didn't want to be involved with his family, but he hadn't moved far away from his aunt and we were knocking on his door within ten minutes.

'I imagine he's at work if he doesn't answer,' said Aaron.

'Yeah, Tara didn't seem to know what he does or where he works. It would have been nice to know, but I suppose we can check with the Department of Work and Pensions.'

I rapped against the door again, louder this time.

Again there was no response.

I pulled a contact card out of my pocket and scribbled a short note on the back asking Lucas to contact me at his earliest opportunity then pushed it through the door.

'Next stop the hospital,' I said. 'See if we can jump-start Matt's memory.'

For the second time in a day we were walking the corridors of the QMC hospital to the room that held Matthew Harper.

Aaron and I entered his room to see him sitting up in bed, finishing his lunch.

'Is it as bad as they say?' I asked, as I pulled a chair up to the bed.

'I suppose it depends on how bad they say it is.' He shovelled the last piece of sandwich into his mouth and pushed the plate away.

I'd already checked with the hospital; he'd had no previous admissions under his birth name; whether he'd had any under a pseudonym was another matter we might never know.

'To be honest,' I said, 'it was bearable when I was in here. I think you're safe.'

He picked up the small ice cream tub and pulled off the lid.

'How's the leg?' Aaron asked.

'Still painful,' Matt said spooning a dollop of ice cream up to his mouth. 'But they have me on regular painkillers so it's not so bad. I can cope.'

'And your head?' I asked.

With his spoon still in his hand Matt rubbed at his temple with the heel of his hand. 'I have a dull headache, but they've said that's to be expected and they're keeping an eye on me.' He went back to his ice cream.

'Look,' I said, 'we have some news you might be interested in, but you have to tell us if it's too much and you want us to stop, okay?'

The spoon paused halfway to his mouth. 'This sounds serious. Do you know who I am?'

I looked to Aaron then back to Matt. 'As a matter of fact, we do know who you are. It's complicated though and will be emotional for you, so, like I said, if you need us to stop, let us know and we'll continue another time.'

Matt put the spoon down on the narrow table over the bed. 'I want to know everything.'

How to tell a young man he'd been missing, along with his mother, for the last eleven years? I supposed the only way was to say it straight.

'Okay,' I started. 'We know your name is Matthew Harper and you're nineteen years old.'

Matt silently mouthed the word Matthew then looked to Aaron then me and asked. 'Matthew?'

'Yes,' I answered. 'You're also called Matt or Matty. It depends on who you're talking to.'

'So that means I have family and friends.' It was a statement rather than a question.

'You do have family, Matt. I don't know about your friends. I'm hoping that might be something you could fill in as your memory starts to come back.'

'You want to know who my friends are?' His eyebrows furrowed.

'When you're ready.'

'You said you knew who I was, that I'm Matthew Harper.' His forehead was crinkled and his eyes were darting between me and Aaron.

'There are some missing details. The information we share with you today, we're hoping will prompt that memory of yours and fill in those details for us.'

He went quiet.

He picked up his spoon and started to eat the ice cream again. This was difficult for him and we hadn't even given him the hard truths yet. I worried about what we were doing to him. How fragile he was. His doctors had told us to go easy on him and, at any sign of distress, we were to stop. We were walking a fine line, needing information if he could provide it and also caring for his welfare. We waited him out as he ate.

'My family,' he said. 'Who are they? Why aren't they here?'

'Your aunt, Tara, is speaking with doctors to see if they'll allow her access. With the amnesia they want to make sure you're fit to see her and we're still trying to contact your brother to let him know.'

'And my parents?'

'Matt, this is where it gets complicated. Are you sure you're ready for some difficult news?'

'I want to know everything,' he said and put the tub and spoon back down. 'You can't imagine what it's like to live with no idea who you are, where you're from or what you've done with your life. Who loves you, who you love, if you're a success or a failure. If you love life or are trying to escape it. If memory loss is a good thing for you because life has been horrific or if it's hiding all the wonderful things. There's no way to know. I have no idea, no inkling. There's no sixth sense about this. It's a complete blank page. Emptiness. Nothingness. It just stretches out in front of you, this bland space. Whatever you have to tell me, it will take away that awful feeling of not knowing anything. Even if it's the smallest thing, it's a mark on my page. A mark I can look at, examine, and focus on and know I have a past and then know I can have a future.'

When he put it like that I had no choice but to go ahead. 'Your mother brought you up as a single parent since you were six months old.'

He blinked. This was all new to him.

'You have an older brother who is now twenty-nine.'

He blinked again.

'We have no idea where your mother is at this point in time, Matt.'

His mouth opened but nothing came out.

'You both went missing at the same time.'

His mouth closed. Like a goldfish.

The next sentence was the kicker.

'You both went missing together eleven years ago and no one has seen either of you since, until you ran in front of my car last night.'

His mouth opened. It closed. It opened again.

'How are you, Matt? Do you need me to fetch a doctor?'

He had been pale when we walked in but now he was the colour of putty. The palest grey. The whites of his eyes shone out. A sheen of tears glistened under the harsh strip light. Silence lay over the room like an oppressive weight.

'Matt?' I prompted.

His glassy eyes found me and he shook his head. 'Eleven years?' he whispered.

'I'm afraid so. You went missing with your mum when you were a young boy.'

'What happened to me?'

'We have no idea. We're hoping you could help us with that.'

Tears slipped from his eyes and tracked down his cheeks.

'Does anything come back to you?' I asked.

He shook his head. His hands went up to his face. His sleeves dropped away and down his arm and it was then I noticed it. I hadn't seen it before now. There was something on the inside of his right wrist.

I stood. 'Matt, what's that on your wrist?'

He narrowed his eyes. 'Where?' He held out his hands palms down.

I gently took hold of his right hand and turned it over. There on the inside of his wrist was a homemade tattoo in blue ink. A simple mark. Matthew Harper had a circle tattooed on the inside of his right wrist.

10

The first thing I did when we returned to the station was make myself a green tea. We'd been out for most of the day and yet there was no sense of having progressed anything. Tara had nothing new to offer that wasn't on the original missing person file. A file we needed to assess and go over ourselves. We hadn't been able to locate Lucas Harper. And Matt had needed to rest after our conversation. After our mind-bending disclosure. It hadn't jogged his memory but had upset him immensely. His doctors had insisted we leave and let Matt rest. He'd no idea where or when he'd got the tattoo of the circle on his wrist and didn't know what it represented. My hopes that providing him with information would trigger at least some small memory had been dashed. Yes, the doctors had warned me it didn't work that way. The mind was delicate and could not be manipulated that way.

With my mug of green tea in hand I walked to the incident room for a briefing. We needed to gather and assess what we had so far and decide where to go from here.

Aaron was already at his desk, head down, tapping away at his keyboard. He would be updating the system with our day's visits and their outcomes.

I moved to the front of the room and took a deep breath. I was desperate to get to the bottom of this case. It was my fault that Matthew Harper could no longer remember what had happened to him. If I hadn't have been distracted by the conversation with Zoe and my dad, my reflexes may have been faster and I may not have hit him as hard when he ran out in front of me. Plus, it was a case I remembered from when it first started eleven years ago. I was a young DC and was on the periphery of the investigation. It was a huge case, a mother and child going missing, and I'd been tasked with taking statements from some of the people who claimed to have seen them in various places. These never amounted to anything as far as I remembered. Eleven years though, it was a very long time to be missing and then to return. What had Matt been through? Was he scarred for life? Was that one of the reasons his memory wasn't coming back, it was protecting him from the bad things that had occurred in the eleven years he had been gone? He'd said as much himself today; he had no memory of if he had a good life or a bad one. I couldn't envisage a scenario where a child missing for eleven years had a good life. The blood that covered him told its own story and that was a story of someone else who needed our help and quickly, if the amount of blood was anything to go by.

We needed to figure this out.

The incident room was noisy. I brought it to order with a quiet cough that rippled through the room bringing silence in a wave. All faces turned to me. People stopped typing, writing, and hung up phone conversations. It was time to work this problem through.

'Thanks, everyone. I want to do a briefing to see where we are with this investigation and to make sure we're heading in the right direction.' I placed my tea on the desk I was perched on. 'As you're aware we've identified John Doe as Matthew Harper. The Matthew Harper who went missing with his mother eleven years ago. Aaron and I have been out to speak to his relatives to inform them and to see what information we could obtain from them. Tara, Matt's aunt, was overwhelmed by the news and couldn't provide much in the way of details from when Matt and her sister went missing. She stuck to the story she told eleven years ago that Sharon asked her to take care of Matt for her for a couple of days, so detectives at the time had a working assumption that Sharon Harper planned to walk away from her family. Tara didn't agree to take Matt which scuppered Sharon's plans and from there there's a fork in the road on what they thought might have happened. They assumed that Sharon had either decided to take Matt with her, or she had killed Matt and gone alone. There was no evidence to back up any of this other than she had made some serious withdrawals from her bank account in the run-up to the time she asked Tara to take Matt. We now know she didn't kill him. What we need to know is where she took him for all this time and where she is now. I want the hardcopy file of the original investigation in this office as soon as possible. It's one thing to read it from HOLMES but I'd prefer to see the originals of statements and pocket notebooks.'

HOLMES was a great piece of kit but I still liked to hold a piece of paper in my hand to read from. I seemed to assimilate the information better.

'I put in a request,' said Ross. 'It should be on its way over.'

'Great, thanks.' I picked up my tea and sipped. My throat was dry. 'We were unable to contact Matt's brother, Lucas. He wasn't at home so we left a message requesting he call as soon as he picks it up. He was only a young man when his mum and brother went missing, so this is going to be a huge shock to him. I don't want to tell him over the phone so, as soon as he rings we'll go out and see him. I'm not sure what he'll be able to tell us about that time eleven years ago. He might remember something his mum said, or something she did that was out of the ordinary. We'll have to wait and see on that one.' I looked around the room. 'Who's been dealing with the CCTV for the accident?'

Ross piped up again. 'I've been out and gathered the CCTV in the area and from the direction he ran from. I've viewed that first and I'm trying to trace a path backwards to see if I can figure out where he came from. I'm using shop cameras as well as street CCTV.'

'Good job.' I looked to Martin and Pasha.

Pasha smiled. 'We've been visiting the people who gave state-ments eleven years ago. A lot of people were involved so we're only at the tip of the iceberg, but we want to see if anyone wants to add to or amend their statements. The people we've spoken to so far are curious as to why we're bringing this up again now—'

'You didn't tell them.'

'Oh no. We said we were reviewing the case and checking to see if anything had been missed or if we could do anything further, a missing persons' case is never closed. This appeased most of them.'

'Most?'

Pasha looked down at her pocket notebook. 'Yeah, there was one guy, he grumbled that we don't have enough cops to police the streets and current crimes, never mind crimes from so long ago, so some-thing must have happened for us to be opening this can of worms.'

She tapped her pad with her pen. 'He wasn't the nicest of chaps.'

'Everyone likes to moan about something and he has a point. Quite astute really. Did you get anything from your interviews?' I looked at Martin, who was leaning back in his chair.

He shook his head. 'The majority of them said they'd given us what they knew at the time and could offer us nothing new. If anything, they said their memories had faded rather than clarified.'

Missing person cases were notoriously difficult. No one paid any attention to the world around them, or the people who played bit-parts in their lives. People came and went and unless you were directly engaging with someone, you were invisible. It was a sad state of affairs. The statistics for missing people each year were horrifying. They could disappear from their lives and not one person knew where they had gone. In some cases someone would know because there would be a body. A murder. A killer. A person walking the world free and clear because the rest of the world was too busy getting on with their lives to notice the small things around them.

'If anyone has time I'd like you to research circles.'

There were some confused faces.

'The meanings of circles. I'm not sure if there will be one,' I said.

'It's just Matt Harper has a home-made tattoo of a circle on the inside of his right wrist and he, as with everything else, has no memory of how he got it or what it means. Maybe we can help out with the latter part of that.'

11

By the time I left work that day we were no further forward and Lucas Harper hadn't made contact. I was confused by this. Maybe he had an aversion to the police. He didn't have a police record but we weren't everyone's favourite people. We would have to follow up tomorrow. There was no way we could allow Matt to be back and for his brother to not know. If Tara had managed to inform him then I was sure he would have made the call to see what information we could provide.

The apartment was cool. I was too tired to cook – which was a regular feeling, so I texted Evie and asked if she wanted to come round to share a bottle of wine and a takeaway. She replied that she would have loved to but she was already in a restaurant with Sam, could we do it another evening? I smiled at the message and told her we could and to enjoy her night.

Evie has been seeing Sam for a few months. She'd met him when they'd bumped cars at traffic lights. Before Sam, Evie had been relationship shy but he seemed to be changing that. She wasn't showing signs of being ready to bolt from him. On the contrary she was thrilled every time she knew she would be seeing him. I was pleased for her. She deserved some happiness in her life.

I was still too tired to make my own dinner so ordered a pizza and opened another bottle of red wine while I was waiting and went to change out of my suit.

Half an hour later I was sitting on the floor, open pizza box at my side and a half-filled wine glass on the other side. As far as I was concerned this was a pretty good way to spend an evening. I leaned my head back on the sofa as I chewed BBQ chicken pizza and closed my eyes. Before I'd left work I'd heard from the accident investigation department who said they'd cleared the scene from the other night and that I couldn't have avoided Matt Harper. I had not been driving recklessly. According to the measurement of skid marks on the road and a CCTV video they'd viewed.

No matter that I'd been cleared, I still felt responsible that he couldn't remember what had happened to him for the past eleven years. If I hadn't hit him, he might be able to tell us where he had been and whose blood covered his clothes. This was what concerned me the most. Someone had lost a huge amount of blood and was in dire need of medical attention. There had been no knife wound victims taken into the hospital in the last two days, no injuries that would warrant the blood loss. Whoever needed attention was still out there.

Waiting for us to find them.

I took another bite of pizza. Time was running out for the mystery person involved with Matt Harper.

I was in the office the next morning by six-thirty. My sleep had been disturbed. This case was niggling at my mind. It wasn't often that we had a case where the people involved were still alive, but because of the complexities of this one Kevin Baxter our DCI had decided to let us run with it. Plus we had no idea if we were dealing with a murder or not. We didn't even know if Matt Harper should be a suspect or a victim. We needed more information and we needed it quickly.

It wasn't long before the incident room started to fill up. It appeared that everyone else had a similar idea.

At eight-thirty my mobile rang.

'DI Robbins, it's Lucas Harper, I have a note through my door requesting that I contact you. I'm sorry, I don't know what this is about.'

I was in the incident room and it was too noisy so I stepped outside into the corridor. 'Thanks for calling. I don't want to go over it on the phone. Is it possible I could come by and see you this morning?'

There was silence.

'I can promise you're not in any trouble,' I reassured him.

'Okay,' he said.

Half an hour later Aaron and I were standing on the doorstep of Lucas Harper's home again.

'He didn't push you to find out why we wanted to see him?' asked Aaron as we waited for the door to open.

'No. He was quiet and reticent, but the fact we're standing here is—'

The door opened and a man with broad shoulders and thick arms stood in front of us. It looked as though he worked out. I studied him to see any resemblance to Matt but this man was older, more weathered, whereas Matt was young, fresh-faced still. Though most of the time he just looked terrified.

'Lucas?'

'Yes.'

'DI Hannah Robbins and this is my DS, Aaron Stone.' I held out my hand and Lucas took it. His muscles rippled under his sweater as he shook my hand and then Aaron's.

'Come in won't you.' He stepped aside and we entered his home and walked into the living room behind him. It was clean, but sparse. There was a couple of sofas and a television and nothing else. No photographs on the wall, no tables, no signs of a computer or other personal knick-knacks.

Lucas waved to one of the sofas for us to sit. We did. He stayed standing. Over us. I waited. Silent. He pushed his hands in his pockets.

'What is it you wanted to see me about?' he asked.

'Would you like to sit?' I asked. I hated the unevenness of the conversational setting.

Lucas stared at me some more then sank down onto the other sofa never taking his eyes from mine. He wasn't combative as such, but he was staking his authority in his own home. He didn't like that we were here when he didn't know what this was about.

'Lucas, have you heard from your Aunt Tara at all over the last twenty-four hours?'

His eyebrows raised. 'No. Should I have?'

I shook my head. 'It was a possibility. I didn't know how close the two of you were.' I was getting the answer to that question now.

'What's going on?' he asked again.

'Two days ago a young man ran in front of a car.' I was repeating the same story. I cut it down. 'A bump on the head meant he had no memory of who he is or what had happened.'

Lucas shrugged. His mind not even starting to make a connection. It had been that long.

'A DNA test confirmed him as being your brother Matthew Harper.'

Lucas jumped out of his seat. 'I don't believe you.' He took a step backwards. 'Matty is dead.'

I shook my head again. 'No, Lucas. He's not. I can promise you that. DNA doesn't lie. He's alive and he's in the QMC being treated for a broken leg and his amnesia.'

Both his hands went up to his head and he scrubbed them through his hair leaving strands standing to attention at varying angles. 'Matty?'

'We need to ask you some questions, Lucas,' Aaron said at the side of me.

'What about? I don't know where he's been, what he's been doing.' His hands had slipped down to his face now and he was rubbing away at his cheeks as though he could maybe rub meaning into the situation. His world was no longer making sense.

'We know that,' I said. 'What we want is to go over the time Matty and your mum went missing again.'

His hands dropped to his side. 'You said Matty...'

'I'm sorry,' I said. 'We don't know where your mum is and, as I said, Matty doesn't know anything. The doctors said his memory should hopefully come back but it could take time.'

He dropped back onto the sofa with a soft thunk and let out a deep sigh. 'What do you want to know?'

'What do you remember about the day your mum and Matty went missing?'

'Nothing much out of the ordinary. I got up for work. Mum was already up. She was making Matty's lunch for school. She asked if I could finish early to have Matty when he finished school. I told her I couldn't. It was a new job. I didn't know the people well enough to start asking for stuff like that yet. She sighed and accepted it. I went to work. When I got home the house was empty. They never came home. I think Tara reported them missing. I was eighteen. She was my mum, I presumed Matty was with her and they were fine. I still thought that for the first week. I thought she'd taken him off for a week's skive off school. She could be a little rash like that sometimes. Didn't like to play by the rules, Mum. Hated all the *have to* do this, *have to* do that stuff. You know, the way society expects certain things of you. Expects you to behave in certain ways and bring up your children in specific ways. She was a bit of a rebel. It wasn't until the second week I began to worry that something had actually happened to them. Tara was great of course. Didn't let me fester on my own but eventually I had to stand on my own two feet. I was an adult and I had to behave like an adult. A bit like my mum had taught me to. Of course there was all the publicity I had to try to avoid and live my life away from it. The press were interested in me for a while. The boy who had been left behind. But as I showed little interest in interacting with them they soon started to leave me alone. And I've been that way ever since.'

Lucas had been looking at the floor but lifted his head and looked from Aaron to me and back to Aaron.

'You never heard from either of them?' asked Aaron.

'Not once. Like I said earlier, I presumed they were dead. It was kind of easier that way than continuing to think they were going to walk through my door one day. That way lies craziness, let me tell you.' He barked out a laugh. 'And yet here you are.' He waved a hand around the room. 'Matty is back from the dead.'

His eyes glistened. 'He'll be how old now?'

'He's nineteen,' I said.

'A year older than me when he went. He's a grown man now, not the little guy I remember.' He looked off into the corner of the room.

'You never got any ransom demands or proof of life from anyone at a later date that you might have failed to tell us about at the time because you were told not to?' Aaron pushed.

Lucas shook his head. 'Honestly, I saw Mum that morning and that was it.' He looked to me. 'You say he's been in an accident. Is he okay?'

'He's broken his leg and has memory problems but other than that he's doing fine,' I said.

Lucas puffed air between his lips. 'I can see him?'

'I think so. You need to speak to the doctors at the hospital. I'll give you their contact details. Your aunt also has the details. We saw her yesterday.'

'I don't see much of Tara. Not since all this happened.'

I didn't know what to say. Families were difficult. I could see how a tragedy could divide a family this way. Maybe Matt returning would allow some changes to be made.

I stood and Aaron followed suit. 'If you remember anything else about the time they went missing, no matter how small, please do get in touch.'

'You've no idea how many times I've run through that day in my mind over the years. Nothing has changed in what I said at the time. Nothing is going to change just because he's back. He's going to be the one who can help you, not me.'

I moved towards the door. 'You have my card anyway. We want to get to the bottom of this and now Matt is back we're renewing the investigation in an attempt to locate your mum. I'm sure you'd like to see her again.'

'Of course. She's my mum. But if you couldn't do anything first time around then I don't see how you expect me to believe you'll do anything different second time around.'

It was a dig at the police investigation and one he was entitled to. I was pushing him and he was feeling helpless. 'Thank you for your time, Lucas. We'll keep in touch to let you know how things are going.'

The door closed behind us with a slam.

12

Matthew Harper lay on his bed staring up at the cracked white ceiling, the sounds of the ward beyond seeping through his open doorway. He had a name now. Matthew Harper. It wasn't a name he recognised. There was nothing familiar about the sound of it. He spoke it aloud. The way it rolled over his tongue was not familiar. He shortened it to Matt and still he didn't recognise himself. It felt alien and random. Not a part of him. Matthew Harper was another person. Had to be. It just didn't fit him.

The disjointed feeling itched at him. It clawed at the base of his brain. He hated the not-knowing and, even worse, being given information that felt false. Were they testing him? Was that it? Had they given him a false name so he could tell them his real name? If they had, it wasn't working. It only served to confuse him more.

There was a knock at his door and one of his doctors walked in. He couldn't remember her name either but not because she didn't exist, because she clearly did, but because he had seen so many people over the last couple of days. Her dark hair was tied in a pony-tail at the back of her head and it swung as she moved. It made her look younger than she probably was.

'Matt,' she said as she walked over to his bed and he wanted to scream at her that it wasn't his name. They'd told him they had DNA evidence that he was Matt Harper. But he couldn't help but feel they were messing with him. 'I have someone here to see you. I'll only allow this to be a short visit, but it's an important one.' The grin on her face was huge. She was pleased with herself. Matt was still annoyed with her for using the name he hated.

'Your Aunt Tara is here. She's missed you for the last eleven years. You've obviously changed a lot in that time and I'm presuming she will have changed too, but she's desperate to see you. How do you feel about a visit?'

He shook his head. He had family. This whole situation was surreal. Seeing this woman might help. It might knock some memories loose. He might even remember his actual name. 'Yeah, yeah, of course.'

She patted his arm. 'Great. Remember, this is going to be taken at your pace. When you've had enough just say so and Tara will leave.' She moved back towards the door, leaned around the frame and talked quietly to someone. A woman appeared in the doorway.

She was average in every possible way. Average height, average weight, average hair, average face. Her hands were clasped together in front of her. She was biting her bottom lip and her eyes were damp. She had zeroed in on Matt and was standing stock still in the doorway. 'Matty,' she whispered.

'Come on in, Tara,' said the doctor.

Tara took a couple of steps further forward. 'Matty,' she whispered again, staring at him. 'Is it really you?' She reached a hand out towards him and Matt wanted to recoil. He didn't know this woman. He was not property.

She must have seen the expression on his face because she dropped her arm. 'I'm sorry.' She looked horrified and stopped where she was. 'I can't believe you're here again. It's been so long. You were only so high,' she placed her hand at waist height, 'when I last saw you and look at you now. You're a fully grown man. Oh Matty. What has happened?'

He shook his head and continued to shake it. It was one thing to not connect with your name but this was another thing entirely. To have a woman in front of him telling you she was related and she remembered him as a child. Reminding him that he had a huge swathe of his life that he didn't remember. She could be anyone. If they were lying about his name what else would they lie about? They could just as easily lie about this woman. She could be anyone. She could be a nurse from a different ward asked to do this to help him remember.

He couldn't do this.

He shook his head more violently.

The doctor peered at him. 'Matt?'

He continued to shake.

The doctor looked at Tara. 'I think this is a bit much for him. We might have to leave it for another time, I'm afraid.'

The woman called Tara looked from Matt to the doctor and opened her mouth. She took a step closer to Matt. He slid up his pillows.

The doctor took the woman's arm and started to guide her towards the open door. 'I'm sorry, it's not what you wanted but it looks as though it's too much for him. We need to do this in his own time.'

Tara turned back to him. 'Matty?' It was louder this time.

Matt clamped his mouth shut. He didn't know the woman and he didn't recognise the sound that came out of her mouth.

Tears started to slide down Tara's face as she pulled against the doctor's guiding arm and back towards Matt. 'I know it's been a long time. Just let me sit with you. I won't talk if you don't want me to. I'll sit quietly. I need to be near you, know you're okay and safe. Matty, I thought you were dead. Please.' The last word was back to a whisper.

He was an adult now, he knew this and yet he was covering his ears with his hands. The whole bizarre situation was smothering him and he wanted to hide from it. The doctor was firm and marched the woman out of the room, closing the door behind them, leaving blessed silence in their wake.

Matt removed his hands from his ears and breathed out. She had thought him dead. If she was real and she did know him she had thought him dead. No wonder she was upset. But that alone was too much to bear. To be the returning child from the dead. How much pressure did that lay at his feet? What would be expected of him? He couldn't give her any answers. He couldn't tell her where he had been all this time. He couldn't tell her he remembered her from before because he hadn't.

He dug back into the deep tunnels of his mind to search for any memories that he might hold at all and he couldn't find anything. The last thing he remembered was running in front of the car that hit him and before that everything was gone. All of it.

Voices rose from behind the closed door. One voice, upset and anxious, and then soothing tones, quieter and muted.

Matt would have to see her next time. See if she could give him some answers. Tell him about his life before he disappeared. Now he knew about her he could prepare for her visit and not show her how unsettled he was by it all. He needed answers and maybe this Tara could provide them.

13

The incident room was humming with the sound of working officers and staff when we returned from seeing Lucas. There were empty mugs on desks and signs that a few had stopped for lunch as plastic tubs and crisp packets were balanced on the corner of desks, having not yet made their way to bins. They reminded me I was hungry. There was a salad in the fridge that I'd brought from home but I didn't have time to stop and eat it yet. We had plenty of work to be getting on with.

'Okay.' I clapped my hands together to draw the team's attention. Heads popped up. 'Do we have the paper file of the original missing person report yet?'

Martin pointed at a couple of boxes on the floor beside him. 'Yes, arrived about thirty minutes after you left.'

'Anything of interest in it?' I'd studied the electronic version but was interested if there was anything different in the paper copies.

'A couple of people said Sharon had started to behave strangely prior to their going missing.'

'Strange how?'

'It was vague. She was a single mum for a lot of years and had found it hard going, wanted to find some meaning in life, something more to it than scrubbing and cleaning and feeding. Sounds to me like she was depressed.'

I considered what this meant to the investigation. 'We need to go back to those people again and clarify what they said and try to get more detail from them. She obviously didn't take them both off to kill them – it wasn't that kind of depression, so what did she take them off to do? And how did she manage to stay off the grid?' It was something people rarely achieved in today's world. 'Has anyone looked at the meaning of circles yet?'

Pasha waved a quick hand in the air before dropping it. This was not a classroom; she just wanted my attention. 'What is it, Pasha?'

'The circle is a huge area of symbolism. It can mean different things, depending on who you're talking to and how their culture has adapted it.'

'Give me some examples then.'

Pasha looked down at her notebook. 'In Zen Buddhist philosophy, the circle stands for enlightenment and perfection. In Chinese symbology, it represents the heavens. Circles are also seen as protective. For instance, in occult practices you stand inside a circle and nothing outside that circle can harm you. It can represent God, the self, eternity, totality, wholeness and the rhythm of the universe. It's a defence against chaos. I could probably find a lot more relating to the circle but that's what I've got so far.'

'There's a lot of possible reasons for having a tattoo,' said Ross.

'It kind of marries up with what Martin was saying about Sharon wanting something other than the life she had,' Pasha countered. 'Maybe she found it and took Matt along for the ride.'

'We need to find Sharon,' I said. 'If Matt is alive then there's a good chance that Sharon is too.'

'And what happens to her, boss?' asked Ross.

It was a good question. 'I don't know,' I admitted. 'It depends on what she has to say, where they've both been this past eleven years. She had a young child she was responsible for and, as far as the state is concerned, Matt Harper didn't have an education or access to medical care. He didn't have his vaccinations. I know there's the new HPV one for teenage boys now. Whether she would have said yes or no to them, they would have had to have been offered but because no one knew where they were that wouldn't have happened.'

'So we're working on the assumption that Sharon took Matt away, rather than they were both taken by an unknown person?' asked Martin.

'Again, it's something I don't know. It's possible she took him willingly. It may be they were taken against their will and Matt has escaped. We won't know more until Matt gets his memory back or until we find Sharon. Until then we don't work on assumptions, we work on the evidence we have and we keep an open mind. But we need to work quickly to locate where Matt was kept because someone is bleeding heavily there.'

This fact looped through my mind. 'Has the DNA come back on the clothing yet?'

'Not yet but we're expecting it any time soon,' said Martin.

'Okay. Anything else come up while I've been out?'

'Yes,' said Ross. 'I was checking the CCTV from you running - I mean from Matt running in front of your car.'

There was muffled laughter as Ross had come close to saying I'd run Matt over. I wouldn't have objected to the slip. I did feel awful for what had happened.

'I followed the cameras the direction he had come from and found he abandoned a vehicle, the next street over. It looked like he had been driven off the road. The car was front-ended into a lamp post. It may be he was already dazed and incoherent before he even fell in front of your car, boss.'

'What about the car that drove him off the road?' I asked.

'It waited a minute and when Matt got out and started running the driver of the following Astra started to run after him but Matt was legging it. The Astra driver couldn't keep up. He stopped, changed direction, returned to his vehicle and left the scene. Seemed he didn't want to be found there. You might have injured Matt but it looks like you saved him from a world of trouble.'

'Do we have a licence plate for the car doing the chasing?'

Ross looked miserable. 'No. The plate was covered with dirt. The number wasn't distinguishable. Maybe deliberately obscured or perhaps just filthy.'

I rolled my eyes. It wasn't a great help to us. 'So Matt's covered in blood and yet he's the one being chased.'

'Maybe they're friends of the person Matt had hurt?' offered Pasha.

'Maybe,' I conceded. I turned to Ross. 'Is Matt's car still there?'

'A police aware sticker has been placed on it as far as I can gather but other than that it's still in place. It hasn't been recovered yet.'

'Good. Let's get the Crime Scene Unit out to it please. Bearing in mind we have no idea what offence we're looking at we treat the car like a potential crime scene. Also ask uniform to go and guard the scene. Email me the location, Ross, and I'll head out there as well and have a look.'

His fingers flew over the keyboard as he did as was requested. 'Done. You think there's maybe a body in the boot? It all seems a little weird if you ask me. He's covered in someone's blood and he's running from something.'

'I suppose it's an angle we'll have to consider.' I wrapped up the briefing and walked to my office. On the way I grabbed my salad out of the kitchen and ate a few mouthfuls.

Aaron entered as I shovelled another forkful in. 'Care for company to check out the vehicle?'

'Sounds like a plan. I could use someone to bounce ideas off. This is a strange case, Aaron.'

'Just work it as you would any other case. I know you feel personally involved because of how it started but you didn't do anything wrong, Hannah. He ran in front of you and from what Ross said, he was having problems before you collided with him anyway. You were just the icing on the cake of his day.'

'You're right. Emotionally, it doesn't connect as well. I feel responsible for him now.'

Aaron pushed his hands in his pockets. 'Well, let's go and see if we can get a step closer to resolving this then because you won't settle until we do.'

14

There was a light drizzle in the air as we pulled up on Station Street behind the car that was abandoned on the pavement. It was the kind of rain that soaked you through without you realising it. I fastened my coat before I got out of the car and pulled an elastic bobble out of my pocket tying my hair back out of the way.

'Someone left in a rush,' Aaron said at the side of me.

The old Ford Mondeo was front-end crushed up against the lamp post but miraculously there was very little damage to the post. I'd seen some snap in half when hit by a car but this one can't have been hit at speed because all that had happened was a slight dent in it where the car had impacted. It would need replacing once the vehicle had been removed. The council were never happy when this happened and we didn't know who was responsible. Even though we knew Matt was the culprit this time, he didn't have a life or job where he could be billed for the damaged post.

According to the incident log the attending uniformed officers had created, the registered keeper of the vehicle was unknown. The last logged owner had informed the officers he had sold the vehicle six months previously. He provided us with the details and we'd follow up on it but I didn't hold out much hope of it going anywhere.

'Shame we don't have a clear CCTV image of them as they left the car but that camera isn't ideal on the junction with London Road. We were lucky to get as much as we did. We seem to be coming up against a lot of dead ends in this case.'

Aaron opened his door to the damp outside. 'It was dark and he knew what he was doing with the baseball cap. Maybe the vehicle itself will help us though.'

I followed him out of the car, a shiver running through my body as the sheen of rain hit me. I wiped my face with my hand. I'd be glad when April and its showers were over and the better weather started. Not that we could count on British spring to bring brighter times.

We walked over to the car and I pulled a pair of gloves out my pocket and snapped them on. Aaron did the same. I peered into the front passenger side window. 'Keeps it tidy.'

Aaron was around the other side, looking in the back. 'Nothing I can see in the back either.'

'We have to hope there's something in the boot, or something we can't see that CSU can recover that will further this investigation.' As I finished the sentence a crime scene van pulled up behind our car. 'And talk of the devil.'

Aaron straightened to see who had turned up.

The driver's door opened and Aditi popped out.

'Hey,' I greeted at her. 'Do you ever have a day off?'

'I could say the same to you.' She walked around to the rear of the van and came back carrying a big black case. 'How you doing after the other night?' Her eyes ran over me, checking me out.

'It wasn't me who was injured, Aditi.'

'No, but it's not a pleasant experience either.'

I hunched my shoulders in an attempt to stop the rain running down the inside of my coat. 'I'm okay. Thank you.' I wasn't going to talk to Aditi about the nightmares, the images that flashed before my eyes.

She took the message loud and clear. 'So, what do we have here then?'

'Matt Harper, the young man I hit, was being pursued which is why he ran in front of me. First of all he was being chased by car. This is the one he was driving. We're wondering if there's any evidence in the vehicle concerning where he's been or where the blood may have come from. We need to get it open as soon as possible.'

She widened her eyes. 'We can either recover the vehicle to the garage and open the boot there or, if you're concerned someone may be alive in the boot, we can open it right now to make sure... save life and limb and all that.'

'We want the boot open now. I'm not risking the possibility someone is bleeding or freezing to death in there and we waited.'

Aditi patted the boot lid with her gloved hand. 'I'll arrange recovery of the vehicle, no matter what we find in here.'

She walked back to her van and returned with a long metal stick with a bend and a loop at the end. I looked around. There was a little traffic and no one was paying attention to what we were doing.

Aditi bent over the boot of the car and set to work. She pushed the stick in and jiggled and focused. Her teeth gripped her bottom lip as she listened. Eventually she gave the rod a quick tug and the boot lid popped. Aaron and I stepped closer. I inhaled sharply, not knowing what we were about to find. Was the reason for all the blood on Matt Harper inside this car? Were we about to arrest him for murder?

Aditi lifted the lid of the boot and the three of us peered inside.

There was no body.

The next stop was the previous registered keeper of the Mondeo. Aaron was driving. Aditi was organising recovery of the car. It would be forensically examined back at the garage.

I took the elastic out my hair and ran my hands through the tangled mess. The rain had done me no favours. It was knotty and unruly. I left it loose in the car so it could dry off. I pushed the blue gloves into the side of the door, making a mental note to put them in a bin later. As the department DI, I was responsible for making sure the pool cars were kept clean and roadworthy. I couldn't take my team to task for untidy cars if I was one of the culprits for leaving rubbish in them.

'I really thought we might find a body in that car,' I said to Aaron. 'The way Matt was trying to escape from the other car and was fleeing that frantically he ran in front of me. Something bad had been going on and my mind went to a body being in the boot.'

'You weren't alone. I had my suspicions but I don't pin my hopes on things the same way you do.'

'No, you're right there. I was definitely amped up that we'd find someone.'

'Disappointed?' Aaron asked without taking his eyes off the road.

I considered his question. Was I? I enjoyed the start of a new murder investigation but it didn't mean I wanted people to die so I could work. 'I don't think so. I don't want someone to be dead. It's possible that whoever that blood belonged to is still alive.'

'The longer it takes to identify them the less likely it is that we're going to find them alive though,' he said.

'You're right. We need to know what happened and as Matt isn't telling us, or can't tell us, we need to find out our own way.'

Aaron pulled up outside Dean Burton's address. It was a narrow terrace on Catmanhay Road, Ilkeston, that looked little cared for. All the curtains were closed. The wheelie bin was in front of the door which opened straight onto the pavement. I tied my hair back again and climbed out of the car then looked up at the first floor. 'In bed or not at home?' I asked.

Aaron rapped on the door. 'Maybe he doesn't like visitors.'

The drizzle had stopped and the remaining chill seeped into my bones. I was ready for a warm cup of tea and some decent food inside me. The salad hadn't done anything to help my hunger. Who was I kidding in trying to eat healthily? I hated it. I preferred proper food I could taste and that filled my stomach.

Aaron knocked on the door again.

There was a mumbled, 'Who is it?' from behind the door.

'Police, Mr Burton. Can you open up please, we need a word,' Aaron shouted loud enough for the street to hear. It usually did the trick as no one wanted their neighbours to know their business. The letter box flicked open and a couple of fingers poked out, along with an overriding stench of overripe feet and a kitchen bin that hadn't been emptied in months.

'Let's see some ID,' a disembodied voice said behind the fingers.

I rolled my eyes at Aaron then held my warrant card up to the narrow opening in the door. 'DI Hannah Robbins and DS Aaron Stone. Can you open the door please, Mr Burton, or would you like us to conduct our business through your letter box?'

There was another mumble and this time I couldn't make it out, but we heard the metallic scrape of a keychain being pulled back and then the twist of a key in a lock. The door opened. Darkness greeted us. It was lighter on the street than it was in this man's house. And the fumes that escaped with the opening of the door were factory strength. I took a step back, composed myself ready for what I was about to encounter, pulled back my shoulders and entered the dark hole that was the home of Dean Burton.

Aaron followed behind me. Once we were both inside, Burton closed the door behind us and the gloom enveloped us. I could barely see my hand in front of my face.

'Do you mind if we have a light on, or open the curtains?' I asked. 'It's a little dark in here.'

Again Burton mumbled but shuffled towards the other door in the room where there was a light-switch and soon a dim glow lit up the centre of the room we were standing in. The floor was littered with takeaway boxes and cartons and empty cans of beer and cider. Ashtrays overflowed on the arms of a couple of sofas and newspapers were piled nearly waist high at the side of the television. I nearly jumped as I saw movement out of the corner of my eye but it morphed into a cat and I watched as it slinked past me and out of the room. Heavens knew where its litter tray was.

'Mr Burton, I know some uniformed officers have been to ask you about the Ford Mondeo you used to own, but we need to ask you some follow up questions if that's okay?' I said.

Burton scratched at his groin then sniffed his fingers. 'I told them everything. I sold that car six months ago. I filled in my paperwork. I done nothing wrong.'

'We know that, but the vehicle has been involved in an accident and we want to know what you remember about the person who bought it from you.'

Burton shoved his hand down his jogging bottoms and scratched again. I winced but kept my face straight. I wouldn't be shaking his hand when we left.

'It was a long time ago, you know.'

'I understand that, but whatever you can remember will be helpful.'

'What they done?' he asked narrowing his eyes at me. 'Is it bad?'

'Like I said, it would be helpful if you could remember what they looked like. Did they give you their name?'

He shook his head. 'Can't remember nowt like that. He was a young man, dark hair, well-built.'

'Any scars, tattoos, piercings? Any identifying marks of any kind?'

Again he shook his head. Something flew off as he moved and I shuddered again. I couldn't wait to get out of here. I felt as though I needed a bleach bath.

'What about the way he spoke?'

'Like I said, there was nothing about him that stood out. Look, I'm sorry I can't help you further. If I'd known police were gunna knock at my door six months later I'd have taken a photo of the guy.'

We thanked him and left the house. As soon as the door opened and I stepped outside I heaved in a huge gulp of air.

'Oh my God.' I didn't need to say anything else. Aaron was breathing deeply as well. I wanted to strip off my coat and spin in the coolness of the damp air.

'Well, that description covers half the male population of Notts,' I said as we climbed back into the car.

'I don't think it describes Matt though, do you? He's not exactly well-built. So, he was driving the car but someone else bought it. It's a step forward, though only a slight one.'

'You're not kidding. Let's hope CSU find evidence in the seized vehicle because we're running out of lines of enquiry.'

15

I finally managed to get Evie to myself for an evening. I was exhausted so instead of going out she came to me.

'Pizza and red wine?' I perched on the arm of the sofa ready to pour drinks and arrange food.

'You're not cooking for me?' She grinned up at me.

I rose and strode towards the kitchen where I grabbed a couple of glasses out the cupboard. 'I would but it'd take too long and I know how impatient you are.' I poured red wine into the glasses and carried them back into the living room.

Evie took one and drank. 'Thanks, sweetie. How's things in your world?'

I hadn't told her about Zoe yet. I let out a deep sigh.

'You still feeling bad about that accident?'

'Shall we order the food and we'll talk about it?' I suggested.

'You know what I like.'

I tapped out the order on my phone and dropped into the seat beside Evie. Her auburn curls were loose around her face this evening. She wore a pair of black leggings and a sweater and she looked fabulous. Her face was scrubbed clean of make-up but she was glowing; dating suited her.

'I want to know more about your love life,' I said.

Her face lit up, her eyes sparkling. 'There's nothing to tell. We're still taking it steady and seeing where it goes.'

'I've never seen you last this long with a guy, Evie. You look blissed out. I'm so happy for you.' Usually, Evie dropped a guy the minute it looked like it might get serious. She reared away from real relationships. This was different.

'Like I said, we're seeing where it goes. No pressure. And it feels good so we keep doing it.'

'I bet you do.'

She laughed and slapped me on the arm. 'Get your mind out of the gutter, but...' She winked.

It was my turn to laugh.

'It's always nice to hear you laugh, Hannah. You don't do it enough.'

'I'm always at work,' I reminded her.

'You work too hard. You need time for yourself. You haven't dated anyone since Ethan.'

I shrugged. 'I haven't had the time.'

'My point exactly. And how are things with the family?'

While I was telling her about Zoe and my dad the pizza arrived. It was a good distraction from the look Evie was giving me. I brought the box to the sofa and sat back down.

'What are you going to do?' she asked.

'I haven't had a lot of time to think about it with work being so busy.'

'Hannah, this is your family. You know the saying that when you die you're never going to have written on your headstone, *didn't spend enough time at work*. That applies to you as well. Work goes on twenty-four seven. Your family, they are finite. As Zoe has told you. You need to address it and not put it off. Spend time with them, talk to them. Especially if it helps you make this decision.'

I rolled my eyes, I couldn't help it.

'Don't do that.'

'I'm sorry, you're right. I do need to think about it more. I'm so conflicted where Zoe is concerned though.'

'The real question is, do you want to lose her? In a total sense?'

I took a gulp of my wine. Evie stayed silent and shovelled pizza into her mouth, letting me mull over what she had said.

It was eleven by the time Evie left. Later than either of us had initially intended as I wanted an early start again. Time slipped past us when we were together.

I lay in bed and looked at the ceiling, aware of how alone I was. Evie would be tucked up in bed and whispering sweet nothings on the phone to Sam, no doubt. How long had it been since Ethan and I split up? It had to be about eighteen months. Not long after my injury. I pushed him away at the time I needed him most. There had been no one since. Instead I used work to fill my life. I had my friendship with Evie, that was true, but even that was shifting now she was settling into a relationship with Sam. She was doing her best to make sure she still had time for me, I could see her doing it and I loved her all the more for doing so. But I was a big girl and this was my own life. I needed to live it myself.

Could I live with myself if I allowed Zoe to die? Was my anger with her that big and out of control? She was my sister, family. Deep down, there had to be love for her.

I rolled over onto my side and curled into the quilt, wondering how Matthew Harper's family were going to cope with his return after eleven years missing, believed dead.

16

I rubbed my eyes. They were gritty and tired already and I'd only been in the office forty-five minutes. The original missing person file was on my desk and I was trying to read my way through it. The previous team had done a comprehensive job once they realised the mum was missing and hadn't just decided to take her youngest son for a day out and was late returning.

The case had been high profile at the time, with lots of media attention. Mother and child both missing together. No signs of foul play. Just disappeared into thin air. A massive team was assembled in an attempt to locate the missing pair. To no avail. They hadn't been seen on train platforms and though the mum had a passport the youngest boy, Matthew, didn't have one. Their images had been aired on every television channel and yet no one reported having seen them. There were a couple of supposed sightings but they were always followed through and found to be a different mother and child. The public were engrossed in the story and we'd fielded calls day and night and yet nothing of substance came in.

Sharon had left her mobile phone at home and the team had examined it. They weren't as technical as we were nowadays, but they had accessed the call log and text messages and accounted for everyone she made contact with. No one knew where she had gone or had any idea she had plans to leave.

There was a knock on my door and Aaron walked in. 'See anything?' he asked, inclining his head towards the file.

I shuffled the papers around – as much as I could. There wasn't a lot of room on my desk due to the other paperwork balancing on there. I pulled a statement out of the pile. 'I'm interested in this one.'

Aaron dropped into the chair in front of my desk. He looked over the piles of paper at what I was holding in my hand.

'Andrea Mayfield, a friend of Sharon's.' I waved the statement. 'I'd like to speak to her and go over her statement again.'

'What does she have to say?'

'She talked about the changes in Sharon before she went missing. The way she felt there was more to be had out of her life. I want to know how she expressed this. What she felt she could do to get more out of her life. It's like the team acknowledged that she was unsettled but didn't dig deeper. They'd uncovered a potential reason for her to go but didn't ask Andrea what kind of life changes she was interested in.'

Aaron's hands went up to his tie and he fiddled with the knot making sure it was straight. Why was he worried?

'What is it?'

'You think we failed?'

'It was a divisional officer who took the statement. They will have considered what they had was enough to say Sharon had left of her own accord rather than anything nefarious happening. They probably didn't expect it to go on as long as it did.'

'I'll make a call and see if she can come in this morning.'

'Thanks, Aaron. I'd like to talk to her myself if that's okay?'

'You're sure? I can get Martin to do it.'

'I ran this boy over. The least I can do is try to get to the bottom of what happened to him. I feel...' I dropped the statement paper back on the desk and shook my hands in front of me. '...Edgy. Like I've too much energy running through me and I need to release it.'

Aaron rose from his chair. 'I'll get on it.' He walked out the office quietly closing the door behind him.

Two and a half hours later and Andrea Mayfield was sitting opposite me in a witness interview room. She was a tiny woman, only about five foot tall. She looked anxious. I offered her a drink but she told me she'd finished one at home and was fine thank you very much. Her manners were polished.

'Thank you for coming in so quickly this morning,' I said as I leaned back in my chair in an attempt to make the meeting look relaxed. 'I appreciate you may have had plans for the day that we've disrupted.'

She shrugged. 'I phoned in work and told them I had to come here and I'd be late. The officer who phoned said it was important.'

I made a mental note to thank Aaron later. It was often difficult to get hold of people on a weekday because of work. When people like Andrea organised themselves for us this way it was really helpful. 'You're not in any trouble, I can assure you of that.' She was clutching her handbag to her chest as though it was a barrier.

'Okay.' Her voice was quiet, I wasn't sure she believed me.

'You remember eleven years ago you provided a statement in relation to Sharon Harper, a friend of yours?'

Her eyes widened.

'I want to go through it again with you.' I crossed one leg over the other.

'What's happened?'

We hadn't released the information that Matt had returned. We were giving him some peace while he healed in the hospital. He would be inundated once the news broke. I didn't want the information to leak before we were ready.

'We're going over the file to see if there's anything we missed. We do it occasionally.'

She released the grip on the handbag a little, the white lie ringing true to her ears.

'You're happy to go over it?' I said.

'Yes. Of course. Anything to help, though I doubt I can add

anything to what I said at the time. Or if I can even remember what I said when I made the statement.'

I pulled the paper on the table closer to me. 'That's fine, we have your statement here. I'm not trying to trip you up. We'll go through it and I'll try to dig a little deeper if I see somewhere that might be possible. After all this time a fresh pair of eyes – mine – might be able to see something that was missed before and it might even lead to locating Sharon.'

A weak smile flitted across her face. 'She used to be my best friend.'

'Yet she never told you she was planning to leave?'

Andrea shook her head. 'Not a word. Yeah, I knew she wasn't happy, that she was unsettled but I didn't think anything of it. Don't we all dream of a better life? Doesn't mean we up and leave the one we have, does it?' A sheen of tears misted her eyes. She still missed her friend. Or regretted that she hadn't been able to stop what had happened?

'Tell me about Sharon's unhappiness, Andrea. How did it manifest itself?'

'Eh?'

'What was she saying and doing for you to know she was unhappy with her life?'

A hand let go of her bag altogether and wiped at her eyes. 'She said there was no real peace in her life and it wasn't because of the kids. She said she adored Matty but how could she have peace when there were too many CCTV cameras watching our every move, companies messing with our food and putting who knew what in it? So much noise with the television directing shit at us with the adverts and subtle messages in the programming. It was like she was fed up of real life but I didn't understand what it was she wanted. You can't have kids and not have a TV, can you?'

I kind of understood where Sharon had been coming from. The world was permanently switched on and with the advent of social media and the place it had taken in our lives the noise was astounding.

'What was her answer to these problems?' I asked instead of answering her television question.

'I mean, Matty needed a television, didn't he? As well as books and stuff.' A tear slid down one of Andrea's cheeks. She swiped it away with the back of a hand. Her handbag now sat on her lap. 'She didn't have the answers. Except...' she paused.

'Go on, what is it?'

'Not specific answers but she did have ideas of what kind of world she'd like, if that would be of interest to you?'

'Of course.'

'She wanted to live off the land, away from prying eyes, away from the government and people who were telling her how to live her life. People interfering in her life by adding things to her food, her information stream, her freedom of movement and passage. She wanted to relax as we were meant to, not in this built-up façade of a world we've created.' Andrea looked scared. 'Did I miss something important last time?'

'Did she mention anywhere specific she could do this?' I asked.

'No. Not at all. I'd have said if she did.'

'And she didn't mention any new friends she'd made? Anyone who was influencing her way of thinking?'

Andrea considered this then shook her head.

'What about seeing anyone come to the house that you hadn't seen before? Maybe she fobbed them off as something else but you got a weird vibe off them?'

'Honestly, I can't think of anyone or anything. Though I did see less of her before she went missing so there's nothing to say there wasn't someone influencing her life, I just can't help you with it.'

'You've been very helpful, thank you, Andrea.'

She rose from her chair. 'I think of that poor boy often.' Her face was pale and drawn. 'I'd have looked after him if she'd asked me.' She wiped away more tears. 'I know she asked Lucas and she asked her sister. If she had asked me I'd have said yes. He wouldn't have gone missing then, would he? And he'd have had his life. I think about that all the time. I'd have said yes.'

17

'It looks like Sharon Harper might have been interacting with a third party before she went missing,' I said to the incident room. 'She was unhappy with her life and wanted to make big changes. Her best friend saw less of her but when she did see her Sharon talked about how unhappy she was with the way life was lived in the world. So our aim is to identify who she was engaging with in the weeks before she and Matt went missing. I'll go and talk to Lucas again. If anyone will know, it should be him. He was old enough to see what was happening with his mum.'

The team stared back at me. Ross looked puzzled. 'So she wasn't taken by force, she left of her own accord but we think there was someone else involved?'

'She might not be missing. She might have chosen not to be in contact with her family any more. There's no law against changing the direction of your life and walking away from it. The problem was she didn't answer calls via the media to check on her welfare which caused more concerns about her. But if she did up and go on her own there are certainly questions around Matt. Legally she had to provide him with an education, medical care. Of course she could move him wherever she wanted to, but no one knew where he was, and that classed him as missing because he was a juvenile.'

Ross scratched his head.

'You have a lot to be getting on with. This is a complicated investigation. I spoke to Andrea this morning but I want everyone who made statements eleven years ago to be interviewed again. We're still waiting for the DNA results on Matt's clothes as well as the results of the examination of the vehicle we seized yesterday.'

I left them to it and walked out of the incident room. Aaron followed me. 'Do you want me to send one of the team to talk to Lucas?' he asked. 'There's no need for you to do it, it's what they're here for. It's a follow-up.'

I stopped in the corridor. I understood where he was coming from. This wasn't something I would usually do. It was a team action.

'I need to see this job through myself, Aaron.'

'I know, but you—'

'I put his brother in the hospital. It's my duty to be the one to keep in touch with him if there's any contact to be made.'

A couple of civilian staff came down the corridor, arms filled with folders, heads bowed together in conversation. Aaron and I moved to the side to let them past.

'I get it,' he said. 'Don't pile too much on yourself though because you feel responsible. You have a team. Use them when you can.'

I patted his shoulder, grateful for his counsel. 'They're busy. There's a lot to do. I'm going to call Lucas and ask him to come into the station or I can meet him somewhere neutral if that's easier for him. But for now it's just a phone call. I'll let you know how it goes.'

He turned to go back to the incident room. 'You don't have to take this on alone, you know that, right?'

I was grateful that Aaron was my friend as well as my right-hand man. 'I'm fine, honestly. I'll shout if I need a hand with anything.' And with that I headed into my office.

Lucas's phone rang on and on. I didn't think he was going to pick up but then his deep voice spoke through the handset. 'Yeah.'

'Lucas, it's DI Hannah Robbins. We spoke yesterday about your brother, Matt, returning.'

There was a long silence on the phone.

'Do you remember me?'

'Yeah.'

He was a man of few words today.

'I need to speak to you again. We've spoken with your mum's friend Andrea Mayfield and we've some questions in relation to your mum's behaviour before she and Matt went missing. Would you—'

'Can't you leave this alone? It's been eleven years, for fuck's sake.'

I was taken aback by the outburst. It was unexpected. I'd thought he would want to do everything possible to find out what had happened.

'It's an active investigation, Lucas. With Matt returning we believe there's a chance we can find your mum. Surely you want that?'

'What I want is for the past to stay where it is. No good is going to come of dredging this stuff up. Have you any idea how painful this is for everyone concerned, DI Robbins? You traipse through people's lives like they're there for you to rummage through but they're not. They're not the remains of some long lost puzzle, they're people's emotions and lives and you're trampling all over them with little regard for the pain you're causing.' He was nearly out of breath with the diatribe he'd thrown my way. Did I really treat people like they didn't exist and were solely there for me to pick through? Policing, I admit, is a little like that. Individuals are secondary to the evidence needed to support a case but I was always thoughtful as I worked. Wasn't I?

'I'm sorry you feel this way, Lucas. We don't mean to trample on anyone's feelings, but you have to understand there's a missing person we need to find and your brother had blood on him when we found him. We need to locate where he'd been before he was picked up in the street. Talking to you would be helpful and I can do this in any place that makes you more comfortable and at a time and place that suits you. It's imperative we get to the bottom of what happened.'

I thought about his personal place in all of this. 'Have you seen your brother yet?'

There was a deep huff of air down the phone. 'No. He's not doing so well at having visitors. It's upsetting him. We're having to take it slowly.'

'That must be difficult.' I had just made the understatement of the century to Lucas. No wonder he had verbally hit out at me. 'I'm sorry,' I said.

Another long silence filled the line and this time I waited it out. I looked at the piles of files on my desk and wondered if I would ever be one of those people who could have a clear desk and space to move. It needed to be on my list of things to do. I loved a clear desk and wanted one for myself.

'I can meet you,' Lucas said eventually.

'Thank you.' I picked up a pen and scrabbled around for a clear piece of paper. 'Where and when?'

18

I pulled my coat on and left my office. Pasha was walking out of the kitchen with a tray of mugs.

'On your way out, Ma'am? I've made drinks.'

'Sorry, Pasha. I won't be too long, I'll catch up with you all later.'

Lucas had asked to meet me on an industrial estate – Finch Close. Said he had a meeting at one of the units so would meet me before he went in. I parked the car at the side of the road and pulled the handbrake on. The grey sleet of earlier had dried up and I was grateful for this at least. April was such an unpredictable month. We were waiting for spring to show its face but the dregs of winter were still present.

A car pulled up a little way behind me. I didn't know what car Lucas would be driving. There hadn't been a vehicle in front of his house that I could remember when we went to see him, so I presumed this was him. I got out the car and pressed the locking mechanism and listened as the click click secured the car. I had turned to go to meet Lucas when the world went dark.

I was pulled backwards by my head as something smothered me in blackness. A cloth bag of some description was over my head. The fibres ticked my nose and I panicked, the breath catching in my chest.

My hands jumped up to my neck as I tried to pull the hood off but someone was behind me, pulling it down and backwards. I was yanked off balance.

The breath caught in my chest built up and I started to gasp for air. My open mouth attempted to suck oxygen into my lungs but all that happened was the bag filled my mouth, the harsh material catching on my teeth.

I heaved as panic filled my head but the bag tightened around my throat and the panic escalated. I couldn't get purchase with my hands. It was tight around my airway. I needed to get air into my lungs; the panic was cutting off all sensible thought.

My feet scrabbled against the ground as the backward momentum continued. I was being taken somewhere. There was a click and the sound of metal and then I was falling and hands were pushing me from the front down into something.

I threw my hands out and caught hold of metal. It was the lip of the boot of a car. They were pushing me into the boot of a car. Who the fuck knew where I would end up if the lid closed over me. I had to resist at all costs. I couldn't be taken like this.

I kicked out with my booted feet as my back balanced against the car. I forced as much energy as I could into my legs but they didn't make contact with anything. My abductor must be at the side of me.

Feeling hands on me I didn't even know how many of them there were.

I screamed out with all my might. I was still being dragged by the hood around my head. It was utterly terrifying not being able to see my attackers. To not breathe properly. To panic.

I was a cop and I had to remember this. I had to fight whatever I was up against and not go willingly into this vehicle. I would not end up as another statistic.

My boots scuffed against the tarmac as I struggled against the hands pushing me inwards to the boot and pulling against my neck. All momentum was in towards the boot. I kicked out but still no one was in front of me. I let go of the lip of the vehicle and punched sideways. I was still screaming and shouting. My throat was sore. Like glass smashed and loose on the soft skin in my pharynx.

My right fist connected with something soft and there was a gentle whump and then a fist connected with the side of my head, above my right eyebrow. Pain shot to my brain and I was stunned. Silenced for a moment.

They had me. With another couple of pushes and a final tug on the hood I was inside the boot. My thigh scraped against the lip of the boot as they pushed me in and I kicked out again, but it was a waste of time. There was more than one of them.

I had lost.

I was going to be another statistic.

I felt a prick in my leg.

The panic started to subside. The edges taken off. The world was already dark but then it went silent and black.

19

'Aaron, Lucas Harper's on the line for you.' Pasha held the phone in the air as though Aaron would actually walk across the room and take it out of her hand.

'Put him through,' Aaron said as he finished writing the email he was in the middle of. The phone on his desk started to ring and he signed the email, pressed send and picked up the call.

'DS Aaron Stone,' he said to the caller.

'DS Stone, it's Lucas Harper here. I don't know what you lot are playing at but DI Robbins arranged to meet me. She said it was imperative to the investigation that she talk to me so I took time out of my day and agreed to meet and for what? For her to not turn up. I'm told she's not in her office and as you were the person with her when she came to inform me of Matty's return I presumed you would know what the hell she's playing at. I must say, I don't appreciate these games. I was not happy about meeting her again in the first place.'

Aaron was falling over the words. He didn't understand what Lucas was saying. He'd spoken with Hannah earlier and yes, she'd said she would phone Lucas and arrange to see him again. He understood that part, but after that he was lost.

'I'm sorry, Lucas. What is it you're trying to say?' he asked.

There was a huge huff of air down the phone. 'I'm not *trying* to say anything. I am *telling you* that DI Robbins did not turn up for the meeting she arranged and I am pissed off about it. Where the hell is she and why is she messing with me this way?'

Hannah didn't turn up? She wasn't in her office if the call had come through to the incident room. He couldn't recall seeing her for at least the last hour. It wasn't like her to make arrangements and not keep them, especially with people involved in an investigation. He looked at his watch. It was more than an hour since he'd walked with her to her office. He'd had a drink and rattled through quite a bit of work since then.

'You're sure you got the meeting place correct?' Aaron asked, searching for reasons why the meeting hadn't taken place as planned.

'I set the meeting place, there's no way I could have got it wrong.'

Aaron's brain was stumbling over the idea of not knowing where Hannah was. 'I'm sorry for your inconvenience, Lucas. All I can say is that it's not like DI Robbins to stand a witness up this way, especially one she wanted to talk to as much as she wanted to talk to you. There has to be a very good reason and I'll find out what has happened and get back to you as soon as I know.'

Lucas blew out more air. 'Don't expect me to be as accommodating next time you get in touch.' He hung up the call.

Aaron gently lay down the handset and sat up straighter. 'Has anyone heard from Hannah in the last hour?' he shouted to the room.

Martin shook his head. 'No, is everything okay?'

'I don't know. I really don't. She didn't turn up to meet Lucas Harper and he's pretty annoyed about it. But why didn't she meet him?' He considered his next move. 'Can I get your attention.' The room quietened down. 'Has anyone heard from the boss in the last hour or so?'

'I saw her leaving about an hour ago,' Pasha said. 'I was walking out of the kitchen with the drinks when she came out of her office. She seemed fine. She had her coat on ready to go out and said she'd catch up with me later.'

'Did she say where she was going?' Aaron asked.

Pasha shook her head. 'Sorry, no. And you don't like to question the boss on her movements, do you. It's up to her what she does and doesn't do.' Pasha looked mortified. 'Should I have done something differently?'

Aaron straightened his tie. 'Let's not worry about her. As you say, she's the boss and does her own thing. Something could easily have come up and taken precedence over the meeting with Lucas and she didn't have chance to cancel him. She'll be kicking herself when she gets back though with the mood he's in about it. She could very well have cost herself a line of enquiry there. I'm not sure he's going to be playing ball with us in the future.'

Pasha tucked her hair behind her ear. 'I'll give her a call. See where she is.'

Aaron looked at Martin. 'She's fine,' he said at Aaron's worried face. Aaron might have reassured the team but Martin could tell he was worried. They were a close pair. Hannah had saved his life when he'd had a heart attack at work. She'd done heart compressions until the ambulance had arrived and had worried over him like a mother hen until he was out of the woods and then some more afterwards.

'There's no answer.' Pasha looked worried. 'In fact her phone is off.' She dialled again. 'Definitely off, Aaron.'

Aaron rose from his chair.

'What are you doing?' Martin asked.

'I have to update Baxter and Walker,' Aaron said. 'They'll want to know.'

'You think we might want a little more information before we send the balloon up?' Martin asked. 'If she walks in and we're all in a tizzy looking for her she won't be happy.'

'And if something has happened to her and we haven't reacted, what then? What happens in the time between?'

Aaron was conscious that he was currently in charge while Hannah was – what did he call it, not here or missing? And Baxter and Walker were unaware. He had to make the decisions. The pressure bore down on him. He remembered the heart attack and the crushing weight on his chest and considered how close to the sensation this was. It was more an emotional feeling than the literal weight, but he was worried about getting this wrong for Hannah. He'd rather look a little stupid than anything happening to her any day of the week.

Martin leaned back in his chair. 'Where was she supposed to meet Lucas?'

Aaron turned to Pasha. 'Call Lucas back please. Apologise for bothering him and ask him that question.'

'We can check for her car,' said Martin.

Aaron was grateful that one of them was thinking this through. He had to get his head into order. Hannah relied on him for his level-headedness and now she needed that more than ever.

'He wasn't very happy. Said we were a useless bunch of idiots.' Pasha shrugged. 'But then said he was supposed to meet her at Finch Close industrial estate.'

Ross scratched his cheek. 'Seems an odd place to meet.'

'When I was talking to him, Lucas said he picked the location, it wasn't Hannah's choice,' said Aaron.

Ross jumped out of his chair. 'I'll go look for her car, shall I?'

'Not alone,' said Aaron. 'I don't know what's happened, what's there. Maybe nothing, but I'd rather you didn't travel alone.'

Ross looked around the room. Pasha stood. 'I'll go with him. Make sure he's okay.'

'I can check a car on my own.' Ross pouted at Pasha.

She narrowed her eyes at him. 'I never said you couldn't, did I?'

'Ross, please?' Aaron issued a calm warning. He could do without the bickering.

'Sorry, Aaron. Going now. I'll contact you when we get there.'

Ross and Pasha grabbed a set of keys and left the incident room.

'I'm sure she's fine, Aaron.' Martin tapped the edge of his desk with his fingers. 'She's a capable cop. Like you said, she's probably got tied up with something else, lost signal and not realised she has everyone in a tizz. She'll be mortified when she gets back and realises what's happened.'

'Yeah, but I'll feel better if we get things in motion and if she does stroll in at least we can show we have a working plan if a member of staff is in trouble.' Aaron picked up his phone from his desk, looked at the screen – there were no calls – then pushed it in his pocket. 'I'm going to talk to Walker. Call me if anything changes in the meantime.'

Martin opened his pocket notebook and picked up his pen. 'I'll let you know if I hear anything before you get back down.' He paused, rubbed at his chin. 'She'll be fine, Aaron.'

Aaron didn't know if he was saying that to reassure himself or Aaron.

Walker's door was closed. 'I need to see her. It's urgent.' Aaron told her PA who picked up the phone, spoke quietly into the handset and then told him he could go right in. He was expecting more of a fight. Walker was a busy woman. He was surprised she was even in her office and not at some agency meeting.

He pushed the door open and softly closed it behind him, then stood in the middle of the floor waiting for her to speak.

Catherine Walker was behind her desk, tapping at her keyboard. Her dark bob had grown and was resting on her shoulders. She was a formidable woman. Fought for everything that was right and did what was best for her unit. Even as policing cuts did everything they could to diminish the capability of every unit in the force. She was strong but she could be unpredictable. You never knew which way she was going to jump.

'You're making the place look untidy, Aaron. Please do sit.' She didn't even look up.

Aaron moved to the chairs in front of her desk and took a seat. How was he going to explain this to her? He folded his hands into each other in his lap.

Walker stopped tapping and looked up from her laptop.

'How are you doing, Aaron?' she asked. She had been as concerned about him as the rest of his team when he'd had his heart attack, and she had personally checked on him when he'd returned to work.

'I'm fine, Ma'am, thank you.'

'And what brings you up here today and not Hannah?'

He tightened his grip on his fingers. 'That's the problem, Ma'am.'

She furrowed her brow.

'We have a little situation with DI Robbins that I thought I should appraise you of.'

'Do spit it out then.'

Aaron straightened in his chair. 'She was due to meet a witness about an hour ago.' He looked at his watch. 'Over an hour.'

'Get on with it.' Her face looked etched in stone. As though she had already leapt ahead to where Aaron was trying to go and was not at all happy with the conclusion she had drawn.

'The witness phoned the office to say she hadn't turned up, and her phone is off. No one can get in touch with her. We've sent a couple of officers out to look for her vehicle, at the place she was supposed to meet this witness and we'll know more soon. But I thought you should be aware of where we're at.'

Walker pursed her lips and brought a hand up to cradle her chin. 'You don't know where DI Robbins is and have not known for over an hour. She's out of contact, do I have that correct?'

'Yes, Ma'am.'

'It may be that she's gone somewhere with no signal?'

'It's possible.'

'That you're jumping the gun?'

'Yes, Ma'am.' Aaron felt slightly ridiculous.

'But you don't think so?'

She was giving his thoughts consideration? 'I don't know at this point in time, Ma'am, but thought I should apprise you of events so far.'

'Consider me apprised, DS Stone.'

Aaron rose from his chair. 'Thank you, Ma'am.' He moved towards the door.

'Aaron.'

He turned back to her.

Her arms were folded across her desk. 'I want to know results as and when they come in, do I make myself clear?'

'Yes, Ma'am.'

'I'll update DCI Baxter about this. You get on with your search for Hannah and make sure you bring her back.'

Aaron left Walker's office feeling better about the actions he had taken so far. She hadn't made him feel stupid for worrying so soon. She'd listened to him and taken what he'd said on board. He now had to work to find Hannah and hope they really were just being idiots for going this far.

Back at the incident room there had been no call from Ross or Pasha yet. Aaron had hoped they'd have arrived at their destination by now but that depended on traffic. He sat at his desk and tried Hannah's phone again. Again it went straight to voicemail. This time he left a message requesting she contact him as soon as she received it. If she picked this up, she would call him and they could stop searching for her.

Another twenty minutes passed without contact from Pasha or Ross and then Aaron's mobile phone rang with Pasha's number flashing. Aaron looked to Martin then picked up. Martin stood from his chair and walked round his desk to stand in front of Aaron. Aaron put the call on speaker.

'Aaron,' Pasha's voice came through the mobile phone a little tinny but clear enough. 'We're here. Hannah's car is here. It's parked fine and locked up. There's no sign of any problems but Hannah is nowhere to be seen. I can't see anything that could help us. It's like she's just disappeared.'

20

The raging black hole in his head where his past, his family, his life, his career, his love-life, was supposed to be, was only serving to provide Matt with the headache from hell. No matter what the doctors gave him, nothing helped, nothing eased it. He continued to burrow into the darkness in a search for answers but there was nothing but a gaping void and a steely blade, dug deep inside his brain.

He was staring at the ceiling when his favourite nurse bustled into the room. He could make new memories. Everything that had happened since he had run in front of the copper's car had stayed put, so why couldn't he remember what had happened before he had run in front of it? But here she was, the nurse he remembered and the nurse he liked.

'Hey Matt, I have another visitor for you. Are you up for a visit?' She strode to his bed and straightened the covers wrapped around his legs.

He was desperate to know who he was, find some answers to the questions he had been asking himself, but after the incident with his aunt he was nervous of meeting someone else. Fearful of his reaction.

A reaction he had no control over. 'Who is it?' he asked. He couldn't guess who might be interested in visiting him.

'He says his name is Lucas.' She waited for a response from him.

There was nothing. No bells ringing. No sudden images of best mates out on the lash. The dark void whistled through his head.

'He says he's your brother,' she said again, with a wide smile across her face. It made her eyes light up and he wanted to reach out and touch her cheek.

He connected with her the way he didn't connect with anyone else. Why couldn't he just sit and talk to her? The words that this man was supposed to be his brother did nothing for him. He should be excited, desperate to meet him, to speak to him and get answers from him, but he was so tired.

'I'll let him in, shall I?' she said stepping back and checking his newly tidied bed.

Matt wiggled his feet, feeling penned in. 'Will you stay?'

She let out a light laugh. 'You don't need me to stay, Matt. He's your brother.' She saw his face. 'Look, if it becomes too much ask him to leave or shout for one of us. We'll help you out. You're not in this alone and you don't have to do anything you don't want to. But Lucas might be able to help. And he's desperate to see you. He thought you were dead, you've been gone so long.'

So many times he'd been told it had been eleven years. Eleven years he didn't remember, or those before his disappearance for that matter.

She patted the back of his hand. 'It's okay, Matt. How you're feeling is normal. Take one step at a time.' And with that she left the room. A minute later the door opened again and a man Matt didn't recognise walked through it.

The light from the ward beyond backlit him and Matt couldn't get a proper sense of his face, but he was tall and sturdy. His hands were shoved in his pockets and his broad shoulders were hunched.

He stood in the doorway before coming further into the room and stared at Matt without saying a word.

Matt stared back at him. Nothing clicked into place. No emotions came flooding back. There was nothing there but the void. Still spinning, still consuming everything.

Eventually the man spoke. 'Matty? Is that you?' A deep gravelly voice.

He'd just been a boy when he'd disappeared apparently. He must have changed a lot. 'Yeah, so I've been told.' He only had the copper's word that he was this missing boy, Matthew Harper. For all he knew he could be anyone. He could be the next in line for the throne. Anything was possible at this point.

'You don't recognise me?' the man asked.

'Am I supposed to?'

The man pulled one hand out of a pocket and rubbed his chin.

Matt tried to explain. 'What I mean is, hasn't it been eleven years, wouldn't you have changed?'

The man stepped further into the room. 'You don't remember a thing?'

Matt shook his head. 'I'm sorry.'

As the man came closer Matt's nerves started to gain control again. The fear of people knowing him and him being disadvantaged was so bizarre he just couldn't cope with it.

'What is it?' asked the person he'd been told was his brother. 'Do you remember something?' He stepped closer still until he was at the side of the bed.

Matt's breath started coming thick and fast in his chest. 'No, no, it's not that. I just... it's just... I don't remember you.' He clutched his chest. 'I need a nurse,' he panted.

The man leaned forward and put his face up close to Matt's. 'You really don't remember me, Matty? I'm your brother.'

Matt screamed. 'I don't know who you are!'

The man stepped back, his mouth forming a perfect 'o'. A nurse pushed the door open and ushered the visitor out, while he continued to look back at Matt until he was out of the room. His head shaking in disbelief.

21

It was like radio waves inside my head. Or rather someone trying to tune into a radio station. Fuzzy, unclear, like static. It was pitch black and my body was tense and sore. I couldn't work out where I was. Had I fallen asleep on the sofa and forgotten to set my alarm for work? Or was that noise in my head the sound of my alarm? The pain in my joints from a night on the sofa? Work was going to be painful today.

I struggled to think of what I had on in the day ahead, where yesterday had ended in the investigation. What my plans had been for going forward.

I tried to move my arm so I could rub my face, my eyes, and it wouldn't move. It was locked in place. I rolled my shoulder and though it gave a little my arm was still stuck. Was I lying on it? I tried my other arm but the same thing happened.

I started to panic. What had happened to me in the night? Had I had a stroke or something? I tried to roll over but my arms and legs were locked in position. I realised it wasn't dark but that I still hadn't opened my eyes. Fear gripped at the depths of my stomach as I struggled to process what was happening. I squeezed my eyes tighter shut and then counted to three inside my head and when I hit three I forced them open.

This wasn't my living room. I wasn't lying on my sofa. I hadn't fallen asleep overnight as I'd feared. This was something altogether worse.

Fragments of memories skittered around in my mind and I reached out to them.

There was a street. A car. Something happened. There was a taste in my mouth as... what?

Something had covered my head.

There had been hands.

The taste had been strong as I'd been pricked in my leg.

I'd been drugged.

What day was it?

Was it still the same day?

Where was I?

Who had taken me?

Why had they taken me?

I moved my head as much as I could to check the room I was in. There was a dull throb in the side of my head. I was tied up. My arms and legs secured to wooden posts at the four corners of a bed. This was why I couldn't move. I twisted my head to look up at one of my wrists and saw I was secured by rope. I took a mental inventory of any injuries and acknowledged the throbbing in my temple, a scraping pain in my thigh and my upper right arm was in agony at being locked into position like this. Other than that I didn't appear to be injured.

The room was sparse. It was carpeted and the curtains were closed. I couldn't tell if it was daylight still or if darkness had fallen. The curtains were heavy and blocked out all but a little light. What was coming through could have been the sun or a street light. There was a wooden dressing table with two drawers. One on each side. And a soft chair in front of it. On the dresser was a jug of water and a beaker. Next to the dressing table was a small, narrow, two-door wardrobe and other than that the room was bare.

The walls were covered with a blue floral wallpaper, peeling at the corners.

I could hear no sounds. Nothing to give away where I was.

The fear turned into full blown panic. It engulfed me, starting in the pit of my stomach and flaring upwards until it hit me in the throat and I wanted to vomit.

I heaved and heaved and had to twist myself sideways as I was positioned on my back. I forced my head to the edge of the bed, straining my neck and vomited out yellow bile. I coughed at the bitter taste in my mouth. The yellow puddle on the floor below me created a rancid stench in the small room. I hoped it wouldn't be allowed to fester there for long. Though I wasn't sure what I expected or wanted to happen next. How I thought I was going to escape.

I couldn't wipe my mouth but could taste the bitter fluid on my lips. I twisted again and wiped my mouth on the sheet below me. It was disgusting.

Now I'd vacated my stomach I was more settled and could think a little clearer. Who would have done this to me? The only case I was involved in was the Matthew Harper case but Matt was still an inpatient at the hospital and his aunt and his brother were emotionally invested in rebuilding those relationships. After all, eleven years had passed. We had no real leads. No one to have upset yet. The other case that Martin had been dealing with, it had been going smoothly and I couldn't see this being connected with that either.

I needed someone to come and explain what this was about so I could talk to them and clear it up. I was sure with some common sense I could resolve whatever issue my abductor had. They had a pretty dramatic way of getting their grievance dealt with but if we looked past that and dealt with the issue, then I was positive I'd be out of here before the end of the day.

My face itched and I went to scratch it with my hand and was reminded that I was tied to the bed. Frustration niggled at me, lying prone on a bed at someone else's bidding. I was used to being the one who made the decisions and directed people to carry out my orders. Being out of control was frightening, no matter how much I was trying to tell myself this could be resolved. You don't go to this trouble if you think your issue is simple and can be talked out. I was swinging in my thought processes and closed my eyes and tried to calm myself.

People would start worrying about me. They'd try to contact me and then they'd start to look for me. They'd realise something bad had happened and a full-scale search would be up and running. Even if no demands were made by my abductors. I had to hold on to the knowledge that my team were good at their jobs. They wouldn't give up on looking for me. Even if I couldn't talk my way out of this, they would search until they found me. No matter what it took. Or, I realised, what state they eventually found me in.

22

Aaron straightened his tie. What the hell was he supposed to do now? If Hannah were here she would have everything under control. She'd be calm and collected and know what next steps to take.

The incident room door opened and Baxter strode through. His face a blank mask. Aaron had no idea what he knew at this stage. Baxter looked around the room and made a beeline for Aaron's desk.

'Walker has talked to me. What do we have?' He was short and to the point.

Aaron was grateful there was a supervising officer in the room. 'Her phone has been switched off and her car has been located at Finch Close industrial estate, Lenton, which was where she'd arranged to meet Lucas Harper, the brother of the lad she ran over a couple of nights ago and who turned out to be the lad missing—'

'From eleven years ago,' Baxter finished for him.

'Exactly.'

'We think it's connected?'

Aaron looked at Martin who shrugged. 'We don't know what to think at this stage. It's come out of nowhere to be honest. There's been no warning, no threats made.'

'Check her phone, call logs, text messages, make sure she hasn't been getting threats we don't know about.'

Martin started tapping at his computer. 'On it.'

'I've sent a flatbed out to pick up Hannah's car to have CSU examine it to see if it gives us anything,' said Aaron.

'Good work.' Baxter spun on his feet, looking around the space. 'Someone check social media, make sure this isn't out there being shared and we haven't seen it.'

The door banged open and Evie flew in with Pasha and Ross trailing behind her. 'Tell me it's not true, Aaron.' She glanced at Baxter but ignored him. She wanted answers from Aaron and didn't care who was in her way or what rank they were. 'Tell me she's not missing.'

Aaron's hand went up to his tie. 'I'm sorry, Evie, I can't.'

Tears flooded Evie's eyes. 'What the hell has happened?'

Baxter turned to her and gave her the weight of his stare. 'That's what we're trying to figure out, Evie.' Letting her know he was in charge in this room.

'Someone must have some idea though,' she spluttered. 'She must have said where she was going, who she was going to see, what she had planned. You don't just disappear.' She knew as well as anyone in that room that people could and did just disappear.

'She had a meeting set up which she didn't make,' said Aaron. 'We're trying to move on from there.'

Evie swiped at her face as the tears fell. 'Tell me what you need me to do.' She was the station analyst and could move figures and data around in mere moments and provide information that had evaded others because she'd managed to put it in some kind of order.

Aaron checked his tie again. 'I don't know where to start, Evie. We have no idea what's happened. If this is connected to any specific case.'

'We could assume it's connected to the Harper case because someone knew she was supposed to be meeting Lucas?' suggested Pasha.

'You're her friend, Evie,' Martin said quietly. 'Is there anything in her private life, anything she's told you about that may have an impact on our investigation?'

Evie shook her head. 'No, nothing. I know her sister needs her, but she needs her around, not going missing.'

'There's friction or something there, isn't there?' asked Ross.

'This isn't anything to do with family,' Aaron said. 'Evie is right. Her family need her. This is terrible timing for them.' He let out a deep sigh. 'I have to let them know.'

'I'll come with you. It needs a supervisory officer, Aaron.' Baxter didn't look pleased about the prospect. 'Shall we go and speak to her family.'

Aaron was starting to feel throttled by the tie around his neck as he stood on the doorstep of Hannah's father's house beside DCI Baxter. He fiddled with the knot and then shoved his hands deep into his pockets to stop himself fidgeting. The door was opened by Hannah's dad. He was smiling as though he was in the middle of a conversation with someone and Aaron knew that someone would be Hannah's sister, Zoe.

The smile slipped from his face when he saw Aaron and Baxter at the door without Hannah. A hand went up to his chest and he shook his head.

'Mr Robbins?' Baxter started, but David Robbins already knew Aaron, he knew who they were and was one step ahead of them.

He was looking at Aaron. 'No.'

Baxter looked from Robbins to Aaron and back again. Realised the connection had been made and went quiet.

'Can we come in, Dave?' Aaron asked.

'No,' David Robbins said.

'We need to talk to you,' Aaron said.

'You're here to tell me my daughter's dead.' He leant heavily on the door frame, his chest heaving.

'No,' Aaron said. 'But we do need to come in.' He took a step forward and took hold of David Robbins by the arm, steered him back in to the house. Baxter followed him in.

'She's alive?' Robbins asked.

Aaron manoeuvred him into the living room. Sitting in the corner of a sofa with a thick blanket over her legs was Zoe. It had been a while since Aaron had seen her and he could see the dramatic change in her appearance. How Hannah could not have picked up on it before being told he didn't know.

Zoe beamed at him. 'Hi, Aaron.' Then she saw her dad's face and leapt to her feet, going to her father's aid. 'Dad, what is it?' She took his other arm, taking the care of him from Aaron, and guided him to the sofa she'd just vacated and they both sat down. 'What's happened, Aaron?' her tone was sharp, her eyes pierced him.

'Do you mind if we sit?' Baxter said.

'Who the hell are you?' Zoe said.

'I'm DCI Kevin Baxter. I'm sorry we've had to disturb you this afternoon.'

'Tell us why you have.' She held onto her father's hand.

Baxter and Aaron seated themselves on the spare chairs. Baxter looked to Aaron, allowing him to do this as he knew the family.

Aaron took a deep breath. 'Earlier today Hannah went out to a meeting alone. We lost contact with her and have since established that she's missing.' There was no other way to lay out the facts.

There was a simultaneous intake of breath from both David and Zoe.

'What do you mean she's missing?' her father asked, sitting forward on the edge of the sofa.

'Her phone is switched off,' Baxter elaborated. 'Her car has been found at the place she was supposed to meet a witness but she never turned up. We have no idea where she is. Let me assure you that we're doing everything in our power to locate Hannah and bring her home safely. She's one of our own and this is a top priority.'

Zoe snapped to her feet. 'I don't care if you class her as one of your own. She's not one of your anything. She's ours. She's our family.' She pointed to her father. 'She's his daughter.' She pointed to herself. 'She's my sister. Family. Are you listening to me? You have to bring her home. You lost her, you bloody well find her.'

David reached up and gripped his daughter's hand again. 'I'm sure they're doing everything they can, Zoe.' He looked Baxter in the eye. 'You are, aren't you?'

Baxter shifted in his seat. 'We want nothing more than to find your daughter and to have her home as quickly as possible, unharmed.'

'Why's this happened?' David asked.

'We can't answer that,' Baxter said. 'We just don't know. It's a line of enquiry we're looking into. This has apparently come out of nowhere.'

'You're a bunch of idiots,' Zoe snapped.

'Zoe.' David rubbed his face with his free hand.

Zoe looked at Aaron who was rigid in his seat. 'Sorry, Aaron.'

Aaron inclined his head. Hannah would want him to make this better for her family and not blame them for their reaction. They'd dealt with enough families to know that people were unpredictable and reacted to bad news in a variety of ways. There was no saying what you would get just by looking at the outside of a house or by examining a person's criminal record. Though it was no surprise that Zoe held the police in little regard, even though her sister was a detective inspector. Aaron would do everything in his power to bring her home to her family so she could help Zoe get better.

Zoe's knees slackened and she started to go down towards the floor. Baxter looked horrified. David and Aaron were up like a shot and supporting her back into her seat before she had dropped any distance.

'My daughter has leukaemia, DCI Baxter,' David explained. 'We recently asked Hannah to have the test to see if she could commit to a bone marrow transplant.' He folded the thick blanket that was in a heap on the arm of the sofa over his youngest child's knees and tucked it under her legs. 'So you see, I know you look at family when things like this happen, but we need Hannah, Zoe needs Hannah and she needs her urgently. I love both my daughters. I couldn't bear to lose one of them and I have been losing sleep over that consideration

over recent months. Now you come here and tell me I might be about
to lose them both. That is unbearable. Please bring Hannah home
and save my family.'

23

My watch had been removed from my wrist so I had no way of keeping track of time. I could no longer smell the vile scent of the vomit at the side of the bed, so that meant enough time had passed for me to adjust to the smell, to get used to it. What else would I get used to while I was here? What would I have to adjust to? My mind closed down and refused to even consider the horrors that could come my way as a prisoner tied to a bed in an unknown location.

I stared up at the ceiling and watched as a spider spun a web across the corner the bed was pushed into. It reminded me of the time Zoe had come howling into my bedroom when we were kids because she had found a spider in the pink plastic teapot she was playing tea parties with.

I wasn't much older than her but put on my big brave older sister face, marched into her bedroom, and found the plastic teapot on its side in the middle of the room surrounded by a circle of plastic cups and saucers ready to receive tea that she'd been making.

She pleaded with me to save her tea party and to evict the spider from the pot. I wasn't a fan of spiders but I was a fan of looking good to my little sister so I gingerly bent down and peered inside and low and behold tucked in the bottom was the tiniest spider. Even I wasn't afraid of it.

I picked up the teapot, walked with it to the bathroom and swished the plastic pot with water and swilled it away down the sink returning it spider free to Zoe. 'Here, squirt,' I said, using my pet name for her. She wrapped her arms around my waist and told me I was the best sister ever and she would always love me. I walked to my own room knowing I'd always do anything for my little sister. If I could brave a spider I could brave the world for her.

I closed my eyes and shut out the spider on the ceiling. I still wasn't afraid of spiders, but my relationship with Zoe had morphed into something completely different. Where was that little girl who had adored me so much and where was the older sister who had promised to brave the world for her sibling? How things changed. The scourge of drugs in our world. Would we be as close as we were when we were kids if Zoe had never got involved in the drug world? Should I have been able to help her more?

My stomach rumbled and I realised I hadn't eaten since breakfast. Though I didn't have any idea what time it was, my body was telling me hours had passed. At least my team must now be aware something was wrong when I hadn't returned to the station.

My limbs were stiff from being locked in position, strapped to the bed. My upper right arm where I had been stabbed was excruciating and was driving me to distraction. I could barely think straight.

How long had I even been tied here this way? I couldn't cope. I needed my painkillers and I needed to be released. Allowed to sit up and stretch my arms and legs out. Allow the muscles to breathe.

I started to scream at the top of my voice. 'Hello. Hello. Is anyone there? Let me off this bed!'

It was one problem at a time. I was a prisoner. Getting out of here and getting home was the big problem, the smaller one to deal with first was getting myself untied so I could think straight and figure out what the hell was going on. I had no idea why I was here or who had brought me here.

'Did you hear me? Let me up!' I screamed out again. My neck

throbbed as I strained against my ties while shrieking into the void. I dropped my head back onto the pillow and tears filled my eyes. It felt as though I had been here hours but I had no idea how long I had been unconscious. I needed someone to come in and talk to me. That way at least I would know what I was dealing with. This isolation was hurting me on another level.

'I need my painkillers,' I yelled out, pain dragging through my arm.

Then I heard it and I shut my mouth.

A key in a lock.

A bolt sliding across the door.

Someone was outside and they were on their way in.

I was going to be face-to-face with my captor. I wriggled. Uncomfortable, spread-eagled across the single bed. It most definitely was not a position of power. Whoever was entering held that. I was the weakest I had ever been.

The tears that had filled my eyes slipped slowly down the side of my face.

The door opened.

It was in an alcove to the side of me. I couldn't see the door. I couldn't see who was standing in the gap the open door provided. I couldn't see how many of them were there waiting to come in.

There was no sound.

They were still tormenting me. Dragging this out.

'I just want my painkillers. They're in my handbag. Do you still have my handbag? It was on my shoulder when you grabbed me. I have an old injury in my arm and it still causes me problems which I take pills for and I need them now. Tying me to this bed hasn't helped at all. Can you loosen my ties?' I rambled. One step at a time. I'd asked for two things. My painkillers and being untied. I should have only asked for the one. If I asked for one it was more likely to be granted.

There was no movement.

'I'm sorry, I need my painkillers. The pain, it's making this difficult for me.'

Then she was there in front of me. Artificial light spilled in from the open door. She stepped from behind the wall and stood facing me. The light pooling around her feet. Her face was more terrified than I imagined I looked.

She was young. Somewhere between eighteen and twenty-three. Her blonde hair was straight and fell to her below her shoulders. Her face was devoid of make-up and her eyes were wide like an animal caught in headlights.

'I'm Hannah,' I said from my position on the bed.

She didn't speak, merely stared at me.

I hadn't heard the door close behind her so I had no idea if it had or if there was someone there guarding it.

'What's your name?' I asked.

Her lips parted but still she didn't speak, but she stretched out her arm and flicked the light on in the room. The puddle of light around her feet disappeared.

'Can you tell me why I'm here? What do you want from me? Is someone else here?' I was asking her too much but I couldn't help it. No matter my training on questioning people, it didn't apply when you were kidnapped in the street and woke up tied to a bed.

The girl raised her hand and it was then I realised she was holding something. A strip of pills. It was from my medication box. Tears of relief from my eyes. She had brought me my painkillers.

'Thank you,' I whispered.

The girl walked to the dressing table and poured a beaker of water. She came to the bed, looked down and must have seen the puddle of yellow I had made. She knelt on the floor, I imagined to the side of my mess, and popped two pills into her hand, and moved her hand towards my face.

'Untie me?' I raised my arms off the bed as far as they would go.

She shook her head and with her hand like a scoop put it to my mouth with the two pills in. She was going to feed them to me. I wasn't to do this myself.

I raged inside, shaking at the binds that tied me. 'Just untie me! You've got me locked in here. What do you think I'm going to do?' I raised my voice so if anyone was by the door they could hear. 'What do you think I'm going to do? Untie me.'

The girl shook. Her hand wobbling in front of my face. She was as afraid as I was. Was she a prisoner here as well? Yet she was in here dealing with me, a woman, tied to a bed. It was a strange situation and I wanted to get to the bottom of it. Could this young woman be an ally? Could I trust her?

I looked into her eyes. She was pleading with me to take the tablets. I lifted my head and opened my mouth. She tipped her hand and the two pills dropped in. She picked up the glass of water from the floor and with one hand held my head steady and with the other she very gently tipped some water into my mouth so I could swallow the pills. The beaker was plastic. They had not left glass in the room with me. Once I had enough I clamped my lips to the beaker and she moved it away.

'Thank you.' I was glad I'd be getting some relief from the pain. If nothing else resolved itself today then getting that relief would have to be enough. The plan was one step at a time and I'd abide by that. I'd managed to get what I'd needed. Now I had to think about what I needed next and work out a way to attain it.

The girl lifted the beaker offering me more water.

'What can I call you?' I tried again.

She turned her face away from me.

'You can speak to me,' I said quietly. 'I'm not angry at you.'

She lifted the beaker again. I had no idea when I would be offered another drink. 'Yes. Please.'

Again she placed a hand behind my head, her hand cool to the touch, and tipped the beaker up to my mouth. I sipped on the water, trying not to lose too much down the sides. It wasn't the easiest drinking position. When I'd had enough I closed my lips on the beaker and she pulled it away.

The girl rose from the floor. She was about to leave.

I didn't want to be left here alone in this room, strapped to the bed. She might not be talking to me but her company was reassuring.

'Do you have to go?' I asked. 'Grab the chair, stay a while?'

She walked to the dressing table and placed the beaker back where she picked it up from.

Desperation welled up in my chest. She couldn't leave. She couldn't leave me alone in here.

'Stay,' I tried again. 'Please.'

She turned and moved towards the door.

'We don't have to talk.' Fear was turning to panic and was clawing its way out of my chest. Too big and heavy to be contained. I couldn't catch my breath. The monster inside me was too strong. 'I won't say anything else if you'll stay.' I'd promise her anything if she would stay in the room with me and not walk out and close the door.

She looked at me and sadness filled her eyes. She was leaving. She was walking out.

'Please no.'

The door closed behind her. She was gone.

I gasped for breath. The air thick like soup. I gasped harder, sucking in all the air I could manage. Realised I was hyperventilating and closed my eyes. I had to calm this down. I had to breathe. I'd had a win with the tablets. I also knew I was not alone in here; whatever capacity this girl was in here it was not complete free will.

I had no idea what lay ahead but I couldn't afford to lose my mind.

24

Aaron walked back into the incident room with a large weight on his shoulders. He needed to phone home and let Lisa know he'd be late but at that moment he couldn't imagine leaving work at all until Hannah was back safe and well. How could they knock off duty if they hadn't located her? How could he return to his wife and children, knowing Hannah was out there somewhere, all alone and needing him?

He shook himself. They couldn't think like this.

'Aaron, you need to see this.' Martin was standing at his desk, his face serious.

Aaron took his jacket off and threw it around his chair. 'What is it?'

'We've seized CCTV from the area Hannah was parked. We don't have a full view but luckily we have Hannah's car.'

A chill swept through Aaron as he walked to Martin's desk. Pasha was sitting with her back to him at her own desk, head down, Ross had wheeled his chair up to her and was bent over, talking quietly to her. This didn't look good.

He stood in front of Martin's monitor. 'You ready?' Martin asked.

'Let's see it.' Aaron pushed his hands into his pockets and tensed his shoulders.

Martin pressed a key and the screen came to life.

Hannah was climbing out of her car. She was there, safe and well. Aaron wanted to tell her to get back in her car and come back to the station. That whatever she was doing was not worth it. He needed her back here with him.

From the side of the screen came two figures in hoodies, you couldn't tell gender or see their faces. One had something in their hands and before Aaron had time to figure out what it was the bag was over Hannah's head and she was clawing at her neck.

Aaron gritted his teeth and kept his eyes on the screen. Maybe they would get a facial shot of one of these people.

They pulled at her, the edge of the hood around her neck, and he watched as her feet stumbled backwards. Then there was a third person and an open car boot. It had been reversed up to them. The licence plate was smeared with something, plus the angle was all wrong.

Nothing was helping on this video. He curled his hands into fists.

Hannah tried to fight them off. She lashed out but they had control of her and she took a punch to the head. Aaron winced.

Then she was at the car boot, they were pushing her in. She was fighting with everything she had not to go inside. She used her feet and her hands but she didn't stand a chance. She was blind and choking and being dragged backwards by her throat.

Aaron's hand went up to his own throat. His fingers danced over the delicate skin under his Adam's apple.

She was inside the boot and then one of the figures leant down to her and she stopped fighting. Had they said something to her? Threatened her family?

The car boot was slammed down.

Aaron wanted to vomit.

The incident room was silent.

Everyone had seen this.

There was nothing helpful here. He couldn't even tell what

gender these people were. But there were three of them. They were organised.

'They're a group,' he said, his voice thick with emotion. 'This isn't one person taking vengeance against some slight they imagine she's done to them. This is organised. We need to figure out why.'

He turned to Martin. 'Let me watch it again.'

Martin rubbed his eyes and did as Aaron requested and the scene started again.

Hannah climbed out of the car.

Aaron needed to pay attention to every detail.

There was no one else around. The two figures approached. He checked out the hood. It was black. Material. Looked to have string or rope around the open edges. Maybe a ready-made bag of some description, like the ones posh handbags are kept in. Lisa had bought an expensive handbag for her fortieth and Aaron had been shocked the bag needed its own bag.

Their clothing was pretty nondescript. Jeans or tracksuit bottoms with hoodies. He could see their hands. 'They're white,' he said.

It wasn't a huge detail but it was more than they had a few minutes ago.

The car backed into the frame and the third individual walked in and popped the boot. It reminded Aaron of something. It niggled at him.

'Rewind to the car backing up.' He pointed at the screen and Martin tapped at a few keys and the car slowly backed up to Hannah again who was struggling against the hood over her head.

'I've seen that car before,' he said.

Pasha stood and walked to his side, quickly followed by Ross.

'Show it again?' asked Pasha.

Martin rewound the clip again and the car reversed into the scene.

Pasha wiped her eyes. Aaron saw that she'd been crying.

'Sorry, can you do it again,' she asked. 'It's familiar.'

'You're sure?' asked Ross.

'No.' Pasha leaned in closer.

The car reversed again.

'Again?'

Martin tapped the keys, the car reversed.

'I know!' shrieked Ross. They all looked at him. 'It's the car that was chasing Matthew Harper the other day!'

25

More time passed and the pain in my arm had subsided and the stress my body was under from being tied to the bed was easing.

By now a full scale search would be underway and Dad and Zoe would have been informed. I worried for Dad. He'd been through enough, with losing Mum and dealing with Zoe going to prison, and me and her not getting on. He wouldn't know how to cope with this. He would feel so useless. That was at the bottom of all of the tragedies he had faced. The feeling of not being able to change anything. Being at the mercy of outside forces. And here he was again, waiting for the police to search for and find one of his daughters, who was hell knew where, having hell knew what done to her.

I was lucky in so far that I was still alive and had been treated reasonably well. I'd been given my painkillers when I'd requested them and had not been harmed – if you didn't count the abduction itself.

This isolation was unnerving though and I begged the silence for the girl to return.

Someone was listening because the door opened and the girl entered. This time she was carrying a tray. From my horizontal position I couldn't see what was on it but I could smell food. They were feeding me.

My stomach grumbled. Another need was being met. If they didn't want me to come to harm though, I was struggling to figure out their motives.

The girl placed the tray on the dressing table and left the room.

How was she expecting me to eat it? Was this some new form of torture?

She very quickly entered again, carrying a bucket. I realised what this was for. The mess on the floor at the side of the bed.

'I'm sorry about that,' I said. 'It was when I woke up. I didn't feel good. It may have been whatever they drugged me with, didn't agree with me.'

She kept up her silence and knelt down and cleaned up the floor. The scent of disinfectant rose up and tickled my nostrils, overpowering the smell of food from across the room.

'I'm Hannah Robbins,' I said. 'A detective with Nottinghamshire police, if they haven't told you. Will you tell me your name?' I was desperate to connect with this girl. To know who she was and why she was here, why she was helping these people.

She scrubbed at the floor and didn't look up. She'd obviously had orders and didn't dare disobey them.

That was it, she was following orders.

I had to connect with her though. I was going stir crazy. I needed her to respond to me. To prove to me I existed here. Yes, they were taking care of me but it was as though I was close to invisible. I lay back on my pillow and waited for her to finish cleaning up the mess on the floor. It wasn't a pleasant task she'd been given. If someone was standing guard by the door then I had to be careful how I tried to communicate with her. Because I couldn't lie here without contact of any kind. I would go insane.

When she'd finished she stood and took the bucket and cloths out to the door. The door closed behind her. I looked across at the dressing table. My food was still sitting on the other side of the room. Was it to stay there as yet more torture?

'Hey!' I shouted. 'What about this food?' It was out of my grasp and I was desperate to eat it.

Almost immediately the door opened and the girl returned without the bucket. Common sense told me she had cleaned up and washed her hands. I let out a small sigh. It was so difficult to think straight while I was in this ridiculous position. She picked up the tray and dragged the chair over to the bed. Sitting on the chair with the tray on her lap, she tipped it a little so I could see it. A small pile of scrambled eggs sat in the middle of the plate. Was that all I was getting? I didn't know when I last ate. Probably this morning. I needed more than this. Then I realised something else as I looked at her. 'You're planning on feeding me?' I asked her incredulous. 'You're not going to untie my hands or even one hand, so I can feed myself?'

She shook her head. It was the most I had got out of her and I realised she was now out of sight of the door and hadn't uttered a word. She had communicated without speaking to me.

'You've been told not to speak to me?' I whispered.

Her eyes widened and she looked down at the plate, picked up the fork and dug into the eggs, putting it up to my mouth.

I shook my head, even though I was ravenous and the eggs, though not much to look at, still smelled good, warm and ready to eat. 'Blink twice if that's true, if you've been told not to talk to me.' I didn't know if there were people outside the door waiting for her.

She held the fork in front of my mouth and I lifted my head as far as I could, straining the muscles in my neck, and opened my mouth accepting the fork, not taking my eyes off her face.

Then it came. Two very slow, very precise blinks.

She scooped up another pile of eggs as I chewed.

What was this set-up? Where was I? Who was this girl? Did she need my help or was she a part of it all – and all what?

I wanted to know what they wanted of me, why they had taken me, what their plans were, all things that required more than a blink.

As the plate emptied I looked up at her 'I can help you if you're in trouble. If we work together, I can help you.'

There was a sharp but very short, barely perceptible shake of her head.

Did this mean she didn't want my help? That she didn't need it and wasn't in trouble? Or that she was terrified of being caught talking to me?

I dropped my head back on the pillow, exhausted from straining up to eat the meal in such a weird position. 'Can I have a drink?' I asked.

She walked to the dressing table and brought me the beaker of water and helped me to drink it.

'Thank you.' I was grateful she was here but realised she was about to leave. I had to get a grip of the panic that was threatening to engulf me again. I had to deal with this one situation at a time. I took a deep breath. 'You know I'm here if you want to talk to me.' Where else could I go?

26

I needed the bathroom; I hadn't been since before I left the station. No way was I going to piss myself in this bed. I would not be turned into an animal in such a short period of time. I screamed for someone to come and help me, shouting that I needed to piss. Though I refused to be an animal by wetting the bed it sure felt animalistic screaming and shouting while pulling against the restraints that tied me down.

Eventually the girl entered the room again. This time, the door closed behind her and I heard it being locked. She looked terrified to be in the room with me, as though I were a dangerous animal and not like she was the one with all the power. She held a small key in her hands which were shaking. Her eyes were wide dark pools in an illuminous face.

'I need to go to the bathroom,' I said to her.

She continued to stand there, shaking.

'You need to untie me and take me to the bathroom.' I shook my hands to indicate the ties that restricted me to the bed.

'This is an en suite room,' she said. Her voice quiet. She'd actually spoken to me.

'What's your name?' I asked quickly. I needed to get a connection going with her.

She shook her head.

'You're not allowed to tell me?'

She shook her head again.

'I don't see the bathroom.'

'It's behind your head.'

Ah, the wall I was up against, it went around a corner and away towards the door which I couldn't see. The en suite was the wall I was pushed up against, in the section between me and the door. That was why they had locked the door. In case I made a run for it. 'Untie me, please.'

She took a couple of steps forward then hesitated.

'I won't hurt you,' I said to her, which was ridiculous considering the situation we were in.

She bit her lower lip.

'I need to go to the bathroom. I haven't been in hours.'

'I don't have to tie you back up once I've undone you, so you'll be free to use the bathroom any time you need,' she said.

My right arm throbbed and reminded me it was not comfortable in this position. This was great news. 'Thank you. Will I still be able to access my medication?'

'Of course.'

'And what about speaking to whoever is in charge?'

She bit her lip some more. 'I can untie you.'

'I want to know why I'm here.' This was infuriating. I couldn't hold a conversation from this prone position. The sooner she let me up the better. One problem at a time. 'Just untie me. Thank you.'

The girl put the key in her pocket and went to my feet first. A good move. Leave my hands to last. Her fingers moved gently as she undid the rope around my ankles. It was good to finally pull my legs back together. My muscles relaxed and I let out a breath.

She stood straight and looked down at me.

'I won't hurt you,' I reiterated.

She leaned down and undid my right arm. The arm furthest away from her. The rope had chaffed my wrist, which was now sore and hot. The release was sweet. I let out a deep sigh. Then she undid my other wrist and I was free. I sat up on the bed and swung my legs around so I was sitting on the edge and she jumped back away from me. 'Someone is outside guarding the door, they're there all the time.' She sounded panicked.

'Hey,' I said. 'I said I wouldn't hurt you and I won't. What I want is to talk to whoever is behind this. I don't believe that's you.'

She shook her head again.

'Right now I need the bathroom. Please tell whoever has me here that I want to talk to them. I want to know what this is all about. I'm presuming someone is behind that door waiting for you in case I try anything?'

This time she nodded.

'Okay. I'll stay here while you leave. Thank you.'

'I'm sorry,' she whispered.

I watched her back away towards the door. She unlocked it and closed it behind her, the lock clicking back into place, securing me in my own hell.

The bathroom was sparse and held nothing that could help me.

I walked back into the bedroom and went to the window, opening the curtain, hoping the window would be my way out. Disappointment plummeted into my stomach like a concrete boulder hitting water, deep and fast. Wooden boards were nailed over the glass. No wonder it was so dark in the room when the light was off. They weren't blackout curtains as I'd thought; it was my exit, boarded up.

27

Aaron looked at Ross, shock rippling through him. 'This is connected to the Matthew Harper investigation? Hannah has been abducted because of something to do with the Harper case?'

This was something none of them had expected.

'Let's look at it again,' said Martin, ever the practical and calm member of the team. He leaned forward and pressed the keys for the whole incident to play out before them yet again. 'Anyone recognise the gait or height of those people, now we think we know what investigation it's linked to?' he asked.

'I'm still gobsmacked that she's been taken because of the lad she ran over,' said Pasha, tears again pricking her eyes.

'He ran out in front of her, she didn't run him over,' said Ross.

She stared at him. 'You know what I mean.'

'I want everything we have on the Matthew Harper case sent to me,' said Aaron. 'We need to go over it with a fine-tooth comb. Assess information we may have passed over the first time. There's something important about this case to someone. Hannah was getting too close for that person's comfort by the looks of it and we need to know what that was.'

'I'll get it to you,' said Martin and strode back to his desk.

Aaron scratched at his chin, stubble pricking at his finger pads. He was in need of a shave but this was a strong lead and there was no way they were going home now. Not while Hannah was out there. 'I'm going back to the hospital,' he said.

'At this hour, you think they'll let you in?' asked Pasha.

Aaron looked at his watch. Time was getting on but he hadn't realised it was so late. 'Visiting time has ended but they might let us speak to him. Come on.'

Pasha didn't need asking twice. She pulled her jacket from the back of her chair and followed Aaron out of the incident room at a jog.

The nurse at the desk gave Aaron a stern look and crossed her arms. 'Visitors left nearly two hours ago, DS Stone.'

Aaron opened his mouth and Pasha stepped in front of him. 'We have a delicate matter of life and death. By morning it could all be too late. We only need to see him for ten minutes or so.'

'He's not been dealing well with his visitors,' the nurse said. 'But he copes a lot better with police visits. It's usually been the DI who comes by, Hannah someone. Is she not on tonight?'

Aaron tensed.

'She can't make it to the hospital,' Pasha said. 'But she'd appreciate any help you could provide.'

The nurse looked tired behind the desk. 'Like I said, he does better with police so you have ten minutes.'

Pasha threw her thank yous over her shoulder as she charged towards Matthew Harper's room with Aaron close behind her. She pushed the door open and found Matt sitting up in bed against a pile of pillows wearing earphones. He pulled them out as the door slammed open and surprise crossed his face. He didn't know Pasha.

He pulled the covers further up his body. Then Aaron walked in and he relaxed slightly.

'DS Stone, this is a surprise. Where's DI Robbins this evening?'

Aaron stepped forward, his hands clenched into fists. Pasha held an arm out and stopped him approaching the bed.

'I'm DC Pasha Lal,' she said. 'DI Robbins can't make it this evening but something urgent has come up and we'd like to talk to you about your case, if you don't mind.'

Matthew Harper looked up at the clock on the wall. 'At this time of evening? Would it not have waited until the morning?'

'As I'm sure you've figured out, this won't wait,' Pasha said as she pulled up a chair to the side of the bed. Aaron stood stoically behind her.

Matt rubbed his forehead. 'I'm sorry, I will help any way I can, but I'm suffering with headaches since I was admitted. It makes concentration difficult. That's why I was listening to an audiobook rather than reading. It's easier for me.' He waved an earbud at them. 'Have you tried audiobooks? I've only recently tried them and they're amazing. I've missed, or forgotten so much. One of the staff brought me in an old phone and headphones so I could listen to them.'

Pasha waved her hand at him. 'Yes, they're great.' They didn't have time for small talk.

'What do you know about where you've been?' asked Aaron.

Matt wrapped the wires of his earphones around the phone they were plugged into and placed it on the tall bedside table. 'I've said this before, I have no idea where I've been. I don't remember anything. I wish I did.'

'What about people?' Aaron pushed. 'There must be someone you remember? Not even your mum?'

Matt looked mortified. 'I wish I could remember my mum. Nothing is coming back to me. Why the emergency tonight?'

'You were running from someone,' said Pasha.

'Running?'

Aaron stepped forward. 'Yes, we have you on CCTV running away from someone. Why was that?'

Matt leaned back, away from him. 'Running away? When?'

'When you ran in front of Hannah's car!' Aaron snapped.

Matt's lips parted. 'I have no idea. I was afraid of someone? Do you know who it was?'

'That's why we're here, to ask you who it was,' Pasha said.

'DI Robbins has been abducted by the very same person who was chasing you,' said Aaron. 'Whatever is going on it's all connected to you and we want to know why that is.' He wasn't in the mood to mess around any longer. If Matt Harper was the key then he had to tell them what he knew.

Matt's hand went up to his mouth. 'Oh my God. You're kidding me. DI Robbins has been kidnapped?'

'I'm afraid so,' said Pasha with a little more compassion to her voice. 'We need your help, Matt. You have to tell us what you know.'

Matt's hands went up to his head. 'I can't remember anything,' he wailed. 'Nothing at all. If I did I would tell you. I would never want anything to happen to DI Robbins, especially on my behalf. Oh no, what was I involved with?'

'That's what we'd like to know,' said Aaron.

'I can't even speak to my family, because I don't know them. It upsets me. I don't remember them and they both want to pick up where they feel we left off. Especially Tara. She talks to me like I'm a little boy and I know I was only a kid when she last saw me but I'm a grown man now and I want to be talked to like an adult. Lucas is different and I can't put my finger on it but he unsettles me. It's been so long since he saw me. Maybe he wants to know where Mum is and thinks I should know. He thinks I should hold all the answers as I've been gone so long and I can't help him and we end up staring at each other in this awful silence. The nurses are doing their best to protect me. But I don't see anyone else other than Tara and Lucas. I really can't help you, I'm sorry. I wish I could.' He rubbed at his face.

A nurse walked into the room and took one look at Matthew's face. 'Okay, time's up.'

'We haven't finished,' said Aaron. He wanted to push Matt harder. The lad had to be hiding something.

'Oh yes, you are.'

Pasha stood from her chair. She took Aaron by the elbow and led him to the door before turning back to Matt. 'Thank you for talking to us, Matt. If you think of anything else please do let us know. As you're aware, it's pretty important we get any small detail.'

The nurse tutted and wrapped a blood pressure cuff around Matt's arm talking quietly to him as she did so.

'He doesn't know anything, Aaron,' Pasha said as they walked down the corridor.

'Someone knows something,' he replied. 'And if we don't push we won't find anything and she'll be alone.'

They walked outside. The night was dark, the air clear.

'I can't bear to think of her alone tonight,' he said. 'She's always been there for me and I get to go home to my family while she's who knows where, having fuck knows what done to her.'

28

Aaron and Pasha stood on the doorstep of Lucas Harper's address and waited for him to answer the door. The house was in darkness but they had no qualms about waking him up. Hannah was missing and it was connected to Matthew Harper. Matthew had been no help so the next stop was his brother.

Aaron knocked hard on the door again. Eventually they heard, 'I'm coming, I'm coming. Hold your horses,' through the door and lights were switched on throughout the house. It was coming alive in front of them.

'He wasn't very happy when he phoned the office earlier, was he?' Pasha asked.

'I don't care how happy he is,' Aaron said. 'He could have been having the sleep of the angels for all I care. I want to talk to him about Hannah and if he wants to get all up in our faces about it he can come to the station to talk about it.'

Pasha kept her mouth shut but Aaron knew he was on dodgy territory, he had no idea on what grounds he'd bring Lucas Harper to the station but so long as Lucas didn't know that, he was prepared to be a little heavy-handed with him.

The key clicked in the lock as it was twisted from the other side and the door opened. Lucas Harper was standing before them in tracksuit bottoms, with bare feet and a bare chest. His hair was ruffled as though he'd been disturbed in bed. A large watch glinted on his right wrist in the hallway light. He glared at them, his eyes dark and thunderous.

'What the hell is this? Do you usually go around disturbing people who are sleeping, or is it simply those you have a hard-on for at the moment?'

Aaron stepped forward, placed his hand on Harper's shoulder, pushed back and walked into the house.

'What the fuck?' Lucas Harper raged.

Pasha stayed on the doorstep, staring after Aaron.

'Let's go inside to talk, shall we?' Aaron said. He had got nothing from one Harper. He certainly was not walking away with nothing from the second one. One of them knew what was going on with Hannah and he wanted answers.

Lucas stared at him, then looked to Pasha who gave him nothing no matter what her thoughts on the situation.

Lucas backed down and followed Aaron, still grumbling about the time and the behaviour of the officers at his house. 'I'm going to put in a complaint against you. You realise that, don't you?'

Aaron didn't care. He would happily lose his job if it meant that Hannah was returned safe and well. His mission was to make that happen. She had been relentless in caring about him after his heart attack. She had taken care of his problem with Baxter. He owed her so much.

He found the living room and waited for Harper and Pasha to join him.

Harper sighed. 'What is it you want?' He folded his arms across his naked chest.

'Do you want to go and put some clothes on, Mr Harper?' Pasha asked.

He glared at her. 'You're worried about my modesty after you invade my house in the night?'

A blush crept up Pasha's cheeks. 'You might feel more comfortable.'

He left the room and Pasha stared at Aaron. Aaron looked around the room, searching for anything that would indicate where Hannah was. 'Good call getting him out of the room,' he said.

'I didn't do it for that,' she spat.

Aaron moved so he could get a better look behind the sofa but there was nothing there. 'Thank you anyway.'

Harper walked back into the room a well-worn sweatshirt covering him. His feet however were still bare. 'Well?'

'It's to do with your brother,' Pasha started.

'Matty? And this couldn't wait until the morning?'

'It couldn't, no,' said Aaron. 'Matthew was being chased when he ran in front of the car. He was being chased by someone in a vehicle. An Astra. Do you know anyone with this vehicle?'

'The first I knew Matty was alive was when you lot came to tell me. Why would I know anything about someone chasing him?' Harper rubbed at his face. 'That's what you came to ask me? Who was chasing my brother?'

'Our DI has been abducted and it's linked to your brother's case. What do you know about that?' Aaron asked him, taking a step forwards.

'Today? When she was supposed to be meeting me? That's why she didn't turn up?' He scratched at his head. 'I suppose I over-reacted when I phoned and complained then. I apologise.'

Pasha inclined her head in acceptance of his apology. Aaron stared at him.

'But I can't help you,' he continued. 'I have no idea what happened to my brother, never mind what happened to your DI. The whole thing is a head-fuck if ever I saw one. I mean, come on. He's been missing eleven years, we all think he's dead and he suddenly turns up. I think it's him you want to be asking questions of, don't you?'

'Believe me, we've asked him but he doesn't seem to remember anything.'

'I get that. He's so stressed out with it all. He's not coping with having visitors from his past who thought he was dead. It's not been good.'

'Going back to the meeting you had planned with DI Robbins, do you know why she wanted to talk to you?' Aaron asked.

Harper shook his head. 'She didn't say, she just said she wanted to talk. When I got there I waited but she didn't show. Obviously I know why now.'

'She wanted to talk to you about your mum, Lucas,' Pasha said.

'My mum?'

'We're still trying to get to the bottom of what happened,' Aaron said.

'Right. Okay.' Harper looked around the room. 'Look, do you want to sit, as you're here?'

'Thank you.' Pasha sat down and looked at Aaron who was staring at Harper. 'Aaron,' she prompted. He turned and looked down at her and then sat beside her. Harper sat opposite.

'We've been informed your mum might have been acting a little out of character in the run-up to her and Matthew going missing,' Aaron said. 'What can you tell us about that?'

Harper let out a sigh. 'It was so long ago. And though I was older than Matty, I was still pretty much a kid. I was about eighteen at the time. Yeah, legally an adult, but my mind was wrapped up with myself.'

'Anything you can remember,' said Pasha. 'You never know what could be helpful.'

'Yeah, she might have been a bit weird, but nothing I could put my finger on. I think she was fed up. But aren't we all, at some time or another? I didn't pay much attention to her. She was the adult in the house. I expected her to get on with it.' He paused and looked at his feet.

Aaron and Pasha gave him the space to figure out his thoughts.

'With hindsight I wish I'd said something to her. Offered to help her with whatever troubled her. But I didn't and here we are. Matty is back and can't remember over half his life, and she's still missing and we don't know if she's alive out there or if she died a long time ago and Matty's been alone all this time. It's all a guessing game, isn't it?'

Aaron couldn't give him an answer about his mum but he figured if they located Hannah then maybe, just maybe, they would find the missing link to Sharon Harper. It was like a great big sucking black hole. Everything was lost inside it and no one could see a way through. 'What about new people in her life?' he persisted.

Harper rolled his eyes. 'You do know how long ago we're talking don't you? I remember everything that happened after they went missing because it was extraordinary, but beforehand, well, that was life. I was getting on with living it and as a selfish teenager I wasn't paying attention to what my mother was doing, and I certainly can't remember it eleven years later. Can you? Remember what your parents were doing or who they were friends with eleven years ago?' Harper rose from his seat. 'I can't tell you anything else. I think you need to go. I'm tired. I need to try to get through to Matty again tomorrow. It's exhausting.'

Aaron wanted more. This wasn't enough, this didn't help Hannah. 'We have an officer who has been taken and you're worried you're not getting enough sleep?' He followed Harper's stance and stood.

Pasha looked up at him lips parted.

'I'm sorry about that, I truly am. But I don't have anything. What do you want me to do, pull something out of fresh air that will lead nowhere? I don't know what was happening with my mum and I have no idea what was happening with Matty before he ran in front of that car. I thought my brother was dead, for fuck's sake.'

Pasha rose. 'We're sorry to have disturbed you. Thank you for your time.' She placed a hand on Aaron's arm.

He let out a breath and turned.

'If you think of anything that could help us, please do get in touch,' she said, handing him her contact card.

The night was still when they stepped outside. It was that time when houses slept, more lights were off than on. Birds were silent and cats roamed like predatory ghosts in the night.

They had nothing. Hannah was out there somewhere and they had nothing.

29

Aaron walked into the incident room in front of Pasha and was met by the tired stressed faces of the rest of the team.

'How did it go?' Ross asked with enthusiasm, eager for something to work on.

Aaron shrugged. 'Matthew Harper was no help at all, still saying he doesn't remember anything even when we informed him that Hannah had been taken and it was connected to him and what he was running from.' He pulled his jacket off and walked to his desk. 'What's been happening here?'

Ross's shoulders dropped.

Martin leaned back in his chair. 'We've been working on the vehicle in the video. It's the second time we've been unable to get a full licence plate which makes it the second time we've been unable to identify it. It'll take weeks, possibly months to identify it from the partial. Obviously we're going to work that angle and track it down, but it's not a lead that's going to bring us closer to finding Hannah any time soon. Though it was good work on Ross's part to identify the vehicle.'

Ross frowned, the lines already in his face deepening.

Pasha walked past him to her desk and patted his shoulder.

'Have the CSU come back with anything yet?' Aaron asked.

Martin shook his head. 'Nothing yet. But going by the video we're not going to get anything from her car as they didn't go near it, they grabbed her after she had exited it.'

'What about Matthew Harper's car? Have they been informed this is linked to his case? If anything in his vehicle can tell us where he's been that could help us.' Aaron needed something. Anything. To say they were a step closer to finding her.

'I updated them,' Martin said. 'And they're working on it as a priority, but we've heard nothing back. It takes time to process evidence in their world. But they are putting a rush on it. They're aware this is for one of our own, Aaron.'

'It's not good enough. We know what this is about but still we're no further forward. How can this be?' He wanted facts and information. The flimsiness of the case was frustrating him.

The room went quiet.

'I'm sorry,' he said. 'I know there's nothing you can do to speed them up and they'll be doing what they can. I shouldn't take my stress out on you.'

Evie walked into the room, her eyes heavy and red-rimmed, her hair tied back away from her face, which was pale and dull.

'What're you still doing here?' Martin asked her.

Evie bit her lower lip for a second. 'I couldn't bear to go home while Hannah is still out there. Do you have anything?' Tears sprang to her eyes.

Pasha walked over to her and wrapped an arm around her shoulders. Evie leaned into the gesture and more tears appeared and rolled down her cheeks. 'Please tell me you have something on her by now?'

'We know the case it's connected to,' said Pasha. 'It's a start.'

'But you don't know where she is?' Evie whispered.

Pasha shook her head.

The atmosphere in the incident room was heavy.

The doors opened again and Detective Superintendent Catherine Walker strode in. She looked around the room and with one glance

Aaron saw her take in the silence, the tear-streaked faces, the expressions of loss and grief. He was aware this was her team breaking. This was one of her own missing.

'The news isn't good but don't despair,' she said. 'Hannah is a strong woman, a fighter. If anyone can get through this, she can. She'll know you have her back and will be searching for her. She'll be holding on to that. It will keep her faith. And if she can keep hers then I damn well expect you lot to keep yours. Are you listening to me?' She stopped to eye every single member of her staff and received a silent agreement from each in response.

'The reason I came down,' said Walker, 'was because I think you should all knock off and go home.'

They stared at her. Aaron crossed his arms. He wasn't moving.

'You won't want to, but how are you going to help Hannah if you are burned out? We need you at your best, not dragging your arses behind you. I've brought extra officers in who will run the office through the night and follow up any leads that they come across, but my A team need to be fully rested to find Hannah and bring her back home where she belongs.' Walker looked to Evie, who was openly sobbing, wrapped in Pasha's arms. 'Go home, Evie. You can't do anything here. Get some rest and come back fresh tomorrow. You can get here early. But you need sleep.' She checked her watch. 'It's one am. I'm not kidding around. Go home and sleep.'

'How do you expect us to sleep when we don't know if Hannah's sleeping or if she's being tortured for information?' said Aaron.

Evie's sobs grew in intensity.

'You may not sleep, but you will be resting. It's a direct order that you vacate this building, DS Stone. We're not stopping for the night.'

The door banged open yet again and a group of four officers that Aaron recognised walked into the incident room as if on cue.

'Get four hours and come back,' she tried again. 'But if this thing drags on you're going to be no help to her if you can't think straight. I know it feels wrong to go home while she's still out there. The police don't sleep, but individual officers certainly need to.'

Ross rubbed his eyes as if all the talk of sleep had reminded him he was tired. Pasha shot him a glare and he put his hand down.

'No one will think badly of you for going home,' Walker pushed. The four officers who had entered the room stayed behind her, waiting to be given their tasks for the night.

'We've got you,' one of them said.

Aaron recognised him as Jason Needham, a good cop he'd crossed paths with a couple of years previously during another investigation.

'We'll keep working while you get some rest and you can pick it back up again in the morning when you get in. And if anything of real significance comes up we'll call you all and you can come back and deal with it yourselves. How does that sound?'

That was something he could work with. Jason was a DS and knew what a team was and how they must be feeling. He was aware how difficult it was for them to what was effectively abandon the investigation to get some sleep, so he had dangled a carrot instead of using the stick of direct orders, and told them they would alert them if they found Hannah.

Aaron looked at the rest of the team. They looked wiped out. The day had taken its toll on them. Walker was right, they did need their rest. No matter how he felt about leaving, he had to think of his team as well as Hannah.

'The minute you think you have something solid you call us,' Aaron said. It wasn't a question. He was making a demand. He wouldn't leave until they agreed.

'I wouldn't do it any other way, mate,' Jason said.

Catherine crossed her arms. 'Now go home.'

The team looked at each other. Was it a betrayal leaving while Hannah was still out there? But they couldn't work indefinitely and Evie was not coping well.

'Can someone make sure Evie gets home?' Catherine asked as they moved past her towards the door.

'I'll get her home,' said Pasha, her arms still wrapped around Evie.

Catherine thanked her and turned her attention back to the four new officers in the incident room.

Aaron wondered if Catherine would follow her own advice and leave for the night, or if she planned on staying to oversee the whole thing.

The incident door slammed behind him and he had an awful feeling he had left Hannah behind.

30

Pasha manoeuvred the car through the silent streets. Evie sat quietly in the passenger seat a tissue scrunched up in her hands, her shoulders slumped and her head down.

'Will you be okay tonight, Evie?' Pasha asked.

Evie wiped at her face. 'I can't believe she's gone.'

It wasn't an answer. 'We'll get her back.'

'You can't know that.' Evie was spiralling in pessimism. Lost in the grief of what had happened to her friend.

'Maybe I can,' Pasha said quietly.

Evie turned and looked at her. 'How can you know that? How can you know we'll find her? That she'll come back safe?'

Pasha let out a quiet sigh. 'I didn't say she'd come back safe, Evie, but I did say she'd come back. I've been through this before. I know how hard it is, the waiting and not knowing. It messes with your head. You think all the worst possible things are happening. You blame yourself. You think you could have done something to stop it.' She glanced at Evie. 'But you couldn't.'

Evie sniffed and narrowed her eyes at Pasha. 'Who are you talking about?'

'I don't talk about it, but my brother went missing when I was twelve and he was seven. He was missing for a week and I'd been responsible for looking after him when he went.'

Silence filled the car.

Evie reached out a hand and placed it on Pasha's arm. 'I'm sorry, Pasha.'

'It was my life-defining moment. For all of us, for Darshit and my parents. He's an alcoholic now and I try to support him. I pick him up from his AA meetings every week.'

'You're saying she's going to come back but she's going to be changed.' Evie pulled her hand back.

'I'm saying she'll come back and we have to focus on that. It's all I can do, Evie. I focus on the fact that Darshit returned, otherwise my head would explode. Going through this all over again, it's nearly too much for me.'

Evie put her hand back. 'Oh, sweetie. I'm so wrapped up in myself, I hadn't realised you were struggling to hold yourself together.'

Pasha shook her head. 'It's not why I'm telling you, Evie. I want you to focus on the fact that Darshit was located and I believe we'll find Hannah. We're a great team. There's no option but to locate her.' She didn't know who she was reassuring more, Evie or herself. The emotional pain she'd experienced since they'd realised Hannah was missing was like a sharp blade in her chest that she couldn't dislodge. Every breath she took moved air past the blade. The pain cut deep.

'Does anyone on the team know?' Evie asked.

Pasha indicated and turned right. 'No, and I'd much rather it stayed that way. I don't want anyone feeling sorry for me when we need to be focusing on Hannah.'

Evie squeezed her arm. 'If you need to talk you can always come and find me.'

Pasha stopped outside Evie's address. She hadn't wanted to burden Evie but disclosing her own fears and concerns had worked to get Evie to think about something else and she had stopped sobbing. 'You'll be okay?' she asked as Evie unbuckled her seat belt.

'I hate that I'm coming home when Hannah isn't, but as you say, we'll get her back. I just worry about what state that will be in.' Evie opened the door. 'Thank you for bringing me home, Pasha, and I'm sorry this is so difficult for you. Remember you're not alone. Take care of yourself.'

Evie climbed out of the car and slammed the door closed behind her.

Pasha watched to make sure she got inside safely then considered her own journey home. Her empty home with no one to comfort her. Her insides twisting in knots. A painful reminder of the time they were searching for Darshit.

A detour was necessary. She needed to see her brother. They were as close as they could be after what had happened to them. He'd been found a week after he went missing in a neighbour's house but had never really spoken about it. Not to her, not to anyone she knew. She hoped he spoke about what happened in counselling sessions which he had started when he was a little older. It wasn't something their parents believed in when they were children. Their business was theirs and they would deal with it within the house. But they never did, deal with it. It was swept under the carpet and both children were encouraged to engage with their lives as though the incident had not occurred.

Darshit had responded by turning to alcohol and their parents didn't understand. Pasha however was there to support him as he needed it. She was the one who had turned away from him for an instant and allowed the bad thing to happen.

He answered the door, bleary-eyed. 'You do know what time it is,' he said.

'My DI has been abducted.'

Darshit stepped aside and opened the door to allow her through. He was awake now. Neither of them had forgotten that period of time. He walked to the kitchen and filled the kettle before switching it on.

'You couldn't have done anything.' He said this to her knowing it counted for both occasions, his own and her DI.

'I feel so helpless. It brings it all back.' She sank into his sofa.

'You want to stay here tonight?'

Pasha did. She didn't want to be alone with her thoughts. She was drowning in them and it wasn't going to help Hannah in the slightest.

Darshit handed her a mug of tea. She took it gratefully and wrapped her hands around it, curling her feet up and under her.

'I'm doing okay,' he said.

'I know.'

'She will as well.'

They drank their tea in silence.

———

31

I t was still dark and I had no idea if it was morning or not and my arm was painful again. I'd slept well but, now I was awake, I was considering ways in which I could escape my confinement. The young woman who was caring for my needs didn't seem inclined to engage with me in any detailed way. I didn't even know her name. The people behind my abduction appeared to want to isolate me as much as they could and I had to hold on. I had to keep my physical and mental strength if I was to survive this.

So far no real harm had come to me, so it wasn't about that. Continuing my decision to take one thing at a time I needed to decide what I wanted to achieve today.

My goal was to talk to the person behind my imprisonment. I wanted to know why they had me and what they hoped to achieve. Maybe I could help them. I needed to let them know I had sway.

A headache started to needle behind my eyes. Lack of sleep and stress were building up to create a tension headache like a band around my head. I rubbed a knuckle into the corner of my eye in an attempt to push the headache away.

With my physical condition being so poor I felt compromised.

Run down and not my best. I had to get my act together if I was to get out of here.

I walked to the window. Through the slim cracks between the slabs of wood I could see it was starting to turn light. I couldn't see anything else. The cracks were far too slim. The planks of wood were pushed together too tightly.

I looked around the room again for anything I could use to prise the wood off the window but there was nothing, just the bed, a wardrobe, a dressing table, a bulb in the ceiling and a plastic jug and plastic beaker for me to drink from. They'd thought this through. I wondered how long this had been planned for, how long I had been a subject of someone's thoughts.

Being left alone in the room for such long periods gave me plenty of time inside my own head. It was a space I wasn't used to being in. I was a busy DI with a full complement of DCs. Being responsible for the workload in the office took up a huge amount of my time and concentration. I wasn't one for self-reflection. Instead I obsessed about work. About the victims, the offenders, the families left behind, even my team and what they were going through. It had been a tough couple of years for them and I cared about how they were coping. Look what happened when Aaron had his heart attack.

And on remembering this a flash of panic sparked in my own chest. How would he cope knowing I had been abducted? Would his heart cope with the stress of searching for me? I wouldn't be able to bear it if my abduction resulted in the loss of Aaron. Yes, he was back at work because he was back to full health, but your heart never fully recovers. I'd learned this during all the research I'd conducted during his sick leave. I'd pestered our pathologist Jack Kidner and also spent a lot of time online, gathering as much knowledge as I could about my friend and what he was facing. I wanted to be there to support him back to health and back to work if that was a possibility, which of course it had been. I'd been so thrilled. But if it had been in his better interest to not return I would have talked him into taking the medical advice and a medical retirement, because I know he would have fought against it. He was as dedicated to the job as much as I was.

Knowing his heart was a little more fragile than usual frightened me. I hoped someone was keeping an eye on him. Making him rest if needed. Lisa, his wife, was good about his diet. She made him a packed lunch now he was back at work. But she couldn't control the stress once he was out of the house.

My team was supportive; they would do good by him, I was sure. I had to tell myself that. I was in a fragile position myself. I couldn't take on extra worry... but I couldn't help it. These were my friends.

I lay back on the bed, the silence in the room loud in my ears. Like putting your ear to a seashell and hearing the sea. It roared in my head. I rubbed at my face, tension running through my limbs, firing through me like electric shocks. I needed to get out and stretch. I fully understood what stir crazy meant. It was a physical reaction, as well as a mental one. The body isn't meant to be confined to one tiny place. It needs to roam and move. Energy moves through us at all times and if you don't get rid of that energy through movement then you feel like your limbs are going to explode and detach from your torso.

I jumped up off the bed and paced around the small piece of carpet, shaking my arms out as I pounded in the smallest of circles.

Not only would this affect my team and potentially Aaron's health but I'd only recently been asked by Dad and Zoe to go through a medical procedure to help Zoe survive a disease that would kill her if I didn't do it.

Here I was locked in a small room thinking of my little sister, and all I wanted to do was make sure she survived and that meant going through the procedure. If I got out of here I would do it. Not just for Dad, but for Zoe. I wanted that second chance with her. Anger was one thing but I couldn't cope with loss and grief. It had been nearly too much to bear when we lost Mum and, looking back, it was probably the trigger for Zoe's hard drug use. She was already a light user, but after Mum's death she had spiralled.

How could I refuse her and watch another member of my family die? It wasn't possible. I needed to escape here and get back to her. She was on a ticking clock. She looked drawn the last time I saw her and half the person she had been before. I didn't have the time to be locked up in here. I needed to get back to Zoe so I could give her what she needed and start to put our lives back together. If I didn't survive this, then Zoe wouldn't survive, and Dad was about to lose two daughters in one hit.

32

Aaron walked into the incident room. Jason looked up at the clock on the wall. It was six-thirty.

'Did you get any sleep?' Jason asked. 'I told you we'd call if anything came through you needed to be aware of.'

Aaron rubbed his face. 'I got a couple of hours. It'll do me until we get her back.'

Jason tapped his pen on his desk. He understood Aaron's feelings. Not only was Hannah a cop, but she was Aaron's supervisor, and it would affect him and his team more than anyone on the force.

'Let me sort you out with a brew while I bring you up to date, mate,' Jason said, looking to one of the other guys on his team.

Aaron sat in his chair. 'I'll have a coffee. Thanks.' The officer Jason had looked at was out the incident room immediately.

Aaron looked to Jason. 'How's it been?' He hadn't really slept. He'd tossed and turned and in a half-dream state had talked to Hannah who had asked him where he was and when he was coming to get her. This resulted in him looking at his clock again and eventually rising from bed with a sad look from Lisa who must have felt every twist and turn from him through the night. He knew she would worry about his heart, worry that the stress would bring on another attack, but she would keep it to herself because she knew that Hannah was in the most danger right now and telling Aaron to wind his worry down would do neither of them any good.

Jason looked down at the computer monitor in front of him. 'There was nothing solid we could do through the night...'

Aaron was silent.

'We couldn't knock on doors for witnesses at two in the morning, so we stuck to doing research. Two of us working on the past case of Matthew and Sharon going missing and two working specifically on Hannah's abduction as we're working on the assumption both are linked.'

'And have we got anywhere?'

The officer from the overnight team strode back into the room clasping a steaming mug and handed it to Aaron who thanked him, grateful for the drink and the kindness of this team even if he was a little curt with them. He didn't mean to be. He was frustrated at not being able to help Hannah any faster than they were doing. He turned his own computer on and waited as it loaded.

'We looked for links but didn't come up with anything,' said Jason. He rubbed his eyes. 'Those images have been with CSU all night and they've been working to clear up any fuzziness that may have prevented us seeing the rest of the licence plate but as of half an hour ago it's still a no go. I'm sorry.'

'No demands have come in?' Aaron asked.

'Nothing,' Jason confirmed.

'We've not heard anything from the media?'

The incident room door swung open and Pasha walked in. A woollen hat pulled down over her head and a scarf hid the bottom half of her face. Between them were a pair of sunglasses.

Aaron squinted at her.

'I didn't get much sleep,' she said in answer to his unspoken question. 'This is me still trying to hibernate on the way in.'

'It's good to see you,' he said and turned back to Jason.

'No, nothing from the press, but Walker didn't want them informed yet, did she?'

'No. I was checking it hadn't been leaked by whoever had her.'

Pasha unwrapped the scarf from around her neck. 'It's been quiet?'

'Silent as a mouse all night,' Jason said.

The door banged open again and Ross and Martin walked in together.

'You lot really don't know how to go home and sleep, do you?' Jason said.

They each gave him a wan smile.

'Let me write up a quick report for Walker and then we'll be out of your hair.' He turned to his computer and started to tap away at the keyboard.

Half an hour later and the night shift were gone and the day team were sitting together with mugs in their hands.

'We're going to have to do a press release,' said Martin. 'We've little to go on. Getting the public involved might be the way to go. Let's get them on board and get their eyes to help us.'

'I'm with you,' said Ross. 'I think we should have done it yesterday. The more eyes out there the better.'

'We don't know what they want with her,' said Pasha. 'Walker wanted to wait to see if they got in touch and see what their demands were. She didn't want to antagonise them if it could be avoided.'

As if on cue the incident room doors opened and Catherine Walker strode through, her dark bob swinging around her face. Aaron didn't know if she'd had much rest, but she looked as though she'd had the sleep of the good. 'Morning, guys. Update?' She looked hopeful. Eyes bright, skin glowing.

Aaron straightened his tie. 'There was nothing from the night shift. No one has claimed responsibility or asked for a ransom, either here or to her father – we've not heard from him anyway. We'll follow up in an hour, give him an extra hour in case he fell asleep late.'

Catherine agreed. 'What are you plans for today?' she asked.

Aaron looked around at the team, considered what they had discussed. 'We think we need to do a press conference. As nothing has come in we want the help of the public. Someone will know who has taken Hannah. They'll be acting extremely twitchy, bearing in mind they've abducted a serving police officer, a detective inspector. Someone has to notice that.'

Walker measured the team up. 'You're all on the same page for this?'

They all agreed.

Aaron didn't dare to breathe. They had nothing to go on and he needed something to do. Something that was active that he could get to grips with.

Walker stared them down for a minute. 'Okay, we'll do it.'

Aaron let out his breath.

'I'll do the talking, Aaron. I know you hate them, but I want you there as well.'

His stomach churned but he nodded. He'd do it for Hannah.

'We'll get them here as soon as we can. Let them know it's urgent, anyone who can't make it misses out on the scoop.' Walker curled her upper lip at using the word scoop for one of her missing officers, but it was the world of the press and she needed them. 'I'll leave it with you to organise. I'll get on and write my statement. Let me know what time you arrange it for. Also, best if we have Baxter there as well. Show a united front.'

She strode out of the incident room, practically walking into Evie who was scrolling through her phone as she pushed through the door.

'Oh my God, I'm so sorry, Ma'am.' Evie's cheeks flushed and she stumbled back a few steps.

'It's okay, Evie. They have news for you in there.'

Evie skipped the rest of the way into the room, her eyes wide, looking for information. Pasha updated her.

Evie's face fell. 'But we're no further forward. Hannah is waking up alone, waiting for us.' She paused, then in nothing more than a whisper, 'If she's even waking up at all.'

33

The door clicked open and I pulled myself into a sitting position. The young woman came in with a tray of breakfast. I was hungry and needed to keep my strength up.

'Morning.' I smiled at her as part of my ongoing attempt to build some kind of relationship with her.

She returned the smile and placed the tray on the dressing table. It was a start.

'Is there any chance I can have some more painkillers this morning? I'm not sure how many I have in my bag, so maybe only one?' I didn't know how long I would be here so I had to stretch them out, while keeping the faith that Aaron and the team were working hard to find me. I'd work from my end to get out.

She said she'd collect my pills.

I rose from the bed and walked towards the tray to see what they'd provided this morning. The girl jumped away from me, backing towards the closed door.

'Hey,' I said, 'I'm not going to hurt you.'

Her wide eyes stared at me.

'Why would I hurt you?' I asked as I peered over at the tray. All I had were two Weetabix with a little milk. No tea, just the water I already had. I was hungry, this wasn't enough after last night. I turned my attention back to the girl. She blinked at me as though trying to figure me out. That made two of us.

I sat on the chair in front of the tray. A plastic spoon had been provided for the cereal. They were taking no chances. 'Are you staying with me while I eat?' I asked her.

A twist of her lips told me she was.

'You have to keep an eye on me.'

She moved across the room and sat on the edge of the bed as I shovelled cereal into my mouth.

'Do you think I can speak to whoever is in charge today?' I asked with a mouth full of Weetabix. I didn't care about manners, I cared about sorting out my predicament.

She shook her head.

'You really don't want to talk to me,' I said.

'I can't tell you anything,' she replied.

I stopped chewing and turned to face her properly. Her voice was quiet and soft. Small like the young girl she was. I wanted to wrap her up and take her away from here with me. 'Why not? Why can't you tell me anything? Don't you know?'

'I'm not allowed,' she said. 'Please finish your breakfast.'

'Not even your name?'

'I'm sorry.'

'But why? Why aren't you allowed?'

'Isolation breaks you down, so you're more susceptible to what we say to you later.'

'So, not even knowing your name is isolating me?'

She flicked at a spot on her sleeve. 'I've said too much.'

It made sense, the lack of conversation, the locked room, not being able to connect with her. 'Why talk to me this morning?'

'It's hard watching you, being the one to interact with you and not talk.'

I agreed with her. How they expected someone so young to conform to their techniques was beyond me. They were pretty specialist techniques. I was feeling ... what? How did it feel being in here with no one to talk to? Nothing to do. Being surrounded by nothing but silence.

I finished the cereal as I didn't know when they would feed me next. The girl had disclosed they had techniques and I didn't know if starving me would be next on their agenda. Whoever *they* were.

When I'd finished the girl stood from the bed and walked towards the tray.

'I can have a painkiller?' I asked. My arm now throbbing deep in my bones.

'Yes, I'm sure you'll be allowed it. We don't want to hurt you.'

That, at least, was good news.

'Thank you.'

She left the room with the tray and I sneaked a look out the door as she left. It was a corridor, the edge of another door in view opposite. A guard ready, I imagined, in case I decided to try to leave the room.

As the door clicked shut behind her the fear fluttered in my chest again. The sense of isolation that they were aiming for was working but I wasn't going to let them know that.

I sat on the edge of the bed and waited for the girl to return. I sat and I waited.

And I waited.

34

I don't know how long I had been waiting but it felt like a good couple of hours had passed and the girl still hadn't returned. Worse case scenarios ran through my head but were derailed by the pain as it sliced through my consciousness.

I dug deep with my knuckles into the scar and kneaded, a flutter of release pulsing through the muscles momentarily before the deep throb broke through and took over again. I wanted to bang my head against the wall to distract myself from what was happening to my body. To give it something different to think about. I was so close to causing myself harm to trigger pain somewhere else when I heard the door unlock and open again.

I jumped up from the bed as the girl came back in.

'I thought you were coming back.'

She turned and locked the door behind her. 'I have.'

'I needed my pills.'

She held out her hand. 'I've brought them as I said I would.'

I snatched them from her. 'I needed them hours ago. Do you have any idea what it's like to be in excruciating pain?'

She took a step back.

'Why did you leave it so long?' I stomped to the dressing table, grabbed the beaker of water and swallowed the pills down in one.

'I came back as soon as I could.'

I rubbed my arm and let out a breath. The pills would start to work soon. I could start to breathe again and relax a little.

'You weren't allowed to come straight back?'

'This was the first opportunity I could come,' she said again.

Someone was controlling her. And in doing so was controlling me and what better way to control me than to withhold my painkillers? It would be a moot point soon enough when they ran out though. I didn't know how many I had in my bag but I hadn't put enough in there for a long stay anywhere.

'You were told to keep me in pain?'

'I have to go now.' She moved towards the door.

'I'm not blaming you.' I gave her space and went to sit on the bed. 'I just want to know my situation. Your situation as well. If we've been pushed together wouldn't it be nice if we got to know one another a little?'

She didn't look convinced and continued to back towards the door.

'I don't want to get you into trouble. I'm locked in this small room all by myself.'

She stopped moving.

'All I want is a little company every now and again. You seem to be it.' I tried a smile; it felt like I was fitting it on someone else's face. I was probably scaring her more.

'People will be worrying about me. Do you have any idea how long they plan on keeping me here?'

She bit her lower lip.

'You don't know, do you?' She was in the dark as much as I was.

'I don't want to get into trouble,' she said.

'What does that look like?'

'I have to go.' She was at the door and unlocking it before I could stop her. She was like a frightened rabbit. Someone had a real hold over her.

The day dragged on. I was alone and bored.

I went to the window again and pulled at the wooden panels that were nailed across it. They were solid and secure. Looking around the room I couldn't see anything with which I could leverage a panel away from the edge.

I checked the drawers of the dressing table, but each and every drawer was empty. The table and drawers themselves were made from wood. It was old. Maybe I could break up a drawer and make myself a weapon. If I slid the drawer back into its position no one would know. The only problem was the guards outside. Would they hear me?

But who was I going to use a weapon against? Would I really attack the girl that came into the room? She appeared to be as much of a victim as I was. I didn't want to harm her or even threaten to hurt her. I wanted to help her escape whatever this place was. Take her with me. But I could fashion a weapon and have it for when the opportunity arose. Surely whoever was in charge would not pass up the chance to taunt me at some point. People like that usually liked to show they were in charge. Flaunt their power.

Would I be able to use a pointed weapon when it came down to it? Could I thrust a sharp piece of wood into another person? This was my life we were talking about. I was the one who was locked up, away from life, from family and friends. If that was what it took to escape then I was damn sure I would do anything I could and I needed to be prepared.

Before I could attempt to create a weapon out of the drawer though I needed to find out more about the workings of this place, to know when I was safe to make a little noise when I split the wood apart. The girl could help me figure this out. She wouldn't return until it was time to feed me next.

I had an idea in my head and I was impatient to carry it out. Impatience, I realised, would be my downfall in here.

I lifted my arm and sniffed. It wasn't too bad yet but I needed a shower. I'd been wearing these clothes since yesterday morning. I'd slept in them. There was a shower in the bathroom but I didn't fancy the idea of stripping off when someone held the power of a key to my room over me. The power to walk in at any moment. Getting naked and having a shower was too vulnerable; being clean was not a top priority. Though it might change at some point depending on how long I was going to be kept locked up like an animal.

Animals were treated better; they were given comfort and human interaction. This silence was excruciating, like a damp heavy blanket, suffocating and restrictive. I was desperate for the girl to come back. I wanted her to stay in the room and talk to me. Not even knowing her name was ridiculous!

I turned and paced some more. Anxiety was clawing inside my chest. I needed to get out of this room. The darkness created by the wood across the window was smothering.

I tried to take a deep breath in. Tried to get a grip of myself. I was slowly unwinding and whoever had control of me in here was winning. I couldn't let that happen. I was a detective inspector. If anyone could get through something like this then it was going to be me. I wasn't going to spiral into crazy. That was what they wanted but I wouldn't give them the satisfaction. I'd keep it together.

My chest contracted. I gulped air in as hard as I could.

'Someone!' I screamed. I needed someone. I needed someone to come into the room to talk to me. To acknowledge I was a person in here.

To acknowledge I existed.

35

They'd run press conferences before but this one was different. Usually there were family members sitting at the front of the room, begging for their loved one to return or be returned, depending on whether they thought they had left of their own accord or had been taken against their will. This was as much to assess the family as it was to get the missing person back. To see how they reacted under the pressure of the media spotlight because in a high percentage of cases a person close, was responsible for whatever had happened.

Aaron looked at the detectives milling around behind the scenes, waiting to go forward and talk about Hannah and ask the public for their help. Because this time there was no genetic family, it was police family only. There was no suspicion on David or Zoe. Hannah had been taken because she was a police officer. That much was already clear and there was no need to put her family through the strain of being quizzed by the media when they heard what this case was about.

The press conference would turn into something akin to a shark tank at feeding time. This was the first time in history that a UK officer had ever been abducted. Yes, they had been killed in the line of duty, but abducted? It had never happened. David and Zoe would crumble under that kind of scrutiny. The press would want to know everything about Hannah. They'd want to know about her personal life, her professional life. They'd want to know what had driven this crime. They'd try to look for angles that just weren't there. Yes, the press could be helpful, which was why they were gathered here, but it was a difficult dance. You had to be extremely careful where you placed your feet or you'd lose your toes.

A trickle of sweat slid down Aaron's spine. He wriggled his shoulders trying to free his shirt from his back.

Walker approached him. 'We're nearly ready, Aaron.' Her exterior, calm and steady. Were there duck feet paddling like crazy underneath the cool surface?

Baxter was standing in a corner, his hands shoved deep in his pockets. Aaron could smell the cigarette smoke on him from here. He was less serene than his immediate boss.

Once this was out in the public domain there would be no taking it back. No one knew if they were doing the right thing. If this would help Hannah or if they were putting her in more danger. They'd heard nothing from those who had taken her so had no playbook to follow. They were working blind and it was disorientating. For Hannah, it could be a lot more than disorientating; it could prove fatal. Was that the aim of all this, to have them blind and anxious?

Aaron straightened his tie. Rubbed at his chin, the thin layer of invisible stubble pricking the pads of his fingers. 'I'm ready when you are.'

Walker straightened her shoulders and pushed them back, lifting her posture in the process. 'Let's do this.'

Aaron stepped forward. He was the first one out into the glare of the media storm that was about to erupt.

It was all quiet at the moment, other than a low hum as the journalists whispered to each other, trying to figure out why they had been called in. Not one of them had heard of a crime on the streets, a murder, or child abduction or a large drugs bust, with vans full of police lining a street. They had no idea what was coming and it made them uneasy when they couldn't get a head start on a story.

Aaron sat down, looked out at the waiting faces, all watching the line of officers coming out. Walker sat next to him, Baxter on her other side.

The hum of the journalists went up a notch when they saw the high-level detectives out here to talk to them.

Walker cleared her throat. Aaron clasped his hands in front of him on the table. He needed to keep still and show no outward sign of being overly concerned or worried. They wanted to look as though they had this in hand. Asking the public for help was another tool in their toolkit. They couldn't let on that they were scrabbling for every tiny crumb of information.

The room dropped into silence and waited for Walker to speak.

A few flashbulbs went off and Aaron could feel himself paling under the glare of them.

'We've asked you here today as we need the support of the public,' Walker began.

The journalists had their heads down and were scribbling in notebooks.

'Yesterday afternoon one of our detectives was abducted while on—'

Aaron didn't hear anything else she said as the room erupted. Journalists shouted questions, some put phones to their ears and relayed this information to their offices so it could lead their online stories. But they only had the headline.

Walker closed her mouth and sat still, waiting them out. Aaron knew she would not let this rabble undermine what she wanted to achieve here today. He glared at them and after a couple of minutes they realised they weren't going to get the information they wanted until they were quiet and listened. It was like dealing with a class-room of children.

Once the room was quiet again, Walker started anew.

'Thank you. This can only work if we cooperate. We have important information to impart and I'm sure, from your reaction, you're

interested in hearing it. But for us both to get what we want we need
to work together. I hope we can do that.'

She paused again for effect. Showing the crowd that silence was
what she needed. Aaron was in awe of how she controlled a room.
She deserved her rank.

'As I said, one of our detectives was abducted yesterday while she
was on duty.' She paused again to make sure they were listening and
were not about to launch at her again. Once she was satisfied, she
continued. 'The officer abducted was Detective Inspector Hannah
Robbins.'

Aaron flinched.

There was a collective gasp from the press. They knew Hannah.
They'd been briefed by her on plenty of other cases.

He watched as they all shuffled forward on their seats. Phones
were clutched but this time they stayed silent. Text messages were
sent. Eyes were still forward on Walker as they waited for more information. A lone hand went up at the back.

'I'll take questions at the end,' she said. 'At this point in time
we've had no demands and no one has taken responsibility for this
abduction. The reason for this press conference is to ask the public
for their help. We'll give out the helpline number at the end.
Someone out there will know who has done this. The person who
committed this evil crime against the police, against those who are
here to protect you, will be behaving strangely. It's a big deal to
abduct a police officer. They're unlikely to be going about their daily
life and behaving as though nothing is different. Someone will
notice. If you think someone in your life is hiding something this big,
let us know.'

More hands were going up. Aaron knew what they wanted.
Walker had avoided telling them what Hannah had been working on.
The case was weird enough as it was, without adding this to it.

He heard the quiet sigh escape from her lips at the side of him.
'Hannah' she was personalising her, 'has family at home who are
waiting to hear positive news. With your help we can hopefully give
them what they need.'

Aaron looked at the shocked but expectant faces. They wanted the full story. They didn't want to be used and fobbed off.

Walker inclined her head towards the first hand that had gone up at the back.

'Hugh Robinson, Nottingham Today.' The local paper. 'What case was DI Robbins investigating when she was abducted?'

Silence expanded in the room like an air bubble filling the space.

Walker answered the question. She had not wanted to link these two cases publicly, but maybe it wasn't a bad thing, maybe the case they were working on would be the trigger the members of the public would need to look at those closest to them.

'Hannah,' that personal connection again, 'was working on the Matthew Harper case when she was abducted.' She didn't elaborate or give them any further details.

A murmur went around the room but they kept it low.

More hands were up. Walker indicated another journalist. Another introduction and then the question. 'What leads do you have at the moment?'

'We can't give out operational details, for reasons I'm sure you'll appreciate.' She was keeping her answers as short as possible. 'One more question and then we're done.' She gave a last nod and the journalist pulled her hand down and introduced herself. She was from the local BBC channel.

'Do you believe the two cases are linked? The abduction and Matthew Harper? Or do you think they're separate?'

The flashbulbs were going mad. Aaron was sweating profusely and couldn't wait to get out from under this scrutiny. He may not have said anything but his body language, along with Baxter's, would be assessed, as well as every word that came out of Walker's mouth. This was huge news. He tried not to wriggle at the discomfort of the sweat on his body beneath his shirt. Not long to go now.

'At this stage we are keeping an open mind, but initial lines of enquiry do seem to suggest that the two cases may be linked.'

The room erupted again. They'd been told there'd be no more questions so they would try to bombard Walker to see if she'd answer any that were randomly thrown at her. You could barely make out any questions over the cacophony of noise though.

'Thank you for your time,' Walker said, rising from her chair.

Aaron and Baxter followed suit, Aaron glad to be able to move again.

'If you could publicise the helpline number that would be most appreciated. You will be given a briefing pack on your way out with the pertinent details in it.'

The pack included a photograph of Hannah, her car, the location she was abducted from and the helpline number, as well as the day, date and time of the abduction.

Baxter turned and filed out from behind the desk, Walker followed and Aaron let out a breath as he followed her from the room. Once out he was able to breathe again. He inhaled deeply, the air in the corridor fresh like outside compared to the room he'd left.

They had to wait and see if the press briefing would yield any results. Aaron couldn't bear to think of Hannah waiting for them to find her, while they floundered.

36

The girl came in carrying a tray as usual. The tray held a plate covered by another upside down on top and a clean plastic beaker for water. I didn't hold out much hope for what was beneath the plate.

She moved to the dressing table and gently placed it down. I was grateful she was here. Not just for the food, no matter the blandness of what they were feeding me, but because of her company. Being alone was warping my mind.

I walked over to the dressing table and sat in the chair. The girl perched on the edge of the bed as was becoming routine for us.

I lifted the plate and beneath it was a dish of mashed potato. Mashed potato alone. I nearly heaved but I held myself together. It was mash, for God's sake, I could stomach it. Much as I craved something with a little more substance and a little more flavour. I picked up my fork.

'I'm glad you stay while I eat,' I said to the girl as I dug into the mound of potato.

She stared at me, silent.

'Do you have to stay with me or do you choose to?'

She glanced at the door. This was my chance to ask the question.

'Is there always someone out there guarding me?'

She looked to the floor, back to the door and then finally at me before giving me a silent nod.

'I thought so. Not that I can get out of here. There's nothing to use. You have me locked down pretty tightly.' I wanted to reassure her but I also wanted them to believe that I had given up on any idea of escape, even though giving up was the last thing on my mind. Though I had to admit they had my mind twisted up quite well with the nothing food and the lack of anyone to engage with. I was close to begging them, asking them what they wanted from me if only they would feed me better and talk to me more. I wasn't used to being locked up. I was a police officer; yes, I had some strength, but I wasn't a soldier, trained for combat, trained for interrogation techniques, trained to withstand torture, which is what this was like. I felt pared back, the basic part of me. Which I'm sure is precisely what they wanted.

The room was dark and I rose and flicked the light switch on before sitting back at the dressing table. The mash was claggy in my mouth. I took a drink of water.

'Is there any chance of a change of diet tomorrow?' I asked.

'I'm sorry,' she said. 'I only bring you what I'm given.'

With effort, I scraped the last of the potato off my plate and finished it. I turned to her. 'How long have you been here?' Had she been brought here as I had and stayed, or had she come of her own accord?

She shrugged. 'We don't keep track of time with calendars. That's an outside world thing meant to keep everyone in check. We move to our own time. Live life as we want to.'

Bullshit if ever I'd heard it. A line fed to her to control her. 'You like it here?'

She stood to collect my plate.

Panic rose in my chest again. I didn't want her to leave yet. 'Can you stay a bit longer and chat with me?'

She looked at the door. 'I can't. I have to take your plate back to the kitchen so it can be cleaned.'

She was afraid. She didn't enjoy living here like this; she was being controlled by fear. 'You can talk to me,' I told her.

The girl placed the lid plate onto the tray and picked it all up. 'I'll ask them about your food,' she said.

I tried to control myself. Getting into a state was not going to do me any good, as I'd already found out. I took a deep breath and sat on the bed the girl had vacated.

'I'll see you in the morning,' she said quietly.

I nodded. Mute. Afraid if I spoke I would sob and frighten her.

The door opened, she left and it clicked as it was secured behind her. The silence of the room enveloped me. I shuffled up the bed until my back was against the headboard and wrapped my arms around my bent knees. How much longer could I endure this treatment in here? They had to tell me what was happening and why, sooner rather than later. They couldn't hold me here indefinitely.

Or could they? It seemed that was exactly what they were doing.

I grew tired as I mulled over my situation, my eyelids getting heavy. It was strange how tiring being alone in a room all day made you.

My mind drifted to Dad and Zoe. To getting out of this room. To seeing them both again. To freedom.

37

Aaron stared at the text message on his phone. Lisa was asking what time he would be home and if he wanted her to save some dinner for him.

He shook his head. He had no answer for her. He had no answers full stop, and this frustrated the life out of him.

It was hours since the press conference and not a single lead had come in. No reliable sightings of Hannah since her abduction. No one reporting a family member or boyfriend or husband was acting strangely.

Darkness had fallen and a sense of failure had fallen over the team at the same time. Ross was at his desk with his head in his hands. Pasha was scrolling through the incident logs from the last twenty-four hours to see if anything jumped out at her that might be a sign from Hannah or a clue from the people who had her. She was glued to the screen, her fists rubbing at her eyes. Martin was answering the helpline but it was mostly people claiming to have seen Hannah in her car somewhere but the police had her car. The callers were after police attention so they could claim they were involved in the investigation.

Jason walked in with Catherine.

Aaron flew up from his chair.

'Don't start, Aaron,' she said the minute he was up.

'Not again.' He couldn't bear it.

'We don't know how long this is going to go on. You need a break. You're no good to her without it. Let your team rest, Aaron. This is not a blot on your copybook. This is me looking out for you and your team.'

He couldn't get his head around it. How they hadn't managed to make any further inroads. How Hannah could simply disappear the way she had.

The frustration was building up inside him and he needed to discharge the tension before it exploded. If he was stressed he would usually do some drawing at home but that wouldn't help right now. It would be better for him to get his trainers on and go for a run. No matter how late it was, he needed to get out and pound the pavements. He inclined his head to Walker.

The team looked at him. Saw him acquiesce and each of them let out a breath. They were tired but they were stressed too. He wished he could sort this out for all of them. They all cared as much as he did.

Jason approached him. 'You'll be the first call I make if anything comes in overnight, mate.'

Aaron knew he meant it and nodded. It was all he could do. He had to get home and get out on the streets. He would run and he would run and he would run. He'd run until he could run no more and then he'd run that bit further and then he'd climb into bed beside Lisa for a couple of hours before heading back into work.

38

I'd slept all night. I didn't understand how I was sleeping so well in such circumstances. I'd have thought I'd be pacing around half the night, itching to escape but I was exhausted being penned in this way.

The day progressed pretty much the same as the previous day. I saw no one other than the girl with no name and I ate nothing but bland tasteless food, provided so that I wouldn't starve to death. It was good in one way; they planned on keeping me alive at least. I could hold on to that. But the isolation and desperation were eating away at me. All sense of time and place and people and socialisation was slipping away. The window was locked down tight so there was no real air getting in. I was suffocating in both body and mind. The only thing I could do for myself was keep myself strong by small exercises. Star-jumps, sit-ups and running on the spot. I couldn't allow myself to wither and die here.

It was strange the way the bare bones of the day both dragged and slipped past in a haze of nothingness. Before I knew it the girl was leaving and I was slipping into sleep on the bed again.

Another morning, another day with streams of light punctured the room through the tiny slats between the wood up at the window.

I pushed my hands onto the bed, lifting myself up and caught a whiff of body odour as I did so.

How long had I been here? How long had it been since I'd showered? I needed a shower. Urgh. The thought didn't fill me with joy though.

I was sick at the thought of what could happen but realised I wasn't going to escape or be released from here any time soon. At some point I would have to strip off and take a shower.

I knew there was someone outside of my room at all times. The girl had acknowledged as such, plus I occasionally heard shuffling, the odd conversation as they maybe changed shift. What if one of them decided to come in while I was in the shower, or *because* they heard the shower running? It was a thought I could barely stomach.

So far I hadn't been physically harmed. But the fear still gripped me when it came to taking my clothes off voluntarily.

On the other hand the stench was so bad from under my arms that it was driving me insane. Which would be worse? Staying as I was and getting worse and worse by the hour or taking a shower?

All the facilities were there for me. There was shower gel and shampoo on the side of the bath and a large bath towel on the radiator. There was even a change of clothes in the wardrobe. Not to my taste but they were clean. I hadn't changed yet for fear of stripping in the room.

I put my ear to the door and listened. It was silent out there. That didn't mean there was no one guarding my door, waiting for an opportunity to come in and assault me. Yes, he'd have a battle on his hands, but I'd be at a disadvantage. I'd be naked and slippery wet, plus I was considerably weaker with the rations they'd put me on. It would be easy enough for an average-sized man to overpower me, no matter how hard I fought.

There was no sound, but a prickle ran up my spine as I sensed a presence outside the door.

A decision had to be made. There was no lock on the bathroom door.

I entered the bathroom and stared at the shower head hanging over the bath. Dreamed of the water sliding over me, cleaning me, refreshing me.

It wouldn't take long to shower. I could be in and out before they realised I was even in there, couldn't I?

Dipping my nose down to my armpit again, I made the decision that I needed to get clean. I could barely think straight for the smell that was emanating from me. The human body is not pleasant if you don't take care of it.

I closed the bathroom door and held my breath.

Nothing happened, but I'd been to the toilet plenty of times without being disturbed. It was the shower water that would alert them to my state of undress so I would put that on at the very last minute.

Slowly I removed my clothes and lay them on the floor. Still paralysed with fear I stood naked and strained to hear through two doors for a sign I was going to be in trouble.

There was nothing.

It had been days locked up in this darkened room. Time was a concept I barely understood and only grasped because of mealtimes when the girl came in. I was craving proper food and now I stood naked in the bathroom, too scared to shower for fear of what might happen. They were breaking me down and even though I recognised this I was absolutely unable to prevent it happening. Their control was all-consuming and my power had been completely removed.

I started to shiver. Pimples pricked my arms and legs. I had to do this. They didn't want to harm me. If they wanted to hurt me they could have come in and done it at any time. But maybe playing with me this way was another of their mind games.

I rubbed my hands through my hair. It was like straw. I pushed the heel of a hand into my eye socket. I would not let them break me.

I climbed into the bath, the base of it cool beneath my feet and stood under the shower head, staring at the knob that would turn the water on. Picking up the shampoo in readiness, I took a deep juddering breath. Then I did it, I leaned forward and twisted the knob and with a whoosh the water cascaded down onto my tired and stinky body. I turned and tipped my head under, soaking my hair, and quickly turned the water off, hoping no one had heard. Choosing to lather up my hair while the water was off. My hands worked quickly, kneading into my head, digging in deep to clean as well as I could because I didn't know when I would next be able to do this. Bubbles slid down my face and into my eyes. I squeezed them shut and felt forward for the knob again and twisted once more for the water to rinse away the lather.

It was warm and luxurious. The best I had felt in days. But I wasn't here to feel good. This was a necessity only. Again I switched it off, though if they were paying attention they'd have probably heard it this time, as I washed the shampoo out. I was making an effort at stealth by turning it off.

So with it off once more I lathered my body, paying particular attention to the nooks and crannies that would fester quickly if not cleaned again soon and then cleaned it all off with another rush of water.

Once I was done I clambered out of the bath and towelled myself dry. I felt so much better for having showered but I wouldn't feel safe until I was fully dressed again. I climbed into the loose T-shirt and jersey trousers that had been in the wardrobe and bent over, putting my hands on my knees, weak now I'd rushed through that.

I was a caged animal and was grateful to have been left in peace for ten necessary minutes. How grateful would I turn out to be over the coming days? How far would they be able to break me down? I had to hold onto who I was. Fight for what would come after this. I had to hold on. I slid down to the floor, the pressure of taking a simple shower too much to bear.

3939

Aaron looked through his emails as the team talked. There was a heavy weariness that followed him around but he would not give in to it. With little sleep and long hours his body was functioning as best it could and he was pushing it to its very limits. There would be no slowing down until Hannah was home, no matter how long that took. As long as she was in trouble then he, and the rest of the team, could cope with exhaustion.

He opened an email from Doug, the crime scene manager, that had come through five minutes earlier.

Aaron read it once and then read it again.

'Listen up,' he said, his voice sharp. The team stopped talking and turned to look at him.

'I've had an email from CSU...'

Mugs were placed back on desks. He had their full attention.

'Doug says the blood that was on Matthew Harper's clothing when he was hit by Hannah has been tested and they have the results.'

It was early and they hadn't had a briefing yet but he wasn't going to wait. This was the first lead they'd had in days. The fatigue in his body was now electrified with hope.

The doors to the incident room slammed open and Catherine Walker strode through. It was likely she was as tired as the rest of them but she looked smart and efficient as usual. She hadn't been present during the shift changeover an hour ago. This was the first they had seen of her today.

'Just in time, Ma'am,' Ross said, sitting up a little straighter. 'The sarge has email results from CSU about the clothing seized from Matthew Harper the day the DI hit him.'

Walker raised an eyebrow and looked to Aaron. 'Okay, let's have it then.'

Aaron looked back at his screen. 'They don't have a full match to anyone in the system.'

There was a groan around the room.

'But,' Aaron continued, 'there was a partial match to a family member whose details are on record.'

They looked at him expectantly.

'Richard Pike, St Ann's. Local. He was arrested and charged with an ABH.'

'The blood belongs to someone related to Pike?' asked Ross.

'Yes. Doug says it'll be close relative.' Aaron stood and pulled his coat from the back of his chair. 'Martin, you free?'

Martin rose. No one cared how early it was. If they went now they would catch Pike before he left for work.

'I want to be updated as soon as you're back,' said Walker.

The door opened again and Evie walked in. This was the routine in a morning now. Walker, Baxter and Evie would all come through to the incident room at some point early in the morning to find out what the plans for the day were or to see if there had been any news overnight.

Evie never failed to look hopeful when she entered and Aaron turned away from her as he pushed his arms into his jacket sleeves.

'What's happening?' she asked.

Pasha explained about the email. 'Aaron and Martin are on their way to interview Pike now. It's a lead we didn't have yesterday.'

Evie frowned.

Pasha tapped on her desk with a finger. 'It might not be a direct link to Hannah, Evie, but the Matt Harper case is connected to her and the more we push on this investigation the closer we get to finding her. There's something about this that caused them to come after her and we need to find out what it was.'

Evie put a finger in her mouth and nibbled the skin at the edge. 'I trust you guys. Let me know what I can do to help.'

It was time to go. Martin had to stride to catch Aaron up who was already halfway down the corridor. He had a witness to speak to and he wasn't stopping for anyone.

40

I t was cold out this morning and Aaron hoped that wherever Hannah was, it wasn't outside. He pushed his hands in his pockets as he waited with Martin for Pike's front door to open.

All the curtains were closed and the house looked to be sleeping. It reminded Aaron of the visit to Lucas Harper and he imagined they would get a similar response if they were waking the occupants up. He didn't care though. They were having a better day than Hannah, and that was all that mattered.

The door stayed closed but a female voice shouted from behind it, wanting to know who was knocking so early.

'Police,' shouted Aaron. 'Please open the door, we need to speak with you.'

'Do you have a warrant?' came the response.

Aaron blew air out and raised his voice. 'We don't need a warrant, Mrs Pike. We're not here to make an arrest or search the premises at this time. We only want to talk to you. You may be able to help us.'

'It's early, go away.'

'We can do this through the door if you'd prefer.' He raised his voice even more. 'It's important that the police talk to your husband, Mrs Pike.'

The door opened a crack. 'Keep your voice down,' she spat. 'Do you want the neighbours to hear you?'

Aaron shrugged. 'I don't mind. Do you, Mrs Pike?'

She sighed and opened the door. 'Richard is in bed.'

Aaron and Martin stepped into the house. 'Can you get him, please?'

Mrs Pike pulled her dressing gown tighter around her ample frame and climbed the stairs. Aaron noticed green eyes peering down from the top step at them as she passed by. A flick of a black tail behind the eyes identified that a cat was watching proceedings.

Aaron could hear mumblings coming from a room upstairs as Mrs Pike woke her husband and explained that the police were here to speak with him. There was a chill in the air as no heating was on. It wasn't much warmer in the house than it was outside. Aaron hunched his shoulders as he tensed against the cold.

'Let's hope we can bring this guy around and onside,' said Martin. 'They're not happy we came so early.'

Aaron didn't care about how happy they were, he only cared about Hannah, but Martin was right, they needed Richard Pike to talk to them. And that meant not aggravating him any more than they already had by arriving at this hour.

There was a heavy thud above them. A couple of minutes passed and equally heavy steps made their way down the stairs towards them. He was overweight but his eyes were sharp as he eyed them up on his descent. Dark hair was pushed back away from his face. His feet were pushed into fluffy slippers.

Martin watched as the man approached them. 'Mr Pike, sorry for the early call, it's an important matter that can't wait. I'm sure you'll understand once we talk with you about it. Can we go and sit down?'

He had taken Pike by surprise. Aaron didn't know if the man had been going to give them grief but Martin had won him over and he quietly moved past them, towards the living room.

They followed him. The room was in darkness, the curtains still closed. Mrs Pike followed the group and she opened them causing light to come flooding in.

She then sat beside her husband, still wrapped in her dressing gown as opposed to her husband, who had pulled on a pair of trousers and a T-shirt. The dressing gown parted at the knee, exposing a little too much flesh of her thigh. Aaron focused on Richard Pike.

'What can I do for you?' Richard Pike asked, his voice deep and gruff.

'It's a complicated matter,' started Martin. It was as though he was aware of the tension running through Aaron.

'Spit it out then,' Pike grumbled.

'We seized some clothing from a male a number of days ago,' continued Aaron. 'It was covered in blood and we didn't know who it belonged to so we had it tested.'

The Pikes looked disinterested. Bored by the morning intrusion.

'We had the results back this morning and though it's not an exact match the blood had clear links to someone we have on record.'

Richard Pike raised an eyebrow, guessing where this might be leading.

Aaron leaned forward. 'It was a partial match to you, Mr Pike.'

Mrs Pike looked at her husband. 'They're saying you've been bleeding?'

Richard Pike shot her a look. 'No, you stupid woman.' He rolled his eyes. 'They're saying someone related to me has been bleeding all over some bloke's clothes. They traced him because of the fight I was arrested for when I was little more than a kid myself.'

She opened and closed her mouth.

'Do you have any idea who this relative might be?' asked Martin. 'It's important that we trace them and make sure they're well. It was quite a large amount of blood and we're worried about their welfare.'

Pike rubbed the stubble on his chin but didn't say anything.

His wife looked like she wanted to say something. She grabbed his arm and Aaron watched as she squeezed and stared into his eyes. 'Richard,' she said. 'It could be...'

'It could be who?' asked Aaron.

Richard Pike shook his head. 'I doubt it.'

'But, Richard, what if it is and we haven't said anything?'

'Mrs Pike, you need to tell us what you know,' said Aaron. This case is also linked to an abduction. There are two people we are very worried about and knowing who the blood belongs to and identifying where that person is of paramount importance.'

Mrs Pike squeezed her husband's arm harder. 'Richard?'

'Mrs Pike, tell us what you know.' Aaron didn't have the patience to wait for her to persuade her husband.

She looked at him and back to her husband who shrugged. 'Our son walked out of the house about four weeks ago. It might be him,' she said, her body slumping where she sat.

'You didn't report him missing?' said Martin.

'He's an adult,' said Richard Pike. 'He can come and go as he pleases. He told us in no uncertain terms he was leaving.'

'It sounds acrimonious,' Martin pushed.

'He said he was going to live with a group of friends,' Mrs Pike said.

Richard Pike interrupted. 'Sounded like a cult.'

'In what way?' asked Martin.

Aaron sat on the edge of his seat. Was this the lead they had been looking for?

'He'd met these people and started spouting this hippy dippy shit and then all of a sudden said he was going to give up his worldly goods and go and live with them. He was going to remove himself from the sins of the world. If that's not a cult, I don't know what is.'

'And do you have an address for him?' asked Aaron, hopeful.

Both the Pikes shook their heads. 'He wouldn't tell us. Said he had to cut himself off from the world and that included us.'

Tears filled Mrs Pike's eyes and she turned to Aaron. 'Please find him. If he's in trouble, find him and bring him home.'

Aaron was stuck for words. His one chance at locating Hannah had gone.

'We will find him,' said Martin. 'We'll do everything we can. Any information you can provide will be helpful. A list of items he took, details of people he talked about or you met, anything at all, no matter how small.'

She rose from her seat and crossed the room, picked up a framed photo off the wall on the other side of the room and brought it over. 'This is Andrew. Please find my son and bring him home safe.'

Martin took the photo and looked down at the image. A young man was smiling out at him, on either side were the parents, Mr and Mrs Pike, in better days when the police were not disturbing them in the morning searching for answers and worrying them about their son. Martin obtained Andrew's details then handed them his card. 'Contact us if you think of anything at all.'

'You think he's in trouble?' asked Mrs Pike. 'He's an adult and can go wherever he wants and we can't do anything about it, but you think this blood is his? That's he's in terrible trouble?' She didn't wait for an answer, she turned to her husband. 'We should have done something about it when he left. We should have reported him missing. Done something. Tried to stop him.' A sob welled up in her chest and stopped the flow of words. Her hand flew to her chest and she broke down. 'You hear such dreadful things about these places and my boy, that's where he's gone. And his blood is all over someone's clothes. What have they done to him?'

'Does he have a car?' asked Aaron, thinking of the vehicle in the CCTV image.

'He does. It was the one thing he took with him. He said the group might need a car.'

Aaron's spirits raised again. 'What car is it?'

Richard Pike rubbed his head. 'An Astra'

Aaron and Martin looked at each other. That was the vehicle on the CCTV. It may not have been Andrew Pike behind the wheel chasing Matthew Harper or abducting Hannah, but this was the first tangible evidence they had that it was all connected.

'We need the registration of the vehicle,' Aaron said.

Richard Pike reeled it off and Martin noted it down.

'This is really helpful,' Martin told them. 'We'll let you know as soon as we have any information on Andrew. Please be assured we are working around the clock on this case. You may hear information in the press about it as one of our officers has been abducted by this group. Please try not to be further alarmed. We'll find Andrew and we'll find our officer. They're both being urgently searched for.'

There was a gasp from Mrs Pike.

'What the hell did he get himself involved with?' her husband said, shaking his head.

'We don't know as yet.' Martin put his notebook back in his pocket. 'But be assured this is our top priority.

41

Pasha watched as Aaron and Martin strode into the incident room, eager to get to work on the information they had.

'What is it?' Pasha asked.

Martin filled her in.

'A cult? They really exist and there's one in Notts?'

'So it would seem.'

Aaron was talking to Ross. 'We need this licence plate putting through the ANPR system straight away. Find where it's been. Maybe we can locate an area for it. A home turf.'

Ross took Martin's notebook from Aaron and turned to his computer. 'This car belongs to the person whose blood was all over Matt Harper?' he asked.

'That's the one,' Martin said.

'So it's unlikely he was driving,' said Pasha.

'True. We think something has happened to Andrew and need to locate him as quickly as we need to find Hannah. This cult doesn't sound like good news, whatever it is they're doing.'

'Maybe this is where Evie can help?' Pasha suggested.

Aaron moved to his desk. 'In what way?'

'Well, she's desperate to be involved and maybe she could

research cults and see if there's any intelligence on the system about cults in the Notts area.'

Aaron turned his computer on. 'That's not a bad idea. See if she can do that.'

Pasha jumped out her chair and was out the office in a flash. She found Evie at her desk, her usually gorgeous curly auburn hair tied back in a severe knot at the base of her head. She was make-up free and her face was deathly pale, dark shadows emphasising the whites of her eyes. As soon as Pasha entered Evie bolted upright.

'What is it?' she asked.

Pasha held up a hand. 'Nothing concrete. We're a step closer to understanding what's happening and we need your help.'

Evie shuffled to the edge of her chair. 'What is it? Tell me.'

'It looks like Matthew and Sharon Harper left to live with a cult. The blood on Matt's clothing has been identified as belonging to an Andrew Pike. His parents have said he left them about a month ago to live with a group who told him to leave all his worldly possessions and his family behind. Other than his car. Which happens to be the vehicle which chased Matt and abducted Hannah.'

Evie put a hand up to her mouth. 'She's been taken by a cult? Here in Notts?'

'I know,' Pasha said. 'It sounds ridiculous. I thought these things only happened in the States but it seems they're alive and kicking in the UK and we have our very own version right here.'

'What does that mean for Hannah? What do they want with her?'

Pasha shook her head. 'I have no idea, Evie. Can you do some research for us?'

'Of course, what do you need?'

'Everything you can get on cults in the county. Anything you can find. Intelligence, whispers, sneaking suspicions, conspiracies. You name it, we want it.'

Evie rolled her chair closer to her desk. 'I'll get straight on it.' She turned back to Pasha. 'A cult, they won't hurt her will they?'

Again Pasha shook her head. 'I don't know anything about them, Evie. Only what I've seen on the television and I doubt much of that is realistic. But, no, I don't think they tend to be violent. People join to be peaceful don't they?'

Evie patted the side of her head as though it needed putting back in place when the reality was it was so tightly pulled into the knot there was not a strand out of place.

'I'll get on it, Pasha. Thank you.'

Pasha reached out a hand and squeezed Evie's arm. 'We're working around the clock, Evie, we'll get her back.'

Evie took in a juddering breath and held it. She waved a hand in front of her face. 'I'm sorry. I've cried far too many tears over recent days but it won't stop until she's home.' She clamped her teeth together, clenching her jaw tight.

Pasha's chest tightened and her own eyes stung.

'Work will help,' Evie said at last.

Pasha squeezed her arm again. This was taking its toll on all of them. She couldn't bear to think how Hannah was holding it together.

42

Since I'd been able to shower without being disturbed, I hoped that I could use the noise of the shower and the closed bathroom door – even though it wasn't locked – to make a little noise. I didn't want someone to hear.

This was my first real chance to attempt to create a weapon of some description.

I pulled the top drawer all the way out of the dressing table and took it into the bathroom, closed the door and examined it closely. The wood wasn't particularly thick – which would make it easier to break the drawer apart but it didn't bode well for making a weapon that would be capable of causing harm.

The back panel was probably my best bet. If I removed it I would still be able to push the drawer back into the dressing table without anyone noticing it had been tampered with. I just needed to prise the two sides away.

I looked around the bathroom for anything I could use as an implement. Anything I could apply pressure with. There was nothing. They had been meticulous in cleaning out this room prior to imprisoning me in it. I would have to do this manually and I didn't know how long that would take, if it was even possible, or how much noise I was going to make.

I ran back into the bedroom and put my boots on before returning to the bathroom and silently closing the door again.

I turned the shower on and started by trying to pull the drawer apart with my hands to see if the simplest option would work, but it stayed intact. It was time to get heavy handed with it. I stood on the inside side panel and pulled again. This time it started to give. It was the cheap and cheerful kind of furniture you find in homes around the country. Flat-packed and pushed together at home. I could feel movement in the corner as the drawer started to give. I tugged and pulled and tugged some more and eventually one end of the panel came away in my hands. It took only seconds to pull the other side away.

I now had a piece of rectangular wood. This wouldn't hurt anyone. I needed to change the shape of it, to create something sharp that would dig into skin and flesh should I need it to.

hoping the sound of the shower would cover up what I was about to do next, I balanced the freed piece of wood on the side of what was left of the drawer and using the heel of my boot stamped down hard in the middle of it. There was a slight cracking noise and I winced in terror, staring at the wood then the door.

Nothing happened. No one burst in.

The wood was still intact though. It was cracked but still in one piece. I needed to try again.

I brought my heel down hard and a piece of the wood splintered off. I'd done it.

I quickly turned the shower off as it had been running a while and the room had filled with steam. I picked up the splintered-off piece of drawer. It was jagged, and as I'd hoped, narrowed slightly at one end. It wasn't particularly dangerous-looking but it was enough for me to be able to use as a weapon should I need to. It was more than I had ten minutes ago.

Now I had to hide it for when it came time to use it. I looked around the small bathroom for places I could stash it. I could hide it in the side of the bath, but that would be difficult to pull off and would mean I'd be making more noise as I prised the plastic panel off and back on again. There was little in here I could do. I clutched the stake hard in my hand, proud of what I'd managed to do but desperate to find a place to keep it. Then it came to me, the toilet cistern. I lifted the lid off. The water was fairly low. There was a big plastic tube in the centre of cistern that rose up out of the water and if I balanced the stake on top of it, the stake would stay dry and it would be easy to retrieve.

After I put everything away I sat on the edge of the bed, happier with myself than I'd been in a while. I'd achieved something. Who knew when I'd be able to use? But just that I'd been active in creating the weapon made my hope bloom. I didn't have to be locked in this room like a helpless child. I was responsible for my own future. I was responsible for my own escape and no one was going to stop me.

43

The girl came again later that day with my food for the evening. There was no improvement in my diet. I was losing hope that it would change and the girl would not discuss the reasons for the weird blandness of the food I was being given. It was rice tonight. A plate of white rice. It seemed that my evening meal was to be made up of white foodstuffs.

She stayed as long as it took me to eat my meal and as always I tried to eat as slowly as possible, so that she would stay longer. She was far from a chatterbox but I liked the simple fact that she was there. In the room with me. Someone else in existence in this strange world that I currently occupied. I might not be able to enjoy scintillating conversation with her but she gave me the feeling I was not alone and I needed that more than anything. The longer I stayed in the room, the more the real world beyond the wooden slats was forgotten to me.

Had I always enjoyed engaging with people on a daily basis? Did I get pleasure from a diet of my choosing, whether it be unhealthy or not? Did I get to walk in the rain and complain about it at the same time? All these things seemed distant as I was wrapped in these four walls with little conversation and no daylight beyond the slivers that filtered in through the slats of wood on my window. The dull yellow of the bulb in my ceiling warping my perception of the world.

The rice was like glue in my mouth, sticking behind my teeth, all claggy and overcooked. Whoever cooked had not cared how it turned out and had dolloped it onto my plate for me to work my way through. I wanted to ask the girl what she had eaten but would only upset myself if she said she'd had a steak dinner, or lasagne, or other such delight.

No matter how much I tried to drag out the glue eating, I finished the rice and the girl collected my plate and tray.

'You could always stay a little longer...' There was a pleading tone in my voice that I hated.

'I'm sorry. I have to take these back to the kitchen. Maybe another time.' She backed towards the door.

I was about to be left alone again and climbed onto the bed and pulled my knees up to my chest. Like a child hiding from the monsters.

Then she was gone.

But...

If I'd heard correctly, the girl hadn't bolted the door behind herself properly. All I had to do was bide my time and wait for everyone to settle down for the night. Not that I knew how many people there were here but I would wait until it felt right.

There was no clock in this room. No sense of time.

I had no idea how much trouble the girl would get into for leaving the door insecure but that wasn't my problem. I had one thing on my mind and that was to find a way out of this place.

I trusted my team and knew they would find me but I also had to trust in myself. I had the control here this evening and I would grasp it with both hands. All I had to do was get out of the building. Once out I could find a passing car on a nearby road – not that I could hear cars from here, but I would run until I reached one. Or a neighbouring house with a phone. That was all I needed, a phone and I could make contact with Aaron, alert him to where I was and I'd be safe again.

I had no idea what was happening here. The girl hadn't told me anything. I got the feeling she was scared and was simply doing as she was told. I'd be able to help her once I was out. I'd come back for her and get her out as well as finding whoever was behind this.

Tonight, I'd be breaking free from this place and I'd be going home. No more locked rooms. No more scared girls feeding me. Tonight, this was going to end.

I settled on the bed and waited, listened as the old house creaked as it settled down for the night as it always did, the temperature in the room dropping a little. I huddled into the corner to keep warm. I could hear movement from within the building somewhere. But as time ticked by, the sounds grew less and less and my eyelids grew heavier and heavier. My head tipped back against the wall and sleep crept up on me.

With a jerk I was awake.

I couldn't allow myself to sleep. This was my one chance.

I shook my head.

It was time to make my escape.

I pulled on my boots; the ones I'd arrived in. I'd changed out of the jogging bottoms and T-shirt they'd given me to wear and put my own clothes back on that had been hanging in the wardrobe. The suit made me feel more like my work self. More capable. Less foggy. Detective Inspector Hannah Robbins. They didn't smell particularly pleasant as I'd been wearing them days, but I liked the way they made me feel when I had them on.

Next stop was the bathroom. I collected the wooden stake from the toilet cistern and pushed it up my sleeve. I didn't want to use it but it was there if I needed to, just like our safety equipment was with us at work should the need arise.

I was ready to go.

I walked to the door and touched the handle. Was I sure everyone was asleep?

As sure as I could be. I had to take my chance or stay here and wait for my team to find me, no matter how long that took, and I had no idea what plans they had for me here. I couldn't wait.

The door opened with a slight click and I found myself on a large landing. No one was guarding my door. Night-time they probably presumed I would sleep. How wrong they were.

Five other doors, all closed, surrounded me. I moved to the top of the stairs and tipped my head to listen. There was no sound. I started my descent.

With each step I was terrified that the stairs would creak and give me away. I moved slowly. Fear beating a drum in my chest. If I was caught I would have to assess my chances of coming out on top of a fight, or whether I would have to submit.

I placed my hand on the wall for balance in case I had to jump off a creaking floorboard. The wallpaper was cool under my touch, night stripping the heat of the day from the air.

At the bottom of the stairs there was a corridor that ran in two directions and I couldn't see where it went. Which one was a way out? I had to make a choice.

I went right.

The house was dark but there were lights outside shining in. If I couldn't find a door I could use a window. I just had to hope they didn't have the house alarmed.

At the end of the hallway was a door; I pushed it open into a huge square kitchen and at the other end was another door.

My escape. It was an outside door.

I'd made it.

The house was quiet, everyone appeared to be asleep, but I needed to keep the noise down as I didn't want to have a chase on my hands.

I started to shake, whether this was adrenalin kicking in I didn't know but I was nearly out.

I was so close.

I twisted the knob and opened the door. Fresh air hit me in the face and I staggered back a step. From behind the corner wall a figure emerged, a small circle of light in his hand where he held a cigarette.

'Hello, DI Robbins. I didn't expect to see you tonight.'

44

Aaron could hear Lisa on the landing arguing with Kyle in hushed whispers about what time he should be going to sleep. Kyle was fifteen now and said he was old enough to stay up. His mother still wanted him to be refreshed for school the next day. The hushed tones were because Kyle's sister was only thirteen and was already asleep.

Aaron couldn't bear the sound of them bickering and had put his earphones in. He was in the bedroom tying the laces on his trainers when Lisa stormed in.

'That boy is going to push his luck too far one of these days.'

Aaron didn't have a response for her. He had nothing to give his family at the moment but he pulled one of the earphones out as courtesy.

Lisa looked down at her husband. He was wearing his running gear. 'Where are you going?'

He pulled his fluorescent jacket from the bed and shoved his arms in and zipped it up. 'I'm going for a run.'

There was a quiet sigh. 'Like I've just said to Kyle, you can't function properly without sleep and that goes for you as well, Aaron.'

He moved past her. Trying to block the sound of her voice from his head, wishing he could simply place the removed earphone back into his ear.

With hands on her hips she rolled her eyes. 'Will you be careful?'

'It's just a run, Lisa.'

Downstairs he grabbed his car keys.

Lisa followed him down, slippers slapping on each step. 'Why do you need your car keys?'

'Different route tonight. I need a change.'

'Aaron, will you please talk to me?' She was frustrated.

He opened the front door. 'Don't wait up for me.' And with that he was gone. He didn't have the time to get into a long conversation with Lisa about his health. Hannah didn't have the luxury of taking care of herself right now so why should he be stopping to worry about himself. He'd do that when she was back and safe.

Tonight he wanted to check something out. Something that might look different in the night-time than when they were there through the day. He didn't want to say the team had missed a vital piece of evidence, but he was going to have a look around himself tonight.

It wasn't long before he pulled up at the edge of Lenton industrial estate. The place Hannah had been abducted from.

It was well lit, street lights dotted at intervals along the road that ran through the estate.

Aaron climbed out of his car and pocketed his keys. He did a couple of stretches then set off at a steady jog, keeping it slow so he could have a good look around as he moved through the area.

The buildings were low level constructions. Many had metal spiked fence-posts protecting the boundaries with closed up gates in the evening from what Aaron could see. There didn't appear to be any that were operating at this time of the day.

Aaron wasn't sure what he was looking for, he just knew he couldn't sit around at home and brood on the investigation in the comfort of his home while Hannah was who knew where. It didn't feel right.

As his feet pounded the concrete he wondered how the abductors knew Hannah was going to be there when she was. How many people had known she was going to be there at that time? He didn't think it would be a long list. Did this mean it was a crime of opportunity and if so, what kind of opportunity. But they'd already linked it up with the investigation into Matt Harper. None of it was adding up. He couldn't make sense of it.

He ran round the industrial estate three times in total before he gave up and recognised that he wouldn't find anything that would help him determine where Hannah had been taken.

45

T he man standing before me, looking ever so relaxed, not the slightest concerned that I'd got out of my room, was none other than Lucas Harper, Matthew Harper's older brother. The one who had not gone missing when his mother and his younger brother had gone. I didn't understand this.

'Lucas?'

'I imagine this is a little bit of a surprise to you,' he said as he sucked on the cigarette in his hand, smoke spiralling into the air around him.

Could I take him out and move past him? Continue my plan to get out of here? I'd come to a standstill, shocked by Lucas standing in the way of my escape. I could go hand-to-hand with him and fight my way out of this place. I didn't see anyone else in my way. Plus I had my stake if it was necessary.

'What are you doing here?' I asked as I weighed up my options. Now I was outside I could see we were pretty much in the middle of nowhere. I couldn't tell how far away the closest house was or the nearest road. They really had found the perfect accommodation to keep someone locked up. I looked back at the building I'd come running out of. It was a huge place, possibly a hotel in a past life.

'I suppose there is a lot to fill you in on, but not if you're planning to leave us?' he held out his hand holding the cigarette, opening the grounds for me to run past him.

I was torn between wanting to know the truth about what was going on and wanting to get back to the comfort of my home.

'Why are you doing this?' I asked.

'I supposed it depends on which part of this you are talking about.' He threw the cigarette butt down and ground the glowing end out with his shoe. 'Are you talking about the growing movement we have here, or your unfortunate incarceration?' He did sound a little saddened by the second part.

I felt the stake in my sleeve. I was going to leave.

'How did you manage to get out tonight anyway?' he continued. 'Do I need to have words with Ruby?' He looked totally untroubled.

This made all thoughts of fighting my way out of here stop in their tracks. That was the girl's name. Ruby.

'No. You can't blame her for this.' I didn't want to get her into trouble. I had no idea what trouble meant for her here but it didn't sound like a good thing. 'I managed to get out on my own. You would if you were locked in a room with no one to talk to and no idea what was happening. Why wouldn't you allow Ruby to talk to me?'

He laughed. 'It's part of the process, Hannah. It acclimatises you to us.'

'Us?'

'Yes, us. There are many of us here and we want you to fit in. Taking it one step at a time has been the best way to do it.' He tipped his head to the side. 'You didn't think we wanted to hurt you, did you?'

I had to get out of here. I'd come back for Ruby. I inched the stake forward. 'How was I supposed to know what to think when you had me locked in a room with no one to talk to and tied to the bed being fed like a child?' I spat at him.

'We untied you though.'

They had and I'd been mercifully grateful for that simple act. Not that I would admit that to him. 'What do you have here? Why am I being held against my will?' I needed some answers before I made my move.

'I'll tell you what, it's late now and you should be in bed. As you've made the first step out of your room I'll talk to you tomorrow and fill you in more. Get some rest. There's a lot to discuss.' He took a step closer to me.

I raised myself as tall as I could. This was decision time. I was capable of holding my own no matter the gender of my opponent. I pulled my arm back, ready to lunge.

'Come now,' he laughed. 'You're not actually thinking of fighting me, are you?' He looked behind him into the dark. 'Thomas?' And from the gloom stepped a tall well-built man. I dropped my arm. I was exhausted. There was no way they were going to let me go tonight.

I could put up a fight and end up battered and broken, or I could go back to my room and try to recover and gather my energy for a better time. I raised my hands, stake firmly back down my sleeve. 'It's okay. I'm going back.' I turned around and started to walk back the way I had come.

'I look forward to our talk, Hannah,' Lucas said as I moved away from him.

Thomas followed me. Once I was returned to my room he made sure it was locked and bolted.

I lay on the bed and allowed sleep to wash over me; closing my eyes, a heaviness enveloped me. Lucas Harper was here and he seemed to have some level of control if Thomas was doing his bidding. Matthew Harper had been running from something. He'd crashed his car in an effort to get away from whoever had been chasing him. Had he been running from whatever this was? And what was it exactly?

46

Morning came and I was woken by the door to the room opening and Ruby entering. I knew her name. I no longer had to think of her as "the girl".

I rubbed my eyes and sat on the edge of the bed. Still wearing my boots, I noticed.

I didn't know if Ruby knew of my walk around the building last night or if she was in any kind of trouble. She placed the tray as she always did on the dressing table.

'Ruby?' I said from behind her.

She jumped and spun to look at me, her lips parted in an unspoken question, terror in her eyes. I wasn't supposed to know her name. They obviously hadn't said anything to her yet this morning.

'It's okay,' I said. 'I saw Lucas last night.'

Her eyes widened even more at the mention of his name. She backed up to the dressing table until she bumped against it and put her hands behind her to balance herself against the wood. The plate on the tray rattled against the plastic spoon at the side of it.

'It was Lucas who told me your name,' I continued. 'It's okay, you don't need to be afraid.'

My reassurance didn't settle her. She was so afraid of him.

'It's a beautiful name, Ruby,' I said to her. 'I'm glad I have something to call you. It was weird not knowing your name.'

She was frozen to the spot. 'H...h...how?' she whispered.

Did I let her know she'd left the door insecure and terrify her even more? Not telling her would save her the terror but then any punishment would come out of the blue and maybe she needed to prepare for it. Maybe she would even run and escape this place. I had to give her that chance. 'The door wasn't bolted last night, Ruby. I left the room and—'

Her hand shot up to her mouth. 'Nooooo.' She started to shake. Tears filled her eyes. I moved closer to comfort her. I hated that I'd caused this pain, but she had a decision to make. I reached out and touched her arm. She let me, her eyes searching my face.

'I'm sorry,' I said. 'I had to try.'

The silent tears that ran down her cheeks told me more than any words could. I didn't understand what this place was and what was happening and I really needed to find out. I hoped that when Lucas had said we would talk he meant it.

I took Ruby's hand and pulled her towards the bed. She followed like a small child, reminding me just how young she was. What was she doing in a place like this?

We sat on the edge of the bed. 'What are you afraid of?' I asked her.

She shook her head.

'Talk to me, Ruby, let me help you. We can help each other.' It would be great if I could get Ruby onside. Though how I was going to help her I had no idea. Maybe I could talk to Lucas. If he was in charge, maybe I could advocate for her.

'I'll be punished,' she finally said, wiping away the tears with the back of hand. 'If it was my fault you got out of your room last night then I'll be punished.'

'What does that look like?' I asked.

She clasped her hands in her lap. 'Don't worry, they don't believe in violence here.'

And yet she was still afraid. They still had power over her. It was a strong will that exerted this kind of power without the need for violence to keep people in line. Was Lucas that strong a person? I'd only met him a couple of times and now I was locked up like this I wasn't sure my previous assessment of him was true. I needed to talk to him again and see what all this was about. What was behind it.

'I'll talk to Lucas,' I said. 'He told me last night we would talk. I'll ask him not to punish you. I need you to be okay.'

She twisted her fingers together.

'What is this place?' I asked her.

She looked down at her hands as she twisted them and I didn't think she was going to answer but eventually she spoke. 'It's a community,' she said.

A community. 'How many people are here?'

Her eyes rolled up as she worked out some numbers. I waited for her, aware that she needed to be leaving. She was never this long in the room. She waited for me to eat and then she left and I hadn't even started eating yet. 'Let me eat while we talk,' I said as I moved over to the dressing table and picked up the plastic spoon. This was the most open Ruby had been. It seemed that knowing her name and potentially getting her into trouble had broken the barrier she had put up around herself when she was in the room with me. Whatever the reason, I was grateful for it. I needed all the information I could gather.

'There are about thirty-four people,' she said when she'd finished counting.

Thirty-four. That was a lot of people to be involved in the kidnap of a police officer. 'Do they all know I'm here?'

'People are unsettled, but Lucas said everyone had to know because he needed to make this area out of bounds.'

This was a cult. I was being held by a cult. I needed to find out more.

I pushed the cereal into my mouth and thought through the implications of this number of people being involved in the kidnap of a police officer. It was huge. The CPS and the press would have a field day. That's if they ever found me. I clung to the information that Ruby had given me that they were non-violent and hoped that they stayed this way as far as I was concerned.

47

S oon after Ruby left the room with the empty plate and mug, there was a knock at the door. This was unusual. I wasn't used to anyone knocking. What should I do? The door was locked; it wasn't as though I could open it.

'Hello?' I shouted.

The lock was turned and the door opened. A young man stood in the doorway. He was about Ruby's age, with a complexion that in the outside world would cause him no end of anxiety. Here, I didn't know if it would bother him. 'Can you come with me, please?' he asked with quiet politeness.

I presumed there was no option to refuse this request. Regardless, I was intrigued to know where we were going and who I was about to see. This was an opportunity to get some answers to my many questions. I walked towards the door and the young man spun on his heel and turned right. I followed. The rest of the doors on the corridor were, as they were last night, closed. I had no idea what was behind them. Though Ruby had said, this area was out of bounds to the rest of the community while I was here. I hadn't heard sounds of life in my time here.

We descended the stairs I went down the previous night. Instead of heading outside, we turned down another corridor and eventually ended up in a large space filled with tables and chairs. At the far end of the room was Lucas Harper.

He really was the person in charge.

I'd bumped into him last night but I hadn't believed he was behind all this. He could have just been in the right place at the wrong time, or whatever. It was certainly the wrong time for me.

Standing behind Lucas was Thomas, the man from last night.

Lucas smiled as I approached his table. 'DI Robbins. So glad you could join me.'

On the table were cups and saucers and a pot of what I presumed was tea.

'I'm not sure I had any choice in the matter.'

He waved his hand at the chairs and I took a seat opposite him.

'Thank you, Simon,' he said and the young man slipped from view.

There was a smell of cooked eggs and toast. This must be where the group ate.

'Of course you had a choice. What do you think is happening here, DI Robbins?'

I nearly choked. Had he really said that? 'I think I'm being held against my will, is what is happening here,' I said. 'I think I've been locked in a room and only allowed out when someone summons me. I think my first day here I was tied to a bed. I think the girl I know to be Ruby was not allowed to tell me her name until you deemed fit to let me know it because you were acclimatising me to your group.'

He smiled. 'This frosty attitude would have been a lot worse had we not taken those actions, Hannah. Can I call you Hannah?'

'It's DI Robbins.'

'I like Hannah,' he said, picking up the teapot and swirling it before he raised it in front of me as a question. I shook my head. I would not be sharing a companionable drink with this man, though I would sit and talk with him because I wanted answers.

He poured me a tea regardless.

Another move to show me who was in charge of the situation here. I was sure he could make me drink it if he so wished.

'What would you like to talk about?" Lucas asked once he'd finished his ritual of tea pouring.

How did I approach this? If I wanted one thing from this conversation what would it be? I didn't want to waste this meeting and come away from it angry and frustrated which seemed to be my natural state while I was here. I had to think carefully. Consider what came out of my mouth next.

'Can I ask how you find your accommodation?' he asked as he waited for me.

'Restrictive,' I said, to which he laughed out loud. The sound echoing around the room.

'Why am I here?' I finally asked him, not knowing if this was the only question I would be permitted or if I would be allowed more. Or even if he would respond honestly or tell me a story he had made up in his head to suit the situation.

He thought carefully for a moment. The guy behind him hadn't moved a muscle. He wasn't watching us. I didn't know if he was listening, he was just there. In case Lucas needed him. In case I became a problem, I imagined. 'You were getting too close to finding out about our existence and it worried us. It worried me.'

'You're in charge?' I pushed for a second question.

'I am now. Dennis Weekes used to be the leader of the group but he died about six months ago and they needed someone else to step up. I took that position.'

'So, this is where Matthew and your mum came all this time ago? Why not you?' I asked two questions at once, hoping he wouldn't notice and would keep talking.

To keep conversation flowing I picked up my cup and took a sip. I'd not wanted to engage with him in such a sociable activity but if it meant he would stay here and talk to me, I would do whatever was needed. It was my first hot drink since I'd been here and I had to admit it was good.

'You ask a lot of questions, Hannah.'

I bridled at the use of my first name by the man who was holding me captive but held myself still. 'Isn't that why we're here?'

His upper lip curled in the approximation of a smile. 'I'm happy enough to give you some information, but mostly about your own captivity.'

'Doesn't that link to what I was investigating? Now I'm here you may as well provide me with those answers.' I sipped some more tea.

'Sharon fell under Dennis's spell. She was hooked by him. You have to understand, she was bringing up me and my brother alone. It was hard for her. Then she had someone telling her they would help her, support her, give her the world. All she had to do was give up the world as she knew it and donate everything she had to the community. She fell for it, hook, line and sinker. She wanted me to come with her but I was too old. I wasn't interested in that shit so she left me. Told me to go to my aunt. She was a weak woman, my mother.'

'Is she still here?'

He laughed. It was hard and brittle. 'Yes, she's still here. Shocked by the turn of events. That I would eventually lead their merry little band. But that story is far too long to go into. It took time and patience and I have my own kingdom. They can't leave but I can come and go as I please. What more can a man ask for?'

He looked so pleased with himself. It was starting to make me nervous how much he was willing to tell me. It worried me about my chances of getting out of here. Ruby said that they didn't use violence but Lucas was an unknown quantity. I had to hope Aaron and the team were getting closer to finding me because I felt unsafe and nervous.

I decided to push harder while I was here. 'The blood on Matthew, whose was it?'

Lucas stood, pushing his chair away with his calves as he did so. 'I think we've come to the end of our little discussion, Hannah. Simon will show you back to your room.'

And just like that, the young man emerged from his previously unseen spot and stood at the side of me, waiting for further orders.

I rose from my own chair. 'I'd like to talk to you again.'

Lucas stared hard. 'I'm sure we will, Hannah, I'm sure we will.' He gave Simon a look, and the lad stretched out an arm to herd me back to my room. I looked at the three men surrounding me. Wondered at the other thirty people in the building. Would I stand a chance of getting out of here? Should I try or submit? They had no weapons. It was them against me. I wasn't restrained. It was ridiculous to just give in when I hadn't been assaulted or threatened. This was my second time out of the room. If I moved quickly maybe I could outrun these men and only have to fight one if they caught up with me.

The decision was made. Simon was to my right. Lucas was turning away. His goon, Thomas, was following him. There was a door behind me, the one we had entered and one to my right which Lucas was heading for. My way out was the door I had come through. I knew through there was a door out of the building.

I smiled at Simon, watched as he relaxed, put his arm down and turned to look to Lucas, and then made my move.

48

The floor underfoot was parquet and my boot squeaked as I made the quick turn and pushed off towards the door I needed to get to. My heart-rate sky-rocketed as fear and adrenalin smashed together in my veins.

I hadn't done much running on the job since I'd come out of uniform but I still kept up my physical fitness by attending the gym as often as I could. I should be able to do this.

My heartbeat pounded in my head. Through the thunder I heard a deep voice shouting behind me. The only words that made it through the jumble were GET and NOW.

I pumped my arms and focused on the door I was heading towards. It was closed but it wasn't locked. All I had to do was get to it. Then I was one step closer to freedom.

My breath came hard as my body recognised the flight situation and gave me everything I needed. I was moving fast. The door was close.

A loud clatter sounded behind me but I didn't stop or slow to figure out what it was.

With a body slam I was at the door, pulling on the handle at the same time I was peeling myself from the wood. Pulling everything in the same direction. I needed it open and I needed to get through it.

I'd made it. I'd made it to the door without Simon or Thomas catching me, but they were on my heels. I swerved around the frame and to the right, into the corridor. There was an exit to the outside world along here somewhere.

A hand clasped on the collar of my shirt. It gagged me at my throat. Pulled me up, taking my feet from under me. My boots slipped on the carpeted corridor, silently sliding forward as I was pulled back by my neck.

My arms wheeled around in a futile attempt to keep my balance. Someone had caught up with me. Someone had me and now was the time I had to fight for my life. I had to escape from here. There was no way they were just going to let me leave. Not after keeping me here so long and Lucas telling me about the structure of the group and about Matthew and Sharon.

It was my only chance.

I was dragged backwards and fell down to the floor, landing on my arse with a crack. Pain sliced up my back to my brain from my coccyx. I twisted to the left with my right hand clenched and already swinging. I couldn't see who had grabbed me but as I turned around on the ground I saw Simon hovering above me. My fist caught him on his chin and he stumbled back, his hand still wrapped in my clothing, dragging my head back with him. I pushed on the floor with my left hand and punched out with my right again. Simon wasn't a fighter. This time as my fist connected his hand released its grip on me and I was free.

I scrambled to my feet as he straightened to his. We were face to face. He had no idea how to handle this. In my eyeline I saw Thomas coming up behind Simon. I had to get away before there were two of them on me.

I punched out again and this time slammed my fist into Simon's nose. I heard a crack and blood poured out. A hand went up to his face and his mouth opened in shock. Then he lunged for me. He grabbed my hair pulling me back and down. I had to get out of this. I raised my fist again and punched once more. Skin and muscle shifted beneath my knuckles but it wasn't enough. His grip tightened.

'No,' he grunted into my ear, bloody droplets spitting onto my face.

I twisted as much as the roots of my hair would allow, ignoring the searing pain in my scalp, and brought my knee up hard with all the force I could muster. The power from my leg vibrated right through to his crown jewels. His hand dropped from my head and I jumped away from him and started to run again.

I could see the exit.

My way out was in sight. I still had a long way to go once I was outside, but I couldn't think about that for now.

In a matter of seconds I was outside. The sun was shining. The sky was lit up, a beautiful powder blue. The brightness made me squint. I pushed on. The gravel under my feet crunched.

Walking to my left was a young woman carrying a pile of books. I heard the door behind me slam open as someone came barrelling out behind me. They shouted to the woman and she froze. Stared at me and then dropped her books to the ground with a dull thud, pages fluttering as the covers fell open. I was crossing her path towards the grass. If she got to me I'd easily overpower her, but I didn't want to hurt her. I imagined the people under Lucas were mostly vulnerable and in need of help themselves. Ruby definitely was.

But like lightning she was moving towards me. I changed direction and skidded sideways. There was a small patch of trees to my right. I couldn't see how deep they went but maybe I could lose myself within them.

I was attempting to outrun three people, four if Lucas had decided to engage in this game of cat and mouse. Though I didn't see him as the type to do the dirty work himself, more the kind to give the orders and stand by and watch them be obeyed.

Simon was grunting heavily behind me. He was persistent. I dug deep for more power to my legs and pushed forward.

The ground beneath my feet changed from gravel to soil as I hit the wooded area. The sky above darkened as the tree canopy blotted out the sun. It was damp and mulchy in here.

I had only run a few steps inside the dark wooded ground when I risked a turn, to see how far ahead I was.

They were behind me. Simon had recovered enough to pick himself back up and keep coming. Thomas was one step in front of him. I had to keep going. Find a road. A house. Someone with a phone.

Then my feet went from under me. I hadn't been looking where I was headed. Something tripped me up and I was falling face first, down into the dirt.

49

Despair hung over the incident room, sucking all the oxygen out and leaving the occupants defeated and heavy.

Aaron prickled in his chair. He would not go down this way. He would not stop fighting for Hannah.

Catherine Walker and Kevin Baxter were standing in front of the team, their faces giving nothing of their feelings away.

'Evie.' Catherine directed her gaze to the rear of the room where Evie was attempting to hold herself together. 'What do you have in relation to cults in the Nottinghamshire area? Do we have any intel on any that may be operating?'

It was the strongest lead they'd had so far. A possible reason for what was happening, bearing in mind they'd had no ransom request.

Evie shook her head. 'There's very little on the systems. Cults are by definition secretive. It's rare people leave of their own free will. It's highly frowned upon and from what I can gather, members of the cult will chase down anyone who tries to leave to return them to the fold.'

'So we think that was happening the night Matt ran in front of Hannah's car?' Ross asked. 'He was trying to make his escape but they wanted him back?'

Baxter looked to Catherine. 'It's one possibility. But until he recovers his memories we're not going to know more.'

'Do we have any registered cults in the county?' Walker pushed.

'It's not an area we've really focused on.' Tears pricked at Evie's eyes. 'We don't have a lot of information.'

Walker waited for her to elaborate.

'No. There's nothing in the system that says there's a cult in Notts,' Evie eventually finished, dropping her head in defeat.

Pasha looked confused. 'Why don't they want members to leave? What are they afraid of?'

Aaron didn't even want to contemplate the secrets they were hiding. How bad it was within the cult that meant they were prepared to abduct a serving police officer.

Evie took a deep breath. 'From what I can gather, it's about lack of control. They hate to lose the control they have over the membership. It's seen as a failure. Plus a lot goes on that isn't accepted by your average society and they want to keep their privacy. Escaping members is not a good look.' She ran a finger below an eye, wiping away any errant make-up.

Walker turned her attention to Aaron. 'Do you think it's worth going to talk to Matthew Harper again, see if he can remember being part of a cult? Being told that's what he was running from might jog his memory.'

Aaron cleared his throat. 'I'm not sure it works like that, but anything is worth trying at this point. I'll take Pasha and go and see him.'

'Keep at your tasks, keep working the case. Hannah is counting on us.' And with that she moved towards the incident room doors.

Ross tutted behind her back. 'Does she really think we don't recognise the stakes of this case?'

Pasha moved past his desk and patted him on the arm. 'She's trying to keep us motivated. She knows we don't need it, but it's all she can do, Ross. I think she probably feels as helpless as the rest of us.'

Aaron collected the car keys. He didn't expect much from

Matthew Harper but it was a line of enquiry they had to follow and he'd jump through any hoop necessary if it brought him closer to finding Hannah.

50

I lay on the ground, stunned. Pain shot from my ankle to my brain. I swore and pushed my hands into the damp uneven ground to try to rise from the dirt.

As I clambered to my feet my ankle screamed in agony. I stumbled again.

Thomas grabbed me roughly by my left arm and tugged me up towards him.

I'd failed.

'I've hurt my ankle,' I yelled.

'You shouldn't have run,' said Simon coming up behind Thomas. His face red where he'd smeared blood across it. He looked down at the ground and swallowed. 'Come on. Let's get back to the house.' He took my other arm and helped take the weight off my ankle.

I hopped a couple of steps then looked back to where I'd fallen. Saw what had made him try to hustle us out of there. It was a grave. A freshly-made grave.

Simon saw me look and pushed us forward a couple of steps. My ankle throbbed. My arm throbbed. Tears pricked my eyes. I blinked them back. I wouldn't let these people see me like this.

'What is that?' I asked.

'It's nothing,' Simon said as he tried to move us further away.

I looked back again. The mound had a small wooden cross at one end. It was someone they had cared about. They had made an effort.

I remembered the blood Matthew Harper had been covered in.

'Who is it?' I tried again as we left the wooded area and once again hit the bright light of the day.

The young woman with the books was standing at the edge waiting for us, her books returned to her arms in a neat pile.

I looked at her. 'Who's buried in the woods?' Did everyone know or was it a secret?

She blanched and turned away from me. She didn't seem surprised, just uncomfortable. So the people here knew what had happened. This was a group secret. Did that mean that Ruby knew? Would she talk to me? Would she tell me? How deep was her fear?

I turned to Simon. 'Where are you taking me? I need an X-ray, I need a hospital.'

'You shouldn't have gone running like that and you wouldn't have this problem, would you? We don't believe in engaging with the outside world so there will be no hospital visits. We'll get someone to have a look at your ankle for you in your room.'

They didn't believe in engaging with the outside world? No wonder we hadn't been able to locate Matthew and Sharon Harper for the last eleven years. Someone within the group must engage with the outside world though for them to have food and medical supplies they might need. I remembered speaking to Lucas Harper outside at his home address and wondered how he worked his way around this, if the rest of the community knew about his other home. Did he adhere to the group rules, or did he just enjoy being the leader of such a fanatical group of people?

We were nearly at the building I had run out of and I had my first chance to take a good look at it. It resembled a run-down hotel, rather than a large country house. I didn't recognise it or remember it from any online searches for hotels so didn't know how long it had been out of commission. It was certainly large enough to house the thirty-odd people who lived here. It also explained the layout of my room, with the en suite.

It took an age to get me back to my room. My ankle had started to swell and the pain was excruciating. 'Can I have a couple of my painkillers, please?' I asked as they lowered me down onto the bed. I wouldn't have many pills left but one wasn't going to be enough to deal with this pain. I needed to get out of here. Especially now I had seen the fresh grave. I had no idea what that meant for my stay.

Simon mumbled a response and backed out of the room. I guessed he still wasn't happy that he had come off worse in a hand-to-hand battle with a female. Thomas glowered at me, no doubt imagining that I would never have got the upper hand if he had caught up with me first.

I lay back on the bed, the pain in my arm competing with the pain in my badly swollen ankle. I needed to take my boot off, even though I was exhausted and just wanted to sleep.

I pulled myself upright and bent my knee. Luckily my ankle boot had a zipper down the side and I undid it and gradually slid the boot off my foot. Pain zapped my up my leg to my brain. I dragged one of the pillows from the top of the bed, folded it in half and popped it under my foot, propping it up. Then I lay back and considered my current position.

There was a body freshly buried in the grounds of this hotel. The likelihood was that it belonged to whoever's blood was all over Matthew Harper. The question was how did they die? These people were supposed to be a non-violent group and yet the presence of so much blood suggested otherwise. If this group could spiral to violence what did this mean for me? How long would they be willing to keep me locked in a room before someone started to shout for a more final decision to be made?

As I was wondering about how long I had here, how long Aaron and the team had to find me, the door clicked as the lock turned. Someone was entering the room. I'd been a bad guest. Was I about to be punished?

51

Aaron walked into the side room followed by Pasha.

He liked Pasha. She was like Hannah in a lot of ways. She had a calm demeanour, though she was still reasonably new to the team and Hannah had a tougher side to her at times as she had to lead and make difficult decisions.

Matthew Harper was sleeping. Aaron had no qualms about waking him. He didn't have time to play games or even be particularly sensitive to people at this moment in time.

Matt rubbed his eyes after Aaron shouted his name at him, rousing him from his slumber.

'We need to talk to you,' Aaron explained.

Matt pushed himself up on his pillows, confusion on his face.

'We're sorry to disturb you,' Pasha apologised for the both of them. Aaron knew there was a reason he'd chosen her to come along with him.

Matt dug a knuckle into the corner of his eye. 'What is it?'

Aaron didn't bother with a chair, instead he towered over Matt. 'We've had some more information that we believe you should be made aware of.'

'Should I be worried?'

Pasha pulled up a chair and seated herself next to the bed. 'We're not here to upset you but again, we do need your help and this might dislodge some memories.'

Matt rearranged the pillows behind him. Tried to make himself more comfortable. 'Okay, what is it?'

Aaron looked to Pasha in the seat below him. Still he remained standing. 'An investigation into the blood you were covered in the night you were found, it led us to a family...'

Matt looked between Aaron and Pasha. As far as Aaron could make out, the look on Matt's face didn't change. He was simply waiting for more information.

'We didn't have an exact match, but the family it did belong to said the match likely belonged to their son, they had no other children. He has left them to go and live with a community they believe is a cult.'

Matt's lips parted silently.

Aaron waited him out.

'I don't even know what a cult is...'

Aaron looked down at Pasha. If he'd been taken as a child and it was the way he was brought up then of course he would never have heard of the phrase. If he had been running, it would have been from something he didn't agree with. But he wouldn't know the concept of the whole. Pasha furrowed her brows in response.

'It's a community separate to the rest of society,' Aaron explained. 'Their belief system is often very different to the outside world.'

Matt's eyes widened. 'And you think I was brought up inside one of these? A cult?'

'It's possible,' said Pasha realising what had happened. 'What can you tell us?'

He shook his head. 'I can't tell you anything. I remember nothing. Did I hurt their son?' His sentences were running into each other. He was getting anxious.

'We don't yet know what happened,' Pasha said. 'We need help, Matt.'

Matt continued to shake his head. 'I don't understand. A cult? Why wouldn't I just leave?'

Pasha rose and reached out, placing a hand on Matt's arm. 'It's never that simple. Cults are complex systems. You were being chased. They don't like members to leave. This may have been the first chance you had.'

'We need a location,' Aaron said. 'Anything you can think of. A landmark. A sound, a smell. Something we can work with.'

'This cult has DI Robbins?'

'We believe so.'

Matt's hands went up to his head and his fingers clawed through his hair. 'Why don't I remember? This is all my fault.'

Aaron wanted to reassure him that it wasn't his fault but it had all started when the boy ran in front of Hannah's car. He couldn't disconnect the link. If this boy had not entered Hannah's life then she'd still be with them. He hated himself for this thought process but could not control his feelings.

'I'm sorry for disturbing you, Matt. If you do think of anything, please do let us know. You understand how important it is.' Aaron turned and walked out of the room, leaving Pasha to smooth things down with him.

Aaron's insides were a swirling mess. They didn't have a single line of enquiry that was taking them anywhere and he was starting to lose his shit.

52

Ruby entered the room, her face pale and drawn. She looked down at me, her eyes travelling the length of my body to my foot.

'You hurt yourself,' she said.

'You could say that.' I propped myself up on my elbows so I could have a better conversation with her. My arm throbbed in complaint.

Ruby held out her hand. 'You only have another four left after these two.' She held a couple of pills still in their plastic covering, cut from the rest of the pack.

'Shit.'

She walked to the dressing table and picked up the beaker of water and brought it over to me. I struggled to sit up.

'Can you get any more meds?' I asked. 'I don't think my ankle's broken but it's a pretty bad sprain. I can't manage it without painkillers.' I took the two pills from her and looked down at them in my palm. I couldn't take both of them, no matter how bad the pain was. I had to make them last. I snapped a pill free from its packet and threw it into my mouth, drank from the beaker and swallowed it down. 'I'm sorry,' I said. 'I'm in pain. I can't manage very well.'

'Why did you run?' She took the spare pill from me and shoved it in her pocket.

I barked out a laugh. 'You expect me to go about daily life here as though I'm a part of your little community?'

Her mouth parted, then closed.

'I'm not one of you,' I said. 'I'm being held here against my will if you hadn't noticed by the fact you have to lock and unlock the door every time you come and see me.' I'd already apologised for being tetchy but I couldn't stop myself. Ruby might be being coerced but she was still one of my captors, preventing me from leaving.

She stood in the middle of the room, arms by her sides, staring at me, eyes wide. 'I don't want you to get hurt.'

'Who's in the grave, Ruby?' I twisted until I was facing her, my feet dangling off the edge of the bed. Pain slaughtered my nerve endings. I jabbed my fingernails into my palms.

Ruby bit her lip. She knew about the grave. She must know who was in the grave. Would she talk to me though? I hadn't exactly been kind to her in the last couple of minutes. I needed to change tack.

'I'm worried. I'm worried about what they might do, what they have planned, or what might happen when they get fed up of taking care of me.' I waved an arm around the room. 'This can only go on for so long.'

She had been pale when she walked into the room; now she was positively grey. 'They won't do that.' Her eyes filled with tears. 'They won't hurt you. They're not like that. We're not like that. I told you before, we're not violent.'

I waved down at my foot.

'You did that yourself, you fell!'

'Over a grave, Ruby. A grave that has been freshly dug. Someone you know is inside that grave.' Was that definitely true though? Had someone turned up here and frightened their little oasis of paradise and they'd lashed out?

'It's not what you think it is,' she said quietly.

'Explain it to me then. Imagine how I'm feeling.'

She looked down at my swollen ankle, at the blocked window,

then back at me. I could see the confusion and fear wash across her face. She wanted to talk to me. I needed to encourage her to do so.

'Look at it from my point of view, Ruby, imagine how it looks to me. You say it's not like that, explain what it is like? Who's out there in that grave? What did they do?'

She shook her head sadly. 'He didn't do anything.'

There was a noise outside. The lock was being turned again. Ruby clamped her mouth shut. I had been getting somewhere and she had clammed up. Had they heard us talking?

The door opened. Ruby backed away until she bumped into the dressing table and put her hands on the edge to steady herself. She looked like a frightened little girl.

An overweight man in his fifties came into view. His face was red and puffy and his eyes dull.

'Hello, Hannah,' he said as he peered down at me. 'Let's have a look what we have here, shall we?'

I shrank back onto the bed, not understanding who he was or what he wanted.

He smiled. 'I'm Dr Christian Chase. I've come to have a look at your ankle, if you'll allow?'

Something I was to be able to make a decision about. I looked at Ruby and she gave a small nod. This man presumably was a doctor of some description. She trusted him to look at my ankle anyway. I waved my hand at my ankle and Christian Chase knelt on the floor in front of me and gently took my foot in his hands. They were cold. I was acutely aware of this man's hands on me, even if I had given him permission.

He touched my ankle lightly, running his fingers along the bones in my feet and asked me to wriggle my toes. All the time Ruby was behind him, having not moved from her position against the dressing table. I did as was requested. My toes moved and I knew my ankle wasn't broken before he rose from the floor and made the announcement.

'It's a sprain. Obviously painful. Keep your foot elevated and don't put pressure on it. We have some paracetamol and ibuprofen. Unfortunately we don't have any crutches so you'll need someone for support should you have to move around. I'll let Lucas know.'

I didn't thank him. As far as I was concerned he was another of the people keeping me locked up here. He was complicit in my detention. He offered me a weak smile before he left the room.

'Ruby, dear, are you coming?' he asked before he closed the door.

She looked at me and to him. She had no reason to stay. She'd given me my tablet. I wanted to continue our conversation but what could she do?

She moved to the door.

Dammit, I hated this place.

The door locked into place and I lay on the bed with my foot resting back on the pillow. Any escape plans were seriously scuppered now I'd sprained my ankle. But I wouldn't give in. I had to get out of here. I would not wait to see if I would be the next person to be buried out in the grounds.

53

A few hours passed. The single painkiller I'd taken from Ruby was doing little to ease the pain in my ankle, but it was better than not having any left at all – which I'd have to deal with in the next day or so. I couldn't bear to think about it.

I lay on the bed staring up at the ceiling with my foot propped up on the pillow. Being crippled this way put my mood at the floor. The situation I found myself in was useless.

The door opened and Ruby came into the room carrying a tray with my evening meal. She gave me a small smile and I grimaced in response. I couldn't see a way out of this now. I had to hope my team were working their way closer to me because my efforts at getting away had failed.

Ruby placed the tray on the dressing table and moved towards the bed to help me over to the plate. With her arm hooked under mine, she pulled upwards as I heaved myself off the bed and she took my weight as I hobbled over to the food.

'How are you?' I asked as I lifted the lid from the plate to stare down at the scrambled eggs. I was getting used to the simplicity of the food they were feeding me.

Ruby looked nervous, her hands constantly moving in her lap.

'Are you in trouble, Ruby?'

She shook her head.

'Talk to me. You can trust me.' I waved my arm around the room with the plastic fork still in my hand. 'Who am I going to tell?' Her face dropped. 'I sure as hell am not going to talk to Lucas about what we say in here. Jesus, Ruby, that man is keeping me locked in a room away from my family, my friends, my job, my life. I owe him nothing.' I looked at this young girl in front of me. 'You owe him nothing.'

She shrank in front of me, her eyes bright with unshed tears.

We only had as long as it took me to eat for us to talk but I put my fork down. 'It's okay, Ruby, you're not in this alone. When I figure a way out of this I'm taking you with me.' I looked up into her eyes. Didn't let her know how low I was feeling about my ability to escape this place. 'Okay?'

A tear slid down her cheek and she nodded.

I had what I needed. I ate some more of the eggs. They'd brainwashed Ruby at some point but putting her in here with me every day had caused cracks in what they had built up and I had finally broken through. I was going to take her away from all this and I'd also save her from prosecution when it all came to a head.

We had to get that far though.

'Tell me about the body in the grave, Ruby.'

She wiped away her tears with the back of her hand then stared at the floor.

'I know it's hard. You're breaking confidences you've been trained to keep, but soon you'll be free of these people and you'll know what real life is like and what it's like to make your own decisions. It will be amazing, Ruby, and we'll do it together.'

I could barely eat for my eagerness to progress with Ruby, to encourage her to embrace her new life before she managed to escape her old one. I was eager for her to have everything she deserved. How long had she been here? As long as Matthew Harper? Had she been indoctrinated from childhood? So many questions. I would talk to her about her life here another time. And we would plan a way out. Together.

'Ruby?' I prompted.

She let out a quiet sigh and looked towards the door.

'There's someone on the other side, isn't there?' I asked.

She nodded.

'Every time?'

She nodded again.

'But the person out there isn't listening. I presume they're to prevent escape?'

Another nod.

'Okay, we can talk quietly.'

'It was an accident,' she said. 'Well... not exactly, he could have been saved, but Lucas...'

'He wouldn't allow it?'

Her voice was quiet, I had to strain to hear her. 'No. He was adamant that we couldn't use outside sources to help him. We didn't do that as a group, he said.'

'What happened?'

'Andrew started having some pain in his abdomen. Christian, the doctor, saw him and said it looked like appendicitis and that he needed to go to a hospital. Lucas said no. Christian said if it burst Andrew would die. Lucas told him to keep an eye on Andrew. The pain got worse, he developed a high fever, the doctor was pulling his hair out. Lucas said the only surgery Andrew was getting was here on the grounds and Christian was to do it.'

I stared at her, unable to believe what I was hearing. 'This guy was in dire need of medical assistance and Lucas refused it?'

Ruby wrung her hands. 'We don't go out to the outside world.'

'Well, you might not,' I said. 'But Lucas sure as hell does.'

'It's so we can run our group smoothly. He does it for us. He can do all the things that are connected to the rule of the overlords who want to control our every move and our every thought. It means only one of us is contaminated by the outside world. He took it on as leader of the group.'

I nearly choked on the soft egg as she spoke and took a sip of water to clear my throat. 'That's very magnanimous of him.'

She looked at me, her eyebrows drawn over her eyes.

'It's very big of him,' I clarified for her. 'So what happened? Did the doctor do the surgery here? How on earth did he manage to do that?' I remembered something. 'And did Matthew Harper have anything to do with it?'

'Lucas made Matt help the doctor. Christian said he couldn't do a surgery on his own. He needed help. He was out of his mind but Lucas wouldn't back down. You have to follow orders or you'll be punished.'

I'd ask her about what that entailed another time, but for now we needed to finish this story. We only had so much time.

Ruby continued, 'Christian was distressed, it was awful. And very quickly it all escalated. Matt tried to talk Lucas into taking Andrew to a hospital. This infuriated Lucas who threatened Matt. The group had already started to prepare a room for the surgery and we had some supplies that had been stockpiled.'

I was incredulous. 'You had anaesthetic?'

Ruby shook her head and rubbed at her face. 'No. Not the proper stuff, but we did have a bottle of gas and air, whatever the real name of that is.'

'You were going to operate on a man with just gas and air?' My incredulity had gone through the roof. What kind of monster was Lucas Harper?

'Hannah, the blood. You should have seen it.'

'You were there?'

'It was the screaming. He was screaming so much. I pushed my way in. The doctor yelled at me to get out, that I was contaminating his surgical field, but not before I saw all the blood. Then it went silent. I think he passed out from the pain. I waited outside the door.'

'Where was Lucas?'

'He was nowhere to be seen. He didn't want anything to do with the messy side of things.'

'And what happened next?' I put my fork on my plate. I'd suddenly gone off my food.

'I could hear the men shouting. Something was going wrong.

Matt wanted to take Andrew to the hospital but I think it was too late...' Ruby trailed off and her face greyed.

A couple of minutes passed before she spoke again. 'Everything was silent and then Matt burst out of the door, his eyes were wild and he was covered in blood. He looked at me but I wasn't sure he saw me. He ran straight past me. I... I... looked in the room, Hannah.'

She was quiet again. I imagined what she must have seen when she looked through the door: the blood, the lifeless body and the defeated doctor. The smell of death and copper and guilt.

There was no time to comfort Ruby, we had taken far too long already. She rubbed at her face again.

'Will you be okay?' I asked her as I piled the plate and lid back onto the tray.

She stood and took the tray from me. 'It brought it all back. It was horrific.'

'You have to try to act like we haven't discussed this though, Ruby. For your own safety.' I was worried for her. I didn't know what this group was capable of, or more importantly, what Lucas Harper was capable of. I wished I had more time to talk to Ruby, to calm her and steady her nerves instead of only having these fifteen-minute slots. It was difficult to really get into anything because as soon as we did we had to end the conversation and Ruby never had time to gather herself. I was sending her back out and she was fragile and emotional and I didn't want her to give herself away.

'Can you take yourself somewhere and spend some time on your own?' I asked. 'Just to get yourself a little calmer and on a more even keel?'

She moved towards the door. 'It'll be time for prayers shortly. Even though I'll be with the group, it's a quiet period where we contemplate what we have here and how well off we are to be away from those who want to control our every move.'

I gave her what I hoped was a reassuring smile while inside I died a little. How could she not hear the irony in what she had said? 'I'll see you again tomorrow. Take care of yourself, Ruby.'

The door opened and Ruby was gone; a click confirmed the door had been locked behind her.

I was alone with my thoughts.

Matthew Harper ran out of the room where they had attempted to do an appendectomy in barbaric circumstances. He was covered in blood, as I found him the night he had run in front of my car. Was this the same night? Was the blood he was covered in the blood of the patient? That was the logical conclusion. Had he been running from this cult at last because it had gone too far for him? Had he wanted out but they didn't want him to leave? Once in, no escaping? How far would they go to keep the numbers of the group here? It was clear they were prepared to let someone die if they needed medical assistance.

I considered this in relation to my own situation and what they planned for me. There was no way they were going to let me leave. The only question was, were they prepared to keep me a prisoner for the rest of my life? Or would they decide on a more final end for me? And, if so, when? How long did I have?

54

Little did I know how soon I would get this question answered.

The following morning, Ruby sat with me as I ate my breakfast.

'Yesterday you said you'd be punished if you didn't follow orders,' I said from my chair in front of the dressing table. 'What does this look like, Ruby?'

She picked up the hem of her T-shirt and started to worry at it.

'I'm sorry if it's a difficult subject. I don't mean to upset you, I just want to understand what life is like. I want to understand the dynamics of the group.'

Ruby picked at a spot on the hem.

I continued to eat my cereal.

'The group is informed about bad behaviour.'

I put my spoon on my plate and waited for her. She continued to fuss at her top.

'You're placed in the centre of a circle wearing only your underwear, and they chant at you. They scream at you while pointing and laughing at how bad you've been and how you need to learn your lesson to be allowed into the community again.'

Jesus, this sounded barbaric. 'I'm so sorry, Ruby.'

She shook her head. 'You're then placed in the smallest room here which I think was once a store cupboard and you're still in your underwear and you're left in there with no food and no water until the leader...' She gulped, her eyes were damp. 'Lucas now, until Lucas deems you have been stripped of your sins enough to learn your lesson and can be accepted back into the group. The room is dark, there's no clock, you have no idea how long you've been in there, hours or days. There's a bucket for you to go to the toilet. I've known people who were left in there for three days. They were hallucinating when they came out. But it doesn't stop him.'

I had no words but she hadn't finished.

'Once you're released you're brought back to the circle where they chant at you about the good of the group and then it's your turn. You have to admit your sins and promise to give yourself back to the group. Once you've done that, you're allowed back to your room to shower and then you have to do your chores to show you mean what you say. There's no time for rest.' Tears were falling down her cheeks.

I left my food and hopped over to where she was sitting on the bed and sat beside her, taking her hand in mine. 'Oh, Ruby, how the hell did you end up here?'

With a gentle shake of her head, she dipped her face to the floor. Her hair fell across her face as tears landed on her feet. 'My manager at work was giving me a hard time. My stepfather hated having me in the house and my mother didn't care one way or another. Lucas promised me somewhere to stay where I'd be cared for, loved for who I was. It sounded idyllic to me. It was what I needed. I gave him every penny I had in the bank and moved in.'

'How much did you have?'

'My dad left me some money when he died. There was fifteen thousand in my savings account.'

There were over thirty people here. If they all gave him their life savings, sold their homes, he was going to be rolling in it. Ruby had told me they lived pretty simply, with chickens providing eggs and their own vegetable garden. I imagined he had some scam going on around the bills for the building.

The door opened and Simon stepped in. Ruby leapt to her feet, I jumped but stayed where I was, guilty looks on both our faces. No one ever came in to this room during mealtimes other than Ruby. My heart slammed into my mouth. It didn't bode well.

'Lucas wants to see you both,' he said, giving nothing away with his expression.

Ruby stared at him. They were obviously friends out of this room – weren't they? Is that what members of the group classed each other as?

'What is it, Simon?' she asked.

He turned back towards the door. 'He wants to see you both. You know Lucas, doesn't give much away.'

I couldn't gauge if he was being honest or not.

Ruby was obviously suspicious and pushed him. 'What did he say?'

He turned back to us with a deep sigh. 'Go and get Hannah and bring Ruby with her.' He pulled a face to ask if she was satisfied.

She looked at me. Her eyes had widened, her lips parted, her face pale. She was terrified of what this meant. I imagined she didn't have many one-to-ones with the great leader of the group and her mind would be going into overdrive with possible scenarios.

I wanted to reach out and pat her arm, or take her hand to reassure her but I didn't want Simon to realise how close we'd become. I wanted the group to continue to believe she was working as part of the community still. In any case, I didn't know if I could reassure her. My mind was doing its own thing, worrying why we were being called to Lucas together.

'I need the bathroom before we go,' I told him. The wooden stake I'd fashioned out of the drawer was hidden in the bathroom and if there was a time to take it from its hiding place, this was it.

'Hurry up. He's expecting us.' Simon poked in his ear then sniffed his finger.

I wrinkled my nose, agreed to hurry and smiled as reassuringly as

I could at Ruby and hopped into the bathroom and closed the door behind me.

I could hear Ruby and Simon talking but couldn't hear what they were saying as the blood was pumping too loud in my ears. I lifted the top off the toilet cistern as quietly and gently as I could and hoped Ruby could keep Simon occupied and that there wouldn't be a lull in the conversation. Ruby didn't know what I'd stashed in here. She had no idea what I was doing so had no reason to cover for me.

There was some mild scraping as I moved the lid and I winced and stilled, waiting for the shout from the room, but it never came. I leaned forward and put my forehead on the wall as a wave of nausea washed over me as my ankle throbbed, and waited for it to pass.

'What're you doing in there?' Simon shouted. 'Lucas is expecting us.'

'Nearly done.' I flushed the toilet providing some noise for me to finish my task and put the lid of the cistern back into place. I pushed the home-made weapon up my sleeve. Splinters dug into my arm as I shoved it roughly up at speed. I winced but dragged my sleeve back straight around it.

'Come on!' A yell from outside.

I turned the tap on. 'Coming.' I rinsed my hands under the running water and rubbed them on the towel before exiting the bathroom.

Simon was waiting, his fingers drumming a beat on his crossed arms, and Ruby was looking even more anxious. Simon's impatience had done nothing to soothe her nerves.

I grabbed her arm and squeezed making out I needed her support to walk, which wasn't a lie. I needed her to try to calm down. She looked at me and I smiled. Simon was already facing the door and striding towards the hallway.

'It'll be okay,' I mouthed at her.

She twisted her mouth in a non-committal way and we walked out of the room.

55

Aaron walked along the corridor towards the incident room after updating Baxter on the investigation. His mood was in his boots it was so low. How could they after all this time still be floundering for real solid leads? His phone vibrated in his pocket.

He stopped outside the double doors to the incident room and pulled his phone from his pocket, expecting it to be Lisa checking up on him. He didn't want to have the conversation with her, even if it was by text, in front of his team. She was worrying endlessly about him. Of course she was worried about Hannah too. Hannah had been there for him after his heart attack, but as Lisa told him quietly in the dark as they lay in bed, her main priority was him, no matter how selfish that was. She didn't want to lose him. Aaron had kept his mouth shut and listened to her worries. He couldn't tell her he was fine. He recognised the stress he was under but there was no way he would pull back on the investigation.

The name on the phone alert surprised him. It was Ross, both times. Aaron's heart jumped in his chest and he pushed the doors to the incident room open. 'What is it, Ross?' he asked, without even looking at the messages.

Ross leapt up from his chair. 'Aaron, I've realised something and it's important.'

'Well get on with it and tell me.' He didn't have the time for Ross's games. He wanted to go and fetch Hannah home.

Ross flashed a grin at Pasha. 'I've been studying the CCTV from where Hannah was taken.'

'Okay.' He didn't need the lead up, just the final bite.

'We've been so busy watching Hannah's car arrive and Hannah being abducted, we missed something.'

Aaron screwed up his face. He'd watched the video multiple times himself. He'd tortured himself with it. He usually travelled with Hannah to meetings and yet this one she had travelled to alone. If he had been there, they wouldn't be looking for her now. He couldn't think what he might have missed. What vital clue they had ignored. He had watched it frame by frame. Analysed every single second of it.

'I don't understand. We've torn apart every still, looking for lines of enquiry. There's nothing else on there.'

Ross's grin widened and Aaron took in a deep breath as his fingers curled in frustration.

'It's not what's there that we missed. It's what's not on the video.'

That made Aaron stop in his tracks. 'What do you mean? What's missing?'

It was Pasha's turn to rise from her chair. They were all excited by what they had found, or what they hadn't found. 'We were so busy looking at Hannah's car and her abduction we missed the fact that—'

Ross jumped in stopping her mid-flow. 'Seriously, Pasha?'

Aaron stomped closer to them. 'It's not a bloody competition. Someone tell me what you've figured out.'

Pasha looked sheepishly at Ross and inclined her head.

Ross rubbed his hands together. 'We missed the fact that Lucas Harper didn't turn up to meet her. But he said he did.'

56

I t took a second for the information to register in Aaron's brain. 'Lucas Harper?'

'Yeah,' said Ross. 'He phoned us up on the day and complained that Hannah hadn't turned up for the meeting. Obviously we know she was there because we saw her on the video. But what we failed to pick up was that Lucas never actually appeared.'

Aaron moved towards his desk. 'There's no sign of his car crossing the CCTV at any point before or after the abduction?'

'None. We've checked half an hour either side of the time he was supposed to be meeting her.'

Martin leaned back in his chair. 'I think Lucas Harper has a few questions to answer, don't you, Sarge?'

Aaron did indeed. 'How the fuck have we missed this?'

There was some spluttering.

'That's rhetorical. I missed it as well. I'm not having a go,' he said. He looked at Ross. 'This was you?'

Ross grinned again. 'Yeah.'

'Good pick up. Okay then. Let's go and speak to Lucas Harper. We need to do a deeper dive on him.' He looked to Ross. 'As you figured this out, you can come with me.'

Ross couldn't hide his excitement. This was the first real lead they'd had since Hannah was abducted.

Aaron turned to Pasha and Martin. 'I want you two to work on digging into Lucas Harper. I want everything. We've messed up badly and I want to rectify that.'

Martin looked up from his screen; he'd already made a start.

'Martin, could you update Baxter and Walker as I'm not hanging around? We need to get moving on it.'

Martin leaned back in his chair. 'I'll get onto it straight away.'

'We might actually...' Pasha couldn't finish the sentence.

'We don't know what we have,' said Aaron. 'Hold on, Pasha. Work the case. Let's see where it takes us. But, yes, it's the best lead we've had.' He could feel her hope. Lucas Harper could hold the answers they were searching for and Aaron could see that was where Pasha's hope was springing from.

It was the weekend. There was a good chance that Lucas was at home.

'There are no valid grounds for arrest,' Aaron said as he pulled up outside Harper's house.

Ross turned in his seat and looked at Aaron. 'You think he'll panic?'

'If he's got something to hide then yes, I think once we've alerted him that we know he never turned up, his next actions are going to be very revealing.'

They climbed out the vehicle and strode to the door. Aaron knocked hard and they waited. There was no response. Aaron knocked again. Still there was no reply.

Ross walked to the front window and peered in. 'I can't see any signs of life. I don't think he's here.'

Frustration rattled at the back of Aaron's brain. 'Okay, let's pay the aunt a visit. See if she's seen him or knows where he might be.'

57

Lucas was sitting at the same table in the dining hall he'd been at the last time I was here. Simon walked in ahead of us, Ruby, and I hobbling behind him and some man I didn't recognise, who had been camped outside my room, bringing up the rear. They didn't want me making another run for it, that was clear. As if I could with my injured ankle.

This time there was no welcome. Lucas watched me closely as we approached.

My apprehension went up a notch.

I had to protect Ruby at all costs.

I kept my eyes trained on Lucas, but swept the room as discreetly as I could. There were no signs of anyone else.

If it came to it Ruby would not fight on my side. She would be too afraid of the consequences.

Lucas leaned back in his chair. 'Thank you for joining me. Won't you both take a seat.' It wasn't a question. He waved to the chairs around the table. Ruby pulled the closest chair out and sat down, clasping her hands in her lap and crossing her legs at the ankle.

Lucas stared at me and waited for me to do as I was told. Simon and the other man hovered behind me. I held my ground for a moment, not wanting to submit to the intimidation. Eventually, I pulled out a chair and sat which was a relief for my ankle. In any case it would be better for me to be on a level with him, and not antagonising him by standing above him.

Lucas looked from me to Ruby and back to me. 'It's come to my attention that you've been having some very interesting discussions.' He turned his attention back to Ruby. 'Things that really should not have been a topic of conversation.'

Ruby coloured and a hand shot up to her cheek. I willed for her to calm down but I knew she was terrified of Lucas and his power over her was absolute.

'I don't understand,' I said.

He tried to use silence to unnerve me but I was used to it as a tactic and held my nerve. Eventually, he spoke. 'Ruby has been spilling her guts about our friend buried out in the wood, has she not?' His eyes drilled into me.

There was a quiet squeak from Ruby. I kept my gaze trained on Lucas, though I desperately wanted to turn to Ruby to reassure her she would come to no harm. I wouldn't let it happen. I moved my hand slowly up and felt the wooden stake dig in my wrist as the tip of it poked out of my sleeve.

Reassured I was armed if this conversation turned I asked Lucas for clarification.

'We have a listening device in your room, Hannah. Is that clarification enough?'

Ruby started to quietly weep. I ground my teeth. I had never hated anyone as much as I hated Lucas and the rest of this blindly-following group right now.

I slowly shook my head disbelieving but at the same time knowing what he said was true. 'I haven't seen anything.'

'You're a police officer, Hannah, you've heard of being covert, haven't you?'

How did he get hold of equipment like this? At this point in time, it wasn't what I needed to worry about. 'Does it matter that I know who's out there and how they ended up out there?' I asked.

'It matters a great deal,' Lucas said, rising from his chair. 'You're a cop. It's your job to investigate cases like that. Ruby has placed us in a very difficult position by giving you this information.'

It was then I saw people moving around behind Lucas, in the kitchen beyond him. They weren't there making the next meal or even cleaning up after the last one. They were packing up boxes.

'What are you doing, Lucas?'

'I'm relocating the group. You and Ruby have given us no choice. We hadn't made a decision on what we were going to do with you. We'd hoped, in time, you would understand who we were and why we chose to live the way we do, but we were mistaken. There's no way you can ever understand us. I put us all at risk bringing you here.'

'You think?' I spat out at him. Fury rose in me like burning hot coal lighting a fire in my belly. I lurched to my feet, oblivious to my ankle.

'You've brought this on yourself, Hannah, with your nosiness and meddling. If only you had stayed in your room and behaved as you should have done, then none of this would have happened.'

Nothing had occurred as yet and my hackles rose at the implication of his words.

A young woman ran in carrying a box. She went straight to Lucas, whispered something in his ear. He pointed back the way she had come, spoke quietly to her and she ran off again.

'What's happening, Lucas?' I asked.

'Like I said, I'm relocating the group.'

'Right now?' I looked at Ruby. She was ashen. She knew nothing of this.

Lucas turned his gaze to Ruby. 'You've betrayed us, Ruby. I feel personally let down by you. I bestowed upon you the great duty of caring for our guest and you repay me by turning on me this way?'

'I... she... we... I didn't.' She bowed her head. 'I'm sorry.'

His face was impassive. There was not a flicker of emotion within him.

'What about us?' I asked.

'What about you?' he asked.

'You're relocating. Does that mean Ruby and I are going with you?' Would my team ever find me if we moved? I dreaded to think how long I would have to spend with this group. Locked up like an animal. Fed when they chose to. Allowed out when they said. Only spoken with when it was the right time. The wooden stake nestled in the crook of my arm.

'Oh no. You and Ruby have a connection so you're staying together. You and Ruby are staying here.'

I didn't like the sound of this. I should be overjoyed that my captor was walking away and leaving me but it sounded too easy. Something was amiss.

'You aren't going to cause us any more problems, Hannah. Once we're out of the building we're done with it. Done with you and done with the building. We don't need either of you again.'

I took a step closer to him and he rose to his full height, not frightened by my attention, unaware of the sharpened stick in my sleeve. 'What do you mean, done with us?'

He laughed. It was hard and brittle. 'I'm going to burn the building to the ground, Hannah, and you and Ruby are going burn with it.'

'Nooo,' Ruby wailed.

I had to make a move. There was no way they were going to lock us back in my room and burn the building down around us. Lucas was so sure of himself. He wasn't afraid of telling us his plans. He had no fear. He was used to his word being law here and nothing going awry. What harm could come of telling the two feeble women of their fate?

I'd soon show him what harm there could be.

I glanced at Ruby. She was paralysed with fear. Shocked that her leader would turn on her this way. Staring at him, hoping that she'd misheard him or that he'd say something else, something that would contradict what he'd said. But Lucas wasn't the contradictory type; he was solid and sure of himself. He knew what he was doing. He'd hoped to bring me into his fold because I'd been getting too close to the investigation, but that didn't work out. Now I'd uncovered their crime with Andrew he had to act and he was sure-footed, unafraid. After all, they'd already been responsible for the death of one man; what would it matter if two more people perished as the hotel burned down? He would walk away without a backwards glance.

I took a step closer to him. There was now only about four feet between us. No distance at all if I rushed him.

58

Tara welcomed them with open arms. They were, after all, her favourite people since they'd come with the news that her nephew was alive after all these years. 'Can I get you both a drink?' she asked, bustling them into the house.

'No, thank you,' said Aaron who never drank in strangers' houses at work.

'I'd love a brew,' said Ross, who Aaron knew loved the hospitality people showed him when he entered their homes.

Tara walked into the kitchen and they followed her and watched as she busied herself filling the kettle and getting mugs and milk out.

Aaron got straight to the point. 'Have you seen Lucas recently?'

Tara tipped the milk into two mugs and put the carton back into the fridge. 'I'm afraid I haven't. It's heartbreaking that we haven't all got together at the hospital.'

'Any idea where he might be if he's not at home?'

The kettle boiled and Tara's hands hovered around it. 'I can't think of anywhere. Like I said before, we've grown distant, I'm afraid. Lucas has isolated himself and does his own thing. It saddens me but he's an adult so there's not a lot I can do about it.' She poured boiling water into the mugs and stirred. 'Why? Is there a reason you need him?'

Aaron was honest with her. 'We want to ask him about the day he was meant to meet our missing detective inspector.'

Tara whipped around to face them. 'Oh yes, I heard about that. I'm so terribly sorry. She seemed like such a lovely woman. It's awful news, awful indeed. And you say Lucas was meant to meet her that day?'

Ross took the mug of tea from her. 'Yes, that was the reason she was there.'

'Oh no. I imagine Lucas feels awful. And you haven't discussed this with him yet?'

Aaron spoke again. 'We have but we need to clarify a couple of things.'

Tara picked up her own mug and turned towards the door. 'Shall we go and sit where it's a little more comfortable?'

They moved into the living room.

'You don't have any idea where he might be?' Aaron asked her again. The frustration clawing at him.

'I'm afraid I don't. I'd love to be able to help you, especially as it's to do with your inspector.'

Ross looked up at the wall. At the photographs in pride of place.

'In happier times.' Tara sounded wistful.

There was an image of a woman with two boys. Ross pointed at it. This is your sister with Matt and Lucas?'

Tara looked lovingly at the photo. 'It is. About a year before they went missing. Before she became disillusioned with life. She was happy then. Happy with her boys and how life was ticking along.' Her voice went quieter. 'Funny how things change.' She perked up again, 'But we have Matty back and look at the photo. Can't you see the little boy in the man we have back?' Her face glowed.

'How's he doing?' Ross asked.

'It's slow going. He didn't want to see me at first. He found it diffi-cult because he didn't know me, but he's allowing me in now and we're talking, so it's promising.'

Ross moved along the wall of photographs, one of Tara with a young man who had his arm around her, the coast behind them.

'A rare day out at the beach,' she said following his gaze.

'It's you and Lucas?'

'Yes. I wanted to try and lift his spirits a little, to show him that life was still out there. We both needed it, to be honest. It was a good day.'

Ross leaned in to the photograph. Peered at something that had caught his attention. 'Aaron?'

Aaron rose from his chair and joined him.

'What is it?' Tara asked.

Ross pointed to the photograph for Aaron.

Aaron turned to Tara. 'The arm around your shoulder, we can see something on the inside of his wrist.'

'Oh yes,' she said. 'It's some bizarre little tattoo he got. A hollow circle. I've no idea what it means. He's had it for ages.'

59

Silence fell over the canteen like a blanket as my heart thudded in my chest. Life had converged into a pinprick point as I stared at Lucas standing in front of me, all secure and arrogant in his plans, with the weapon of my own making tucked up my sleeve. My focus was laser sharp. I knew what I had to do. If I took out Lucas I stood more of a chance of getting the group to back down. He had a tight hold over them. It was unbreakable, but what if he was broken? Out of the picture?

I'd never contemplated inflicting this level of harm on anyone before but it was his life or mine and Ruby's.

I could see his mouth moving; he was talking again. I tuned in.

'It's time. I'm afraid this is where we part. I'm sorry we couldn't have become friends, Hannah. You would have made a great addition to the community.'

This was it. I had to act, here and now.

He turned his attention to Ruby. 'And you, dear Ruby, you are a deep loss, a wound I will—'

I moved. I flicked my wrist up, opening the gap so I could grasp the stake with my right hand. Pulling it out, I wobbled forward, slightly off-balance as I kept pressure off my ankle, but his attention still on Ruby, his mouth moving in his self-gratifying speech.

The stake was rough in my hand. It was not an ideal weapon, it had been fashioned out of necessity out of furniture wood, but I'd done what I could to make it useful. All I needed was some level of force and the slightly narrowed end would do its job.

I raised my arm. There was no time for thought. Lucas's head swivelled back to me. I was aware of Simon and the other man behind me. I had to act before they could stop me.

I propelled myself forward, a primal scream ripping out of my throat, my arm pushing downwards to meet flesh. I aimed for his neck. An arm injury would not help us and his chest was too well-protected by his ribcage.

Lucas's scream bellowed up and met my own.

60

When people say it happened so quickly I now understood what they mean. One minute I was leaping for Lucas with the stake in my hand, hearing both of us screaming in the face of the other, feeling contact of stake and skin, trying to force my arm down as deep as I could. Next minute I'm on the ground face down, arms out wide like I'm on a cross. A huge weight in the middle of my back and someone stamping on my hand. I didn't know if the stake was still in my hand or not. I couldn't feel it. I didn't even know whether my hand was open or closed. All I wanted was for the stamping to stop. There was a searing, blinding pain in my hand.

My focus started to come back. Sounds seeped into my consciousness. Ruby was screaming for them to stop. Lucas was roaring. My only thought was that I hadn't done enough damage if he was still able to make that sound.

Heavy footsteps thundered into the hall. Lucas roared some more. Ruby was still screaming. I could barely breathe with the weight bearing down on my back. Someone was sitting on me. It couldn't be Simon. He didn't look heavy enough to be causing this much pressure. It must be him stamping on my hand in wild panic. I wanted to tell them they'd got me, I wasn't capable of doing anything else to Lucas, but speech wouldn't come, the breath caught in my lungs.

Focus slipped away again and greyness filtered through. The floor was cool on my cheek. I could smell something floral down here, floating through the grey, whatever they cleaned the floor with. The noise and pandemonium slipped away. I wished I could see my dad and Zoe again. I had so much to say, but darkness was taking over.

Someone shouted and I was pulled from the floor into a sitting position, still surrounded by grey, unable to see who was yelling at me.

'You don't escape that easily,' the voice said as they bent down into my eyeline. The grey ebbed away and I could see Lucas. Blood dripping down his T-shirt where I'd caused him some damage. He was holding a gauze pad low down on the side of his neck. I could see the circular tattoo on the inside of his right wrist. The same tattoo I'd seen on Matthew's wrist. My vision fully cleared and Lucas's eyes bore into me. Cold and empty.

'You have some fight left in you.' He crouched down in front of me.

I was being held up by the guy who had been sitting on my back. My hand was throbbing, screaming in pain. Something was broken in there. I risked a quick glance at it, resting on the ground at the side of me, limp and already bruising, dark purple and swelling. This wasn't good. How could I fight with a broken right hand? Because I was not going out without a battle.

'You don't have to do this, Lucas,' I said. My speech slow as the pain invaded my whole being. 'The man in the grave, it was an accident, but if you go ahead with what you're planning then it's something else entirely. You don't want to cross that line.'

He'd already crossed it with Andrew; we both knew that. Not getting medical aid was one thing, but operating in the circumstances Ruby had described took it to a whole new level. Lucas might not have been hands-on, but he'd ordered the action. He was as liable as anyone else.

He laughed in my face, pulled the gauze away from his neck and looked down. There was a puncture mark oozing blood where I had driven the wood into him. He tutted and pushed back down on the gauze and stared at me again. 'You have to make things so difficult all the time don't you?'

I could hear Ruby still sobbing behind me somewhere. At least she hadn't been hurt.

Yet.

'We can talk about this, Lucas,' I tried again.

'It's far too late for talking,' he said. 'You've had your chances. If you genuinely wanted to talk, I wouldn't be bleeding right now, would I?'

He had a point. I'd hit him too low. The stake hadn't been sharp enough and had punctured lower than I'd aimed for. If I'd done a better job with the weapon we might not be having this discussion and I might be talking to one of the other members of the group and talking our way out of here. As it was, he was only injured and just as set on walking away and leaving Ruby and me here to die.

Lucas straightened. 'I don't have time to go through this with you. I wanted to do you the courtesy of explaining what was happening and why, but now I've done that I need to get on. We're about ready to leave.' He turned to Simon. 'Take them to their rooms. Make sure you secure them both.'

'Lucas, no,' Ruby pleaded. 'Let me come with you.' I doubted she wanted to continue living with the community but she would rather do that than die left behind here.

Lucas sneered. 'You're nothing but a disappointment, Ruby. We have no time to put you through the ritual to cleanse you. You left us no choice but to leave you behind with the dead wood.'

He turned and strode from the room.

'Lucas, no,' Ruby sobbed again.

I was grabbed by an arm and yanked to my feet. My hand throbbed like a living breathing animal as it was removed from its resting place on the floor. I closed my eyes and tried to overcome the pain and keep my focus on what was happening.

Ruby was pulled from her chair and she wailed. The fear all-encompassing.

Ruby and I were frog-marched from the room. Ruby's eyes were wild and her face flushed. The group she had given her life to had betrayed her in the most final way possible. She couldn't comprehend what was happening. I was badly injured, my ankle making the task more difficult and the pain screaming in my head from my hand making it hard for me to follow instructions so it was more like a dragging in my case.

The first door we came to was mine. I was pushed inside and fell to the floor onto my knees. I put my hands out instinctively and screamed as my shattered right hand slammed into the solid floor. Tears streamed down my face from the pain. I turned my head quickly to see the door close and Ruby being dragged away. She screamed out for me. She screamed to stay with me. I could hear her screaming as they moved away down the corridor.

I stayed on the floor, nursing my broken hand in my lap. No doctor would come this time to check me over. I was alone waiting for my fiery death.

61

The sounds of people packing up and leaving seeped through my boarded-up window. Footsteps, banging of vehicle doors, the murmur of excited voices. Eventually, car engines fired up and the cult members drove away.

Silence descended.

I wondered if I would still have a sentry outside my door but figured they would be gone by now. No one would want to stay behind.

But what of the threat to burn the building down to the ground?

Lucas could have set the fire somewhere else in the premises and I wouldn't yet know. It would take time for it to spread.

I couldn't just sit here and wait to find out if he'd followed through with his threat. It would be far too late by the time I was aware of fire inside this room. I had to get out, find Ruby and break her out of her room. We had to exit this building and fast.

I looked down at my hand, so swollen it was barely recognisable. My ankle was still painful. I wasn't in the best shape for this but if I was to make my way home to Dad and Zoe I had to move.

I hauled myself off the floor, allowing the silent tears to flow as the agony pierced my brain.

I rattled on the door handle and screamed for the door to be opened, in case someone was on the other side. As I expected, there was no response.

It was time to take positive action.

My ankle was weak and painful but for what I planned meant I needed to steady myself on one leg and it was going to be my sprained ankle taking the weight. I took a deep breath to ready myself.

I pulled the chair in front of the door and held onto it with my left hand, my only working hand, balanced on my bad leg – it was like a comedy of errors with my body – lifted my good leg and with all the energy I could muster I forced it forward, kicking the lock on the door. Pain flooded through me. More tears sprang into my eyes. There was a loud cracking sound from the door but it didn't move.

I gritted my teeth. This was the only way if I didn't want to die, I had to try this again. The tears fell from my eyes as I lifted my leg again and forced my booted foot into the lock. There was another crack, but this time it was visible. The door was giving but it still wouldn't open. Once more I lifted my leg and as I was about to push forward I smelled it. It was unmistakable. The dark dry smell of fire.

Lucas had done it. He'd done as he said he would. He'd set fire to the hotel with me and Ruby inside and he'd driven away and left us here to die.

Fury and fear rose up in me and I slammed my foot into the door one last time and watched as it splintered away from the frame. I moved the chair away from the doorway and yanked hard on the handle. The door was hanging wonkily and took some dragging but eventually I managed to pull it open and I was out in the corridor.

Stopping to listen in case I could hear Ruby shouting, I heard instead the sound of the fire eating through the downstairs space. The angry sound as items heated up, expanded, and were destroyed.

'Ruby!' I screamed at the top of my voice. 'Ruby, where are you?' I needed to find her and fast. Yes I could escape and save myself but I couldn't leave without Ruby. She'd cared for me during my time here. No matter that she had been a part of the community that had me locked in the room. It had been at Lucas's direction. She was as much a victim as me and I wouldn't go without her.

'Ruby?' I shouted again, stopping to listen for a response. Nothing. And all the doors along the corridor were closed. I gingerly moved to the next room along and tried the door. It opened easily. I didn't expect to find her in an unlocked room, but I had to check. I hopped a couple of steps inside so I could look around and called her name. She wasn't here. I hopped out and moved to the door opposite. It was also unlocked. Again I checked and called. Still no sign of Ruby.

How many doors and rooms was I going to have to check to find her?

The flames were burning hot and fast. Smoke was drifting into the corridor. The fire was below but it wouldn't be long before it burnt its way up to this floor. I needed to move faster. Hopping was not good enough. I needed to put my foot down and apply pressure, take the agony and deal with it later.

I lurched along the corridor, checking the rooms, screaming as loud as I could for Ruby, the power in my voice being pushed forward with the pain, but there was no response and no sign of my friend. Because that's what she had become in here, my friend and I wasn't going to leave and allow her to burn to death.

62

The warrant to search Lucas Harper's address didn't take long to obtain. Aaron contacted the office as they were travelling back and Pasha had compiled the necessary paperwork and then visited the district judge at home to get it authorised and signed.

They regrouped in the incident room. The mood was electric. This was a serious lead and could result in finding Hannah at last.

Pasha was shuffling the warrant paperwork into a folder. 'I can't believe we missed it.'

'He was the boy that was left behind, there was no reason to look at him,' said Martin. 'He'd lost his family. We assumed he was thrilled that his brother was back.'

'He had us all fooled,' Ross grumbled, wrapping his kit belt around his waist. He didn't usually wear it but he kind of hoped Lucas would be at home and would put up a fight.

'So he knew where his mother and brother were all along?' Pasha couldn't get her head around it.

Martin pulled his jacket on. 'It looks that way.'

'But why Hannah?'

Martin shook his head. 'That's something we're going to have to ask him. My best guess is she was getting too close.'

They were outside the door soon after and again there was no answer. This time they didn't need a response; they had a warrant. They'd brought a couple of uniformed officers with them because breaking down a door meant someone had to stay with the property until it was secured when they'd finished.

With a couple of cracks from the big red key the door swung open.

Aaron was the first through the door, shouting 'Police' as he entered in case Lucas was inside and failing to respond. The house was empty, silent, hollowed out.

'Okay, glove up, look for any evidence of where he may have taken her. Computers, phones, all paper records, other properties owned or rented, vehicle documents, phone records, passwords written down. We want it all.' Aaron bent down to the search bag and snapped out a pair of blue gloves, pulling them on as he spoke. 'As far as computers and phones go we want to get them back to the station to get them analysed as quickly as possible.' Usually there was a bit of a wait for an examination, but in these circumstances officers were waiting to receive whatever the team found.

Everyone grabbed a pair of gloves and worked the house meticulously. Everything that was seized was logged by the exhibits officer and signed by both the seizing officer and exhibits officer, keeping the chain of continuity. They didn't want anything to go wrong with this case, once they got it to court.

It took three hours to do a thorough search of the premises. They had nearly finished when Pasha came rushing up to Aaron with a piece of paper in her hand.

'I found this. It's an old agreement for a hotel that's no longer operational. Seems the owner sold it to Lucas for a pound.'

Aaron looked at her, puzzled. 'A pound? You're sure?'

She handed him the document. 'I don't know how legally binding it is, but I found it in his bedroom. He didn't want us to find it as it was taped to the floorboards underneath the corner of his carpet. It seemed a bit loose and not as secure as the rest of the room so I lifted it. Found this.'

Aaron looked at the document. It was true; the premises had indeed been passed to Harper for the lowly sum of one English pound. 'The guy who's done this sale is very likely going to be part of the cult, if you ask me. No other reason to sell a building for that price.'

Pasha scribbled her signature on an exhibit label. 'Though why did he need to sell it? He could have let them use it.'

'Greed. Harper didn't just want to use it, he wanted it in his name. He'll be taking everything he can off these people.' Aaron handed her the document back so she could log it with the exhibits officer.

'Think that could be where he's keeping Hannah? Where the rest of the cult live?' she asked.

'It's likely. We need to finish up here and get moving to that location as fast as we can.'

63

The heat was making me sweat. It was like someone had turned the heating up to full and closed the windows, with the sun shining in and a magnifying glass jacking the rays. I had to find Ruby quickly.

The corridor turned right and there was another corridor of doors, all closed. I wiped the back of my good hand across my brow and moved to the first door. 'Ruby,' I shouted.

Over the crackling of the fire below me I heard her. It was muffled. She was behind one of these doors. Which one?

I screamed down the corridor, 'Bang on the door, Ruby, I don't know where you are.' The smoke was getting thicker. Time was running out. The smoke would kill us before the fire even reached us. Which if I stopped to think about it was probably more preferable, but I didn't want to go by either method.

'Ruby!' I shouted again. Then I heard it. Banging against a door halfway down this corridor. I limped to the door and put my hand against it, my ear to the wood. 'Ruby, are you in here?'

'Hannah, oh Hannah, yes!'

'Stand back,' I shouted, coughing as the smoke hit the back of my throat. I was going to have to try to kick another door down but this time I didn't have a chair to balance on and I had a fire and smoke at my back.

I gritted my teeth, balanced on my bad ankle and kicked the lock. It didn't move.

'Again, Hannah,' she shouted.

I was in agony, I could barely focus, but I balanced again and kicked once more. A splintering crack. I had made headway. I bent over double, coughing and hacking up my lungs. I was running out of time. I kicked once more and the door flew open. I tumbled in after it and was caught by Ruby. She started sobbing as she looked at my hand and then my face. She brought a hand up and wiped my cheek. I grabbed her hand with my good one, dragged her to the door and looked both ways down the corridor. The smoke was thick and acrid.

'We need wet towels,' I rasped.

She ran back into the en suite and soaked a couple of bath towels. We each put one over our heads. The towel was heavy, protective. Water running down my face. It gave me an idea.

'Shower!' We had precious seconds but being wet would give us some protection from the flames.

Ruby spun the shower on and jumped under it, spinning until she was soaked, then she jumped back out and helped me in. I did the same with some help from Ruby. With towels over our heads we went back to the door.

By now the corridor was greyed-out with smoke. I took Ruby's hand again and turned left. Maybe there was a door to the outside this way. It was the shortest distance to the end of the corridor. I didn't want to go back the way I'd come. Ruby followed me blindly, like a lost lamb, changing one leader for another. She would need some real support if we managed to get out of here.

Panic was a heavy weight in my chest, battling with the smoke to overwhelm me. With the tips of my swollen fingers I pulled a corner of the towel and placed it over my mouth, looked at Ruby and indicated she should do the same. She copied me instantly.

At the end of the corridor was a glass door leading to some stairs. With my shoulder I pushed on the door. Smoke billowed in from the stairwell. Ruby and I started to choke. I took a step onto the landing, looked over into the stairs, saw fire climbing towards us. There was no way down. We were stranded on the first floor. Flames were spreading fast and a cloud was building in my head. A fuzziness that was threatening to engulf me. I was close to succumbing to the fumes from the fire.

Ruby bent over, gasping. I pulled her back and pushed the glass door closed. From her bent position she looked up at me, eyes wide.

'I'm so sorry,' I heard her say through the towel over her mouth.

I shook my head. The tightness in my chest was taking away my ability to talk. I had to save my breath. I was not giving in now. Barely able to see, I turned back to the corridor, stumbled forward and fell to my knees. My ankle twisted again as I went down. I spluttered out in pain.

We had one chance left. I would not go down like this.

64

Aaron was in the car driving, Martin and Pasha with him. He wasn't waiting for the search warrant Ross had gone to swear out for the next address. The hotel. There wasn't time. Hannah had been missing too long. He had no idea what she had been going through and the quicker he got to the property, the faster he could remove her and get her any medical assistance she might need. As for the son of a bitch who had taken her, Aaron had never been a violent man but he was pushed to his limits right now. Glad to have his colleagues with him.

'You think she's going to be there?' asked Pasha, twitching at the side of him in the front passenger seat.

'It's the closest we've had to a lead,' Martin answered her from the rear.

Pasha rubbed at her face. 'Oh God, I hope she's okay. I don't think I could bear for anything to have happened to her.'

Aaron had been here before. The operation when Hannah had been hurt. It was the worst night of his career. It had taken them all a very long time to recover. He had hoped to never repeat that night and yet here they were dashing through the dusk to get to her. But this time they might not be there in time. Last time, they had been with her during the operation. This time, she'd been alone for days. Aaron shuddered as he thought about what could have happened to her, then closed his mind down and focused on the road. Pasha hadn't been with the team then and didn't go through that trauma. He was sure she was as capable of imagining the worst outcomes.

'She's tough, is the boss,' said Martin. 'If anyone can get through this then it's her.'

Pasha looked hopeful. 'You think she's still alive then? They never asked for anything in return for her.'

'Stop it,' Aaron snapped. 'Of course she's still alive.' He stamped his foot down on the accelerator.

'I'm sorry, Aaron. Of course she is.' Pasha turned and looked out of the side window. A tear slipped down her cheek.

They travelled in silence for fifteen minutes. Each lost in their own thoughts. Afraid of what they were going to find. Then Martin received a text message from Ross. The warrant was authorised and he'd attached a photograph.

'What's that?' Pasha pointed into the distance where an orange glow lit up the grey dusky evening air.

'It looks like street lights,' said Martin, 'but it seems to be moving. A parade? Isn't that where we're heading?'

Pasha peered at the glow. 'It's not street lights or a parade. It's a...' She paused, too scared to say the word. 'It's a fire.' She turned to Aaron. 'Is that where we're going?' Her voice quivered.

Aaron looked at the satnav and then at the direction Pasha was pointing. It certainly looked like it.

Aaron had never struggled to drive as much as he was now. The cars on the road were going too slow for him and he was trying to find safe overtaking spaces but his focus kept being dragged back to the glowing orange fire at the side of them. He needed to block it out until they could get there.

Five minutes later he was bumping down an old road filled with potholes and leading directly to the fire. They could see the blaze. It had taken the entire bottom floor of a large old building. There was no sign of people. No vehicles. No fire engine.

Pasha pulled out her phone and dialled the control room and asked for the fire service to be called immediately, as well as an ambulance. They had no idea where Hannah was but if she was inside...

The three of them jumped out of the car and stood in front of the building.

The fire roared at them and they had to take a step back.

There was no way in from the front. All the doors were burning.

Aaron ran around the side. Two minutes later he was back with the others. Every single doorway was burning. There was no way in.

Which meant there was no way out.

65

R uby pulled me up from my knees, leaning on my shoulder as she did so. Both of us crippled by the smoke we were inhaling through the towels over our faces.

'Back to the room,' I wheezed and we stumbled back the way we had come, Ruby helping me stay upright on my injured ankle.

The door was open and we burst through it, pushing it closed behind us and gasping for breath. I moved straight for the window and opened it. Thank God there were no wooden slats nailed down over the glass. We leaned out and sucked in the clean air, my chest aching.

This was our last chance. 'We have to jump, Ruby.'

She looked down at the hard ground below us. 'Your ankle...'

'It's better than staying in here.'

We both looked back at the door. The smoke was floating in under the door, the room filling with grey death.

'We don't have much time, Ruby. We have to go.'

She was scared. I was scared, but we were out of choices.

'We can tie sheets together and make a rope,' she suggested.

I shook my head and indicated the door. 'We don't have time. We have to go now. We've already inhaled too much smoke. Any more and we could be unconscious before we jump.'

I was aware of how close death was. The world was fuzzy and tilted. I gave her a shove. 'You first.'

Her eyes widened in horror. 'No. Please, you go first.'

'There'll be no way I can get you if you freeze, Ruby.' I shouldered her closer to the window. 'Get out.'

She stepped towards me and grasped me in a huge hug squeezing out what was left of the air in my lungs.

We didn't have the time. I pushed her away. 'Out, Ruby.'

Her face was blackened and tears streaked a path down her cheeks. She clambered up onto the window ledge, lifted her legs over and sat for a couple of seconds.

'Go, Ruby,' I whispered. Then pushed.

She screamed. A piercing sound that broke my heart but she was out of the building. I didn't have the strength to lean out and see how she had landed.

The room was suffocating, the heat bearing down. My chest was so tight I was unable to get my breath. I needed a second to catch some air and then I could climb onto the ledge, lift my own legs over and make the leap.

Just a second, that's all I needed.

The tilting of the room disoriented me. I slid down the wall under the window. Which way was up? The greyness of the smoke fused with the fuzzy blackness on the edges of my vision.

I was so tired.

Just another couple of seconds.

That's all I needed.

Another couple of seconds.

66

Aaron didn't see her until she was tumbling from the open window. There were splitting screams in his head, like stereo, and he realised the tumbling woman was screaming and so was Pasha.

Hannah!

They ran, the three of them, to the crumpled mess on the ground. All Aaron could see was arms and legs. A white towel covered half the woman. There was a dark patch around her. Blood?

Aaron's heart jumped into his mouth.

Hannah.

They got closer. He could see the dark patch around the woman wasn't blood but was wet. It was water. She'd covered herself in water to protect herself.

The heat from the building was blazing hot. They needed to pull her away. The fire brigade still wasn't here but Aaron could hear sirens floating in the air behind them.

'Hannah!' Pasha reached her first. She bent over and pulled away the towel. The woman was young. Her hair blonde. Dirtied from the fire, but nonetheless it was blonde. This wasn't Hannah.

Pasha looked up. 'Where's Hannah?'

Martin bent down and lifted the woman up in his arms. 'We shouldn't move her but she's too close to the building.'

Aaron agreed and Martin gently scooped her up. Her eyelids flickered as he walked away from the building and laid her down on a patch of grass.

The group surrounded her again.

'Where's Hannah?' Pasha asked.

The girl blinked. 'Hannah?' She looked around her.

'Yes,' said Pasha. 'Dark, shoulder-length hair, slim.'

'She's not with me?' The girl tried to push herself up.

'Hey, take it steady,' Martin said, holding up a hand.

But the girl was adamant. She pushed on her arms, winced, cried out but forced her body upright. 'Where's Hannah? She was supposed to be following me.'

Aaron looked from the girl to Pasha then Martin. 'She was in there with you?'

'Yes!'

'She's still in there?'

'There's a lot of smoke. She was supposed to follow me out of the window. She made me go first. She pushed me out. She said she'd follow me. I believed her. She saved me.'

The fire engine and ambulance arrived in front of the building simultaneously, blue lights rotating in the darkness. The orange flickering glow of the fire lighting up the area, with the blue lights slicing up the shadows.

Aaron, Pasha and Martin looked up at the building, up at the open window the girl had tumbled from.

'HANNAH,' they shouted in unison. 'HANNAH, WE'RE HERE, JUMP.'

Firefighters climbed out of their truck, ready to do battle.

Aaron yelled at them that someone was alive and in first floor room.

They got to work.

The team and the girl watched. Nothing they could do but watch and wait. They could only stand here, surrounded by the stench of a scorched building. Listen as it crumbled. The night sky alight with the blaze of orange and blue. Silent tears fell. Hands were held and prayers were whispered.

The firefighters fought and no one knew if Hannah would come out of this alive.

67

There were flashes of information, like someone trying to tune a television channel. Bright orange and blue lights, seeping through the darkness. Blurred faces peering over me with distorted voices all mumbling at once. The sound of sirens above me rattling me to my bones as we bounced over uneven ground. Hands moving over me. A gentle voice as someone worked. Hissing over my face.

All in clips and moments in time.

I had no idea if I was dead or dying, if this was my way out of life, or if this was my way back. I couldn't make sense of anything.

I didn't want to die. I wanted to help Zoe to not die. I'd made my decision. Being taken away from her and Dad had shown me how much I loved them both. So very much.

I succumbed to the darkness and prayed to whoever was out there that I would see them another day. A different day. This day I wanted to go back to my family. The place where my heart and my soul were kept safe.

Sound penetrated the comfort of the darkness. Loud and brash. With light that was electric white.

I was moved and there were more hands. Pain. Then wooziness and the darkness enveloped me again.

I don't know how long I was out of it but I opened my eyes to find I was in a bed in a side room at the hospital. The room was brilliantly bright and I blinked to adjust to the glare.

'Hey,' a quiet voice said from the side of me.

I turned my head. Sitting in a high-backed chair was my dad. I couldn't stop the tears that sprang to my eyes. It was so good to see him.

He was out of his chair in a second and holding my left hand, my good hand, tightly. 'Hey, it's okay, you're safe, Hannah.' He bent his head to hide his own tears but as he kissed my hand they fell onto my skin and told their own story of his pain.

'I'm sorry, Dad.' My voice was hoarse. It didn't sound like me at all. I tried to clear my throat but it was dry and brittle.

He lifted his head. 'You don't have to be sorry for anything, sweet. This is in no way your fault. We're just so so glad to have you home safe. We were so scared for you.' He squeezed tighter and I welcomed the contact. We had each other. It was over.

'You needed me for Zoe and I disappeared.'

He straightened up and wiped the tears from my cheek with his large thumb. 'Zoe was distraught. She was so worried about you. She didn't care about herself as long as you came back okay. You should have seen her with your boss.'

I dreaded to think. She was notorious for talking before she thought it through. We were pretty alike in that way.

'Anything else we can sort out in time,' Dad said.

'I want to help her,' I said. 'It's all I thought about while I was away.' *Away*, as though I'd gone on a retreat or something.

He beamed at me, leant down and kissed me on the head. 'Focus on getting well first. You inhaled a lot of smoke. From what I've heard it was a close call whether they were able to get you out of the building in time. You were in one of the few rooms that weren't alight. You've been so lucky, Hannah.' He let out a juddering breath. 'I could have so easily lost you.' He turned away and his hands went up to his face.

'Dad?'

'I'm okay,' he mumbled from beneath his hands.

'Dad?' I tried again, putting whatever force I could with the little voice I had.

He turned back to me, ashen. Tears had flooded his eyes and his face was stricken.

'I really am sorry, Dad.' I held out my hand.

He pulled the chair up close to the bed and collapsed into it and sobbed over my arm. I squeezed his hand and let him know how much I loved him. I was so glad to be back. My heart broke seeing how much he loved me and the fear he'd had of losing me. I could turn this around and do something good.

Once I was free to leave here I would see the consultant in charge of Zoe's care and I would undergo the procedure so she could get what she needed from me.

I looked down at my dad and hoped I wasn't too late, that Lucas Harper hadn't killed my sister as well as Andrew.

68

The house smelled of baked goods. Dad was in the kitchen. A broad smile filled his face when he saw me in the doorway.

'Hannah, so lovely to see you. Go on in and I'll make you a cuppa. I've just baked some flapjacks as the invalid fancied some. I'll bring one through for you with your drink.'

I smiled. Flapjacks had always been Zoe's favourite when we were kids. I moved into the kitchen and gave him a kiss on the cheek. He pulled me into a tight hug, held it a second or two longer than usual and then let me go. He looked down at my hand. 'How are you feeling?'

I lifted my right hand in the air and looked at my cast and splint. It had been so badly damaged it was taking some time to heal. 'It's painful, but I have a prescription to help with that.'

'And your ankle?'

'That's fine.'

He narrowed his eyes.

'I promise.'

'What about your lungs?'

'I've had the all clear. Stop fussing.'

He turned to busy himself with the kettle. I smiled again. He couldn't be happier. 'You've seen Evie?'

'Yes, she came to the hospital. There were a lot of tears and she wouldn't let go of me.'

'She's a good friend.'

I couldn't agree with him more. I wrinkled my nose in the direction of the flapjacks. 'They smell lovely.'

'I can't promise they'll be as good as your mum's,' he said with his head bent, sorting out cups and plates, 'but it's from the same recipe book, so hopefully they won't be far wrong.'

I rubbed his arm. 'They'll be great, Dad.'

'Go on through. She's desperate to see you.'

I took a deep breath, scared of what would be waiting for me in the other room. My relationship with Zoe had been difficult for so many years. I didn't know how we would move past it and start a new life. The difference now was that I wanted to.

'She's been waiting, Hannah,' he said quietly, giving me a verbal nudge.

I took in a deep breath and steeled myself. This was my sister and I was scared of how this would go. She hadn't been allowed to visit me in the hospital because of the possibility of picking up an infection. They'd tested me and I was a match for her. As soon as this result had come through Zoe had started her chemotherapy to ready her body to receive the bone marrow I would provide her. The procedure was due to take place in the next couple of weeks. But at this moment Zoe's body was weakening even more and this was the first time I would be seeing her.

I walked out of the kitchen, hung my bag on the coat rail and then went into the living room. Zoe was on the sofa, tucked in neatly by a soft blanket, her face in a book.

'Hey,' I said, stepping forward. My heart leapt in my chest at seeing her there. We had come so close to losing her and now I could help her.

She lifted her head and beamed at me, dropping the book in her lap. I was surprised to see she looked pretty much the same as the last time I had seen her. I was expecting her to be much worse. The difference was that hope shone out from her face. Her eyes were alight as she saw me and I could see she was tearful.

'Hannah.' She pushed on the arm of the sofa to lift herself up.

I rushed forward. 'No, stay there.'

But she was up and as I rushed to her we collided and our arms wrapped around the other in a tight embrace.

'I was so worried about you,' she cried into my shoulder. 'I thought I was going to lose you. I couldn't have taken it.' Her shoulders rocked under my hands and tears streamed from my own eyes.

'Zoe, I thought about you the whole time I was there. All I wanted to do was get back to do the procedure for you. I'm so glad I'm able to.'

Her arms tightened. 'I was scared, Hannah.' She sounded like a little girl. Like my little sister. The girl I needed to protect.

'You don't need to be scared any more. I'm back now and safe.'

She pulled back and looked me up and down then shook her head. 'But look at you.'

I didn't know what she meant. 'What?'

'You've lost weight, you're so pasty, your hair is limp, look at your hand. You're a mess. You need some real time off, Hannah. Stay here with me and Dad.'

At that point Dad walked in. It was a good job really because I don't think I could have taken any more of Zoe's honesty.

'Here we go. Tea and flapjacks.' His voice was overly jolly. Did he see me as Zoe did?

He placed the tray on the coffee table and looked at the pair of us. 'Are you both going to stand there or are we going to sit down and have a drink?'

I hugged Zoe again because I couldn't help myself and she squeezed me tight. Then we parted and sat down. Dad moved over to Zoe and tucked her back in then sat in his chair.

'So, you've got some time off work I take it?' he asked pointedly.

I wriggled in my seat. 'I'm thinking of going back in soon.'

Zoe rounded on me. 'You need to take time off to recover. That place can actually function without you. It won't crumble because you're not there. Good as you are at your job.' How could I not see how much sense she talked? But knowing it and feeling it were two different things.

Dad stayed quiet. Let Zoe do all the chiding. Then he asked the difficult question. 'Have they caught him yet?' He was talking about Lucas Harper.

A heavy silence fell over the room and both of them looked at me. Dread filled my stomach. Not only at having to respond to this question but at knowing the answer. 'We have no idea where he was taking the group and we know nothing about the vehicles they were driving. We...' I corrected myself, '*They*, have nothing to go on. I can't blame them for having not caught him yet. They were so busy trying to get me out of the building they couldn't focus on who had escaped.'

The silence played out. It was Dad who eventually broke it. 'The important thing was that they got you out. I don't know how either of us would have coped had we lost you, Hannah.'

I looked at Zoe. Her jaw was rigid, her mouth a thin line, her fists clenched. I caught her eye and held it, wishing for her to break this lock she had on her anger. I understood she wanted harm to come to those who had harmed me, and at the very least, justice to be done, and it was infuriating her that her sister's captors were currently roaming the British roads free. I willed with all my might for her to just be happy to have me.

Through gritted teeth she spoke. 'They deserve to rot, Hannah.'

'I know. We'll get them eventually. He'll pop up somewhere. His image has been circulated to all police forces.'

She looked at Dad and he gave a slight shake of his head. Zoe let out a breath and looked back to me. 'Oh Hannah. I'm just so frustrated. I could have lost you.'

I jumped up and crawled into a ball at her feet on the floor, grabbing her hand with my good hand. 'It's not possible, squirt, I'm stronger than that. It takes more than a wannabe cult leader to do away with me.' I smiled up at her and she grinned at me.

'Only you, Hannah.' She went silent for a moment and I could see the cogs turning. 'What about his brother? The guy who ran in front of your car, what happened to him?'

'Matt Harper. He's gone to stay with his aunt for now. His home was sold years ago. His aunt is over the moon to look after him. He's seeing someone, a therapist.' I shouldn't be telling them all this, but these were extraordinary circumstances. 'They're hopeful his memories will return with time but at the moment he's still struggling. It'll be a long road for him. He doesn't understand where Lucas fits into all this. As far as we can make out, his mum kept in touch with Lucas after she left. He met her a few times, got sucked in himself and though he never left his life, the group liked him and saw him as a natural leader following the death of the original guy. Lucas never wanted to leave the real world behind though, which was why he often stayed at his home address. He knew we would visit him there once Matt had made his escape so made sure he'd be there for us.' I didn't tell them about the parents that had lost their son because Lucas refused to take him to a hospital. He could so easily have been saved. Matthew had wanted to save him and that was working in his favour. Andrew's family were grieving. My family were the lucky ones.

'His mum, where is she? Did you see her?'

I shook my head. 'I never did and as far I know she's still alive but has escaped with Lucas. She's still in thrall to the group. It seems she got the life she wanted after all.'

Zoe grabbed hold of my good hand and squeezed.

'I do need my painkillers though.' I winced as the pain in my bad hand shot through my arm.

Dad jumped up and brought me my bag from the hallway. 'Here, love.'

'Can you pop me a couple out please, Dad.'

He rummaged through my bag with a slightly guilty look on his face, found the pack and popped a couple of pills into my hand. I swallowed them down with the tea he'd made.

'Things could have worked out so much worse,' he said as I

relaxed back onto the sofa at Zoe's legs. 'I'm glad you had that girl to take care of you. Whatever her original part in it, it sounds like she was a support for you while you were there. What's happening to her?'

Zoe looked at my face. 'Dad, I think we should stop talking about it. She needs to rest.'

His hand flew to his mouth. 'I'm so sorry, love. Of course.' He picked up the plate and offered me a flapjack. I shook my head.

'It's okay, Dad. Ruby was a godsend while I was there. A file has been submitted to the CPS for them to make a charging decision in relation to her part in my captivity, but it's unlikely to be in the public interest to pursue it. She helped me in the end. She's being housed in a women's refuge because she fears Lucas could come looking for her if he finds out she's still alive as she knows so much about the cult and she's being supported for her transition back into society, after living under the shadow of Lucas and his weird beliefs for all this time.'

I couldn't talk about this anymore. I was exhausted. I leaned onto Zoe and she stroked my head, her fingers twining through my hair. It was comforting. We had each other.

With eyes closed I thought back to the darkness that had enveloped me in the bedroom at the end, the tightness in my chest as the air ran out and I opened my eyes as a similar pressure started to grab at my breath.

I was safe now. They'd pulled me out of the burning wreckage of a building and I had nothing left to fear. I leaned into Zoe's legs more. Leaned into the sturdiness of my sister, the here and now of where I was. It had been a close call but I had survived.

But, I wondered, at what cost?

OTHER BOOKS BY REBECCA BRADLEY

ABOUT THE AUTHOR

Rebecca Bradley is a retired police detective who lives in the UK with her family and two Cockapoo's Alfie and Lola, who keep her company while she writes. She needs to drink copious amounts of tea to function throughout the day and if she could, she would survive on a diet of tea and cake.

If you enjoyed *A Deeper Song* and would be happy to leave a review online that would be much appreciated, as word of mouth is often how other readers find new books.

To claim your FREE Novella go to the website Rebeccabradley-crime.com

When you Sign up to the Readers Club mailing list you not only receive a FREE novella, but you will also receive early previews, exclusive extracts and regular giveaways. As well as keeping up to date with new releases.

Please look her up, as she would love to chat.

facebook.com/rebeccabradleycrime

twitter.com/rebeccajbradley

ACKNOWLEDGMENTS

This was a difficult book to write. Having Hannah abducted for half a book completely changed the dynamics of a Hannah Robbins novel. I second-guessed myself most of the way through this and struggled with certain sections of the book. I hope you enjoyed the finished product.

I have to thank, as always, Denyse Kirkby for her support in crafting Aaron. Any errors made are solely my own.

My thanks to Jane Isaac, who continues to read my early drafts no matter how much she has on with her own books.

I couldn't put A Deeper Song out without the support of Debi Alper, who edited the novel and took it from messy scrambled idea into something I'm prepared to put into the world. And Helen Baggott who smoothed the final prose out as she proofread it.

To my launch team who read an early copy to support the launch of the book, thank you. To my readers who make all this worthwhile. I appreciate every single one of you. You make up my bookish world.

And finally to my family who support me wholeheartedly as I tap away at my laptop, I love you, and thank you.